LONDON ALERT

Other Books
by Christopher Bartlett
(Print and Kindle editions)

Air Crashes and Miracle Landings
Sixty Narratives:
How, When...and Most Importantly Why

The Flying Dictionary

LONDON ALERT

By
Christopher Bartlett

ISBN 978-0-9560723-4-4

Published

April 2, 2015

by

OpenHatch Books UK

londonalert.co.uk

TABLE OF CONTENTS

DISCLAIMER

All featured characters are fictitious, despite any fortuitous resemblance to actual people. This also applies to the government departments and operations centres, and while the headquarters of the three main UK security establishments, two in London by the River Thames and one in Cheltenham, do exist, what is purported to go on there is also purely fictional, as in the James Bond films.

Details in CIA briefing papers for US presidents about to receive foreign dignitaries are, as far as this book is concerned, merely humorous fiction.

The political views of the Owl or any other of the characters should not be construed as being those of the author.

Had Hollywood had the prescience to make a disaster film showing young men learning how to fly but not how to land, and using that knowledge to hijack four fuel-laden airliners and fly them into iconic US buildings, would 9/11 have ever happened? Had it, Hollywood would have been blamed, just as transpired after the first 'bomb on a plane for insurance' film.

Christopher Bartlett, London, 2015

Chapter 1
Just a Boy

The master had been called away, leaving the twenty or so fresh-faced boys unsupervised and ten-year-old Holt a chance to demonstrate his prowess as a practical joker.

With his giggling classmates looking on, he snapped a piece of blackboard chalk in two. Holding the front half in his left hand and a gimlet in his right, he bored a hole from the break almost right up to the tip. Into this hole he inserted a broken-off Swan Vestas strike-anywhere match from a very old box he had found lying around in his father's shed. He pushed the match in so the head would end up almost at the tip of the chalk.

The boys gathered around him were already chuckling in anticipation as he neatly cemented the two halves of the chalk together to make the break invisible and handed the chalk to the boy standing beside him.

'Quick,' said Holt. 'NT could be back at any moment.'

The long-haired boy grabbed it, hurried over to the blackboard, replaced it on the tray and pocketed the two other chalks, so Nervous Tom – the nickname given to the master unjustly alleged to be a Peeping Tom – would have to use it.

NT was indeed soon back, surprised to find the classroom unusually quiet, with the boys absorbed in their books rather than fighting. Turning away to face the blackboard, he was unaware of their smirks as he picked up the doctored chalk and began to write.

They all waited in expectation, but nothing happened. Soon he would finish writing his instructions for their homework and be finished with the chalk. Holt was wondering whether his hands, sweaty with excitement, had dampened the match head.

Suddenly, there was a loud crack. The tip of the chalk caught fire, shocking the hapless NT so much that he let out a scream and danced around in panic, as if he were being electrocuted with alternating current and unable to let go of the wire. His relief when the flame fizzled out was tempered by the sight of the boys bent double, laughing at his expense.

Two days later Holt was half dozing in the afternoon French class when there was a sharp knock on the classroom door. The master went to it and pulled it open to reveal the headmaster's secretary. They engaged in a brief whispered conversation. His face looking grave, the master turned towards the class and called out, 'Holt.'

'Yes, sir?'

'The head wants to see you. You had better take your things with you.'

With the whole class looking at him and wondering what his punishment was going to be – expulsion maybe – Holt gathered up his textbook and exercise book and shoved them into his satchel. He then followed Mrs Jones, the middle-aged secretary, along the corridor and down the wide staircase to the headmaster's office.

'Come in,' came the muffled voice of the fifty-year-old head in reply to her knock.

Pushing open the door, she called out, 'Here's Jeremy,' rather than using his surname, as she usually did, and indicated that he should go in.

'Hello, Jeremy, do sit down,' said the head, who, although not an awesome figure, still managed to make the boys wither by the way he used sarcasm and raised his brush-like eyebrows to indicate disbelief. He was actually quite a small man.

He pointed to the leather settee facing a similarly covered armchair, in which he himself proceeded to sit. These comfortable chairs were the ones used for discussing embarrassing personal matters, such as the facts of life. For a telling off, one would normally be left standing or sat in one of the hard wooden chairs facing his desk.

'Jeremy, I'm afraid I have some bad news...'

'What's that, sir?'

'Your father and mother were involved in a serious car accident early this morning. They were so badly hurt that they were helicoptered to hospital, where your father was declared DOA.'

'DOA?'

'I'm sorry. That means dead on arrival.'

'What about Mother? How's she?'

'She is in intensive care and I'm afraid in critical condition.'

'Can I see her?'

'Indeed you must. And as soon as possible. Your aunt is at the hospital, and we've arranged for a taxi to collect you and take you there. The school is paying for it, so there's nothing for you to worry about in that regard.'

'How will I know where to go when I get there?'

'Just go to the emergency wing and ask for intensive care. They will probably call your aunt so she can fetch you.'

'Oh,' was all Holt could say. He did not know what to think, other than praying his mother would be okay.

'Mrs Jones will give you a cup of tea while you are waiting. It should not be long.'

The headmaster walked over to his desk to call his secretary on the intercom. In moments she was back, having no doubt expected to be called to take the heartbroken boy in hand.

'It will,' said the kindly woman, 'take over an hour to get to the hospital, so you'd better go to the toilet before collecting your coat and things. I'll make you that cup of tea.'

Even though he was only there for a pee, Holt went into a cubicle so no one would see the tears welling up in his eyes. He remained there for a good ten minutes, flushing the toilet to mask the sound of him blubbing when a boy did come in. Consoling himself with the thought that he would be seeing his mother, he wiped his eyes and returned to Mrs Jones's office, having collected his coat and satchel from his locker.

Fortunately, the boys were still in class, and no one had seen his red face or had an opportunity to ask the nature of his presumed punishment for the chalk prank.

When the caretaker called Mrs Jones to announce the arrival of the taxi, she informed the headmaster, who came out to accompany them to the school entrance, where the taxi was waiting.

She gave him a hug as he was about to climb into the back seat.

'Our thoughts are with you,' said the headmaster before closing the door and signalling to the driver that he should move off.

The journey through busy traffic to the hospital seemed interminable, and Holt began to feel more and more depressed. He had a sinking feeling and wondered whether he was going to be sick. At one point the driver turned to him and asked if he was all right.

'No, not really,' he answered. 'Mum and Dad had a car crash. Dad's dead and Mum is in a bad way.'

'You poor boy. I don't know what to say. What can one say other than that we never know what might happen in life? I'd better keep my eye on the road – we don't want you to be injured as well.'

'If Mum dies, I don't know what I will do. Might as well be dead.'

'Don't say that! There's always something one can look forward to.'

'Can't think what it could be.'

After exchanging a few words with the driver, Holt felt a little better. Anyway, they were arriving at the hospital. He would be seeing his mother.

He also began to feel a little guilty in that he had always taken his parents, and especially his mother, for granted. He had just been beginning to appreciate her, having gone through a period where he thought females were inferior.

'All the best,' said the driver as Holt stepped out of the car. He was so enfeebled, he had to slam the car door shut a second time.

Apart from attending a hospital when he broke his wrist, he had never been to one.

'Intensive Care is halfway down the green corridor, on the left. You can't miss it,' said the receptionist at the main desk.

He didn't miss it and pushed open the double doors leading to another passage. A few yards down there was a window marked 'Reception'. He gave his mother's name and was told to sit down on one of the nearby chairs and wait.

'Your aunt will come for you.'

Holt had never hit it off with the woman, for she was actually the wife of his mother's brother, who unfortunately was away on business in the Far East.

'Ah, there you are, Jeremy.'

'Hello, Auntie. How's Mum?'

'Not good at all. She has internal injuries, ruptured liver and spleen, other complications as well. Good job you've got here in time. The doctors don't think she has long.'

'But...'

'She keeps asking for you...so come along, dearie.'

What an impersonal word. 'Love' would have been friendlier. She might have shown some fake compassion by holding his hand. Though had she done so, he probably would have felt worse.

His mother was in a private room, with all sorts of tubes attached to her. The nurse standing beside the bed said, 'Your son's here.'

The seemingly lifeless figure stirred, and his mother's eyes opened.

'Come nearer. I can't see well.'

'Oh, Mummy...'

'Jeremy. My Jeremy.'

'Dad's dead.'

'I know. Go and say goodbye to him. For you and for me. Promise?'

'I promise.'

'I have not got long, so listen carefully. I've signed a paper making my brother, Harry, your guardian. Auntie Dorothy has agreed to look after you. There will be some money in trust for you, but not much, as there is still the mortgage to pay on most of the house. Oh dear, I feel so tired. Give me your hand and kiss me.'

'Mother!'

'Try and do something in later life of which Father and I would have been proud...'

'I will.'

Holt leant over and kissed his mother on the cheek and squeezed her almost-lifeless hand as she sank back on her pillow.

'I think he should go now,' said the nurse, adding that there was not much more he could do other than say goodbye, which his mother might just be able to hear.

'Goodbye, Mummy,' murmured Holt with tears welling up in his eyes.

Holt's aunt pulled him away by the arm and led him out of the room as the nurse leant over the bed to tend to his mother, who was not responding. The nurse had lifted her eyelids and was shining a torch into her eyes.

Once in the corridor, Holt demanded to see his dad.

'He's dead. Nothing you can do for him now,' snarled his aunt, before adding, 'There's no point – plus I've been here long enough.'

As they passed the nurses' station, Holt turned to face the senior nurse standing behind the desk.

'I want to see my dad. I promised my mum I would say goodbye to him for her as well.'

'He's been stone-dead for hours,' said his aunt angrily.

'I think it would be all right,' replied the nurse, who was actually a sister. 'He's in the room over there...Nurse Barnes, can you take this little boy to say farewell to his dad? Just two or three minutes will mean a lot to the dear boy. Just don't drag it out and get him too overwrought.'

Unsure of what 'overwrought' meant, Holt let the young nurse take his hand and lead him into the room where his father was lying in bed, with his head low because there was no pillow. She pulled back the sheet to reveal his face, which though ashen gave Holt the impression his father was alive.

Gingerly, as befitted the schoolboy he was, he kissed him on the forehead.

The cold sensation as his lips touched his father was a shock he would remember forever.

Chapter 2
More Than a Boy

The school had a bursary to help boys in difficult circumstances and agreed to let Holt stay on without the fees being paid for the term and a half remaining until summer.

'It will give you time to find your feet,' had said the headmaster.

It did in a way, and especially at the beginning, because everyone was so kind. A couple of boys had told their mothers, and they invited Holt to their homes for the weekend. There, he was showered with attention, compassion, and even love, which was a far cry from what he received from his aunt. However, after five weeks, when things were getting back to normal, a tremendous feeling of loneliness overcame him. Gone for a time was the laughing boy playing practical jokes.

Even though his mother and father had had to struggle to pay the mortgage on the house and the school fees, they were considerably richer than his uncle and aunt, who with the connivance of the solicitor had moved into his parents' house. Just about able to find the money to pay the mortgage using some of the money earmarked for Holt, they did not have much left to spend on him. He could not expect any more holidays abroad.

That was not strictly true, for the first summer, the brigadier's family next door invited him to join them on their holiday in France. What made the holiday with them especially enjoyable was the presence of their vivacious daughter, Samantha. She was a year older than he and, as a girl, so much more mature, and he was well aware she was quite out of his reach. That did not prevent the sight of those bronze thighs emanating from her tight shorts being a mixture of pleasure and torment. Yet, unlike many attractive girls that age, she never put him down or ignored him. In fact, she always listened to what he had to say with interest.

Unfortunately, the brigadier had retired from the army, and the family soon after moved away, down to Hampshire.

After a year at an ordinary secondary school, Holt was accepted at a grammar school. Without seeming to do any work he managed to pass exams with top grades. The trouble was that apart from his unrequited interest in the opposite sex, he had lost his appetite for life. In fact, it was not just sex that he lacked but emotional contact.

His mother's dying wish that he do something in life of which she and Dad could have been proud haunted him, but becoming increasingly withdrawn and lonely, he could not focus on anything.

The mean-spiritedness of his aunt, which had rubbed off on his uncle, a decent but disappointed man, did not help matters. They would run down anyone who was successful and would even try to nip any aspirations Holt might harbour in the bud. Of course, they did it subtly. Their favourite phrase seemed to be 'We thought you would have…done the sensible thing' – i.e. not done it. Another was, 'Aren't you getting above yourself?'

Although very able, he could neither draw nor dance. The former ruled out an obviously noble career in medicine, as boys doing that did biology, which meant dissecting animals and drawing them lying in foul-smelling formaldehyde.

Not being able to dance – maybe he got so stressed and frustrated he could not get the rhythm – made getting to know girls nigh impossible. Anyway, they found the tense vibes emanating from him off-putting, in addition to finding his conversation too serious.

He got through school virtually unnoticed, apart from the times he played the odd practical joke. He was not viewed as a swot, because he did not need to swot. He tried to keep a low profile and had already left the school when the A-level exam results confirming he would get the expected scholarship to Cambridge came out. By then he had grown quite tall, but remained thin rather than elegantly slim.

In freshers' week at Cambridge, he even found a Jewish girl with whom an intellectual and then a physical spark was lit. She was his first proper girlfriend, which meant things did not go according to plan the first time – she had to go fishing for the condom he left behind.

At the end of freshers' week, just when, for want of a better word, he thought he was getting into his stride, she decided he was not a suitable partner either socially or physically and ended the affair.

'You need more experience, but not with me,' she had cuttingly said.

Trying to recover from that put-down, he had consoled himself with the thought that the inevitable break-up would have been even more painful had the relationship been more established. He would be a hindrance for someone as socially ambitious as she. Indeed, why she had taken to him in the first place was something of a mystery. Perhaps it was because she too had been on unfamiliar territory.

From then on he put all his energies into his studies, getting a double first in pure mathematics and physics.

Such qualifications do not lead to a specific job and only proved he was capable of many things. With no idea of what he should do for a career that would have made his parents proud, he went to see a London-based head-hunter called James recommended by his tutor.

After they had talked for a while, the nattily dressed man with highly polished shoes reassured Holt, saying, 'With your qualifications, I would have no difficulty in *ultimately* placing you. You don't need to worry.'

'Really?' replied Holt. 'That's good to hear.'

'Yes. But – and it's a big but – you need to sort yourself out emotionally first. Otherwise, you won't settle anywhere and soon pack it in, leaving our client unhappy, not to mention yourself in a quandary and even depressed. Not only that, it would forever damage your prospects.'

'How do I, as you say, sort myself out? See a shrink?'

'No, that would do more harm than good. What you need is emotional experience – partly to make up for the loss of your parents. You need to interact with ordinary people, a wide range of people, in a relaxed setting. I don't mean sex, although one never knows. I sometimes think young people learn more in human terms dealing with clients in a restaurant than they do in some intern placement in a legal office gained through their parents' connections.'

'I don't feel like working as a waiter. Isn't there something more exciting I could do?'

'Yes. Have a gap year. Travel.'

Holt's eyes lit up at the idea. The last time he had fun on a foreign holiday was with the brigadier's family years back.

'I like the *idea*.'

'That's what I did,' continued James. 'Best thing I ever did.'

'I haven't...enough money – gap years are for rich kids.'

'Jeremy, I wasn't so rich. I got a job for a few months and saved up.'

'Um.'

'I tell you what. In view of your exceptional qualifications and in the hope that you stay on our books, our partnership will lend you ten thousand pounds, repayable in five years' time. If in the meantime you get jobs through us, we may well find our way to writing it off. Not a bad idea, eh?'

'A great one! I like it.'

They discussed the details and came to an informal agreement, whereupon James called Accounts to tell them to make out the cheque, ready for Holt to pick up on his way out.

'See you in ten months' or so time,' he said as they shook hands.

'Oh, by the way,' he added. 'Don't try to do too many countries. The main point is to meet people, get to know them – a rolling stone gathers no moss. That said, it's far easier to make real friends, even with English people, when abroad. There are fewer class barriers. Good luck!'

Not having a place of his own to worry about made going away simpler. A friend from Cambridge who had done a gap-year trip prior to university was more than glad to give him some advice, as talking about the trip brought back happy memories and delicious moments.

Taking his advice but not so sure of the fantastic moments, Holt decided to fly to India to see Delhi and the Taj Mahal, then take a boat to Singapore, from where he would take the train to Thailand.

Cambodia. Then California – being technically minded he wanted to see Silicon Valley –Washington and New York. He would take the consultant's advice not to overdo it, and leave out Hong Kong, Japan, and Australia.

He was surprised, on looking on the internet, just how much help and advice there was on gap years for people of all ages. One website, called gapadvice.org, had an invaluable gap-year planning check list. But like the friend who had advised him, he did not want to do a trip organized by others. Having adequate funds made doing it independently much easier and safer, as he could always stay at a good hotel should suitable backpacker accommodation be impossible to find.

It took him some six weeks to make the basic plan, get the necessary inoculations, and do and get the things on that check list. Once on the flight to Delhi, he sat back, expecting the next eight months or so to be plain sailing. He was soon to be in for a shock, one that would make him more wary thereafter.

He stayed at a reasonable mid-market hotel, so there was nothing of concern there, but when he came out of the American Express Bank in central Delhi after changing money, a kid threw some foul-smelling poo all over his shoes. Someone immediately came up to help him, but knowing that it was a trick to rob him, Holt pushed him away and escaped. He finally sought sanctuary in a nearby five-star hotel, thinking he could clean himself up there in comparative safety.

People looked at him in askance as he went into the washroom, some even putting their hand up to their nose, but no one stopped him, and he made it. The Sikh looking after the facilities offered to help clean him up. Feeling sorry for the poor guy, Holt gave him what in India would be an enormous tip and came out not smelling of roses, but not smelling bad enough for people to immediately distance themselves.

He decided a stiff drink was in order and made his way to the bar and sat at a table with no other guests in the immediate vicinity. However, he had hardly sat down when a mother and girl in her late teens, obviously American from the way they were speaking, installed themselves at the adjacent table. He hoped they could not smell him.

'Another couple of days and we'll be out of here,' said the girl.

Holt could not avoid hearing other snippets of conversation and finally could not resist intruding.

'Are you on holiday?' he asked.

'In theory, yes. In reality, we're just waking up from a nightmare.'

'How's that?'

'We wanted,' said the mother, 'to see the Taj Mahal and decided to stay what we thought would be merely a couple of nights at a nearby hotel. When we checked in, the receptionist asked us a number of questions, including whether we had health insurance. "Better to be safe. Some guests have been ill," he said.'

'Were you?' enquired Holt.

'Were we! The first night we were fine and went off early the next morning to see the Taj Mahal, which by the way was fantastic. We got back to the hotel, had a shower, and then dinner. Everything seemed fine. Then in the middle of the night my daughter had terrible stomach cramps and diarrhoea. She felt so terrible, she thought she was going to die, so I called the front desk, who said the hotel doctor would be with us shortly.'

'That was lucky,' said Holt.

'At the time we thought so.'

'What happened?'

'When the doc arrived, surprisingly quickly, he took one look at Sylvia and said it was so serious she would have to go to the clinic. She was rushed there in some kind of ambulance and remained there for ten days, most of the time on a drip.'

'God!'

'Although medical costs are nowhere near those back in the States, the bill was quite sizable, but they said it would be covered by the insurance. We're convinced it was a scam.'

Holt subsequently did some research and found that such cases were quite common. There were even instances of monkeys being trained to bite tourists when ordered, so that a complaisant doctor could order expensive anti-rabies treatment. In fact, the large number of such cases prompted the British High Commission, which is what the embassy is called in Commonwealth countries, to carry out an investigation, but no heads rolled, as the provincial governor's office had tenuous links with the perpetrators.

Holt returned to his lesser hotel a wiser man, hoping no one would notice the smell given off by his shoes.

He did a day trip to the Taj Mahal, which was truly magnificent, and after a couple more days in Delhi took the train to Mumbai. There he was to board a ship for the three-day voyage to Singapore, one of the safest and cleanest places in the world, because the government is so strict.

We won't bore the reader with the details of Holt's subsequent travel, as so many have done similar trips. Suffice to say, staying and eating at establishments ranging from stylish hotels to beachside cafés, in addition to talking to people on the beaches themselves, he did make many friends. Let it be said he did not fully participate in Thailand's full moon parties, as that was not his style.

Culturally it was enriching too. Not only was there Angkor Wat in Cambodia but also museums and art galleries in Washington and New York. On the technical side, he visited a couple of companies in Silicon Valley and the National Air and Space Museum in Washington.

When he returned to England, he was a much more rounded person. He had met girls he liked and where there was mutual attraction, but virtually all had boyfriends or partners in tow.

James, the head-hunter who had advanced the money for his fantastic trip, looked well pleased at the change in Holt and set him up in a job in IT for a securities company in the City.

'I know it is not the perfect job for you, Jeremy, but, like the gap year, it will give you experience of interfacing with people who will come in handy later. For someone of your talents, it will not be too demanding.'

Indeed, this proved to be the case, and Holt was beginning to think he needed to be doing something that stretched him more when James phoned him in the office to say he had some information he could not impart over the phone. Could he drop in on his way home after work?

'I have received a request,' said James, 'for someone with exceptional qualifications to dedicate him or herself to a special task that could save many lives.'

'Really,' interjected Holt, his interest piqued.

'I cannot give you details, as I do not even know them exactly myself. You are a rare bird, and although not many nests would suit you, this one well might, so I put your name forward. It's all very hush-hush, so I could not discuss it with you. I hope you don't mind.'

'Not at all,' replied Holt. 'In a way I'm happy enough where I am, but as you said, it is only meant to be a stepping stone.'

'They will probably contact shortly – they mentioned having to do some checks. Of course, they may well have other irons in the fire.'

Chapter 3
Your Profile Fits

A few days later Holt returned home from work to find a large manila envelope lying on his doormat. He scooped it up, went into the drawing room, placed it on the arm of the bargain-sale black leather sofa, and went into his tiny kitchen to make himself a coffee with his newly acquired machine. It had been an extravagance, but as he had no car, it was a luxury he felt he deserved.

Having taken a few quick sips, he took the coffee back into the drawing room, turned on some soft music, and sat down beside the expected – or rather, hoped-for – envelope. Once comfortably installed, he took the paperknife from the coffee table to slit it open and extract the contents.

There was a long application form and covering letter in it with STRICTLY CONFIDENTIAL stamped in red at the top. The letterhead was simply GIRAFFE, with no address.

The post-paid return envelope didn't have an address either, though it did have a reference number and the postcode W1Z 0XG.

Holt read the letter carefully, and then reread it.

Dear Holt,

We have been advised that your profile fits that required for a very special assignment we have in mind.

Should the prospect of pursuing an activity at which you are obviously gifted while potentially saving many lives appeal to you, please complete the attached forms and return them to us in the enclosed post-paid envelope.

Should all be in order, we will summon you to an exploratory interview, which you should not construe as meaning we will be able to pursue your candidature. Even an innocent relationship or a chance association could rule you out.

Regard this letter as confidential; mention it to no one, not even to a spouse, partner, or family member. Mere suspicion of such an indiscretion could result in undesirable consequences, both for you and even for them.

Dictated and unsigned – Giraffe

Though somewhat daunted by the probing questions and the need to provide numerous references, Holt for the first time in a long time felt a tinge of excitement.

Whom could he cite as a reference?

The brigadier would certainly be willing to provide him with one that would carry considerable weight. He was like a second father, even though they had not recently been in contact.

He had to scrape the bottom of the barrel for some of the other references, though the inclusion of that fleeting girlfriend from freshers' week at university, recently married to a highly successful lawyer – he had, to his surprise, been invited to their wedding – was a clever touch. She could vouch for his apolitical extracurricular activities and unimaginative bedroom style, which was of course why she left him.

On the Monday morning, he left home for work, clutching the envelope containing the completed application form. If he posted it in the box at Bank station near his office in the City, the letter would be delivered earlier than if he posted it out in the suburbs, possibly even that very afternoon.

After changing trains twice, he arrived at Bank, with its dangerously curved platform leaving considerable gaps at places, down which anyone could slip. Indeed, he had done so at another station when trying not to push up against the bottom of a lovely young woman who had dithered on stepping off the train. Fortunately someone caught hold of him, hauled him back up, and he did not slip too far down, though he had grazed his shin so badly that it took more than a year for the skin right on the bone to heal.

Coming out into the open air, he walked the few yards to the post box and slipped the manila envelope through the slit, noting that it had been narrowed to prevent introduction of an explosive device. On hearing the envelope drop irretrievably to the bottom, as there was little mail so early in the day, he told himself that even were he to get a positive reply, the interview would merely be exploratory. He would still be free to back out. But deep down he felt he already was on the first step of an escalator from which it would be difficult to alight halfway up – or rather, halfway down.

The summons to the exploratory interview not only came by return of post but set it for that very Saturday at 10 a.m. That did not leave much time for him to ruminate about what he might be getting into. Perhaps that was their technique: quench the iron while it was still hot; give him no time for second thoughts.

'No need for confirmation,' the letter had said. 'Should you fail to show, we will simply consider the matter closed.'

On the Saturday, he was up early and, after a long shower, prepared a breakfast consisting of scrambled egg, toast, and coffee. Whenever he made scrambled egg, Ian Fleming's 007 recipe would come to mind, though the only parts of the recipe he could really remember were the need to have lashings of butter and a thick-bottomed saucepan. On this particular day, it somehow seemed more appropriate than usual.

While munching away and sipping his coffee, he watched the morning news to catch up on current affairs. No point in getting stupidly caught out over a question on that. One advantage of not having a live-in girlfriend was that he would not have to lie about where he was going and risk her wary questions spoiling his mood.

Selecting the clothes to wear was not difficult, as he only had one snazzy suit – one that had seen better days. It was not that he couldn't afford a new suit, it was just that in his IT work one was expected to dress casually as a techie and not get people's backs up. It reminded him of a comment by a middle-aged-woman friend of his parents. Very brazen for someone with a husband and son-in-law in the Diplomatic Service, she had told them she had an excellent gardener, saying the best thing about him was that he knew his station.

The advantage of working in IT was that one did not have a 'station' and was all things to all people. The staff at his securities company knew his IT department had a program that would pick up on non-PC words in their emails and even detect any large expanses of bare skin on the images they viewed, and that he would usually have a word with them rather than denounce them to Human Resources.

Arriving at a graceful Georgian building in central London for the exploratory talk with five minutes to spare, he stepped into the high doorway to find an elderly caretaker looking at him through a sliding window.

'Mr Holt?'

'Yes.'

'Go right on up. Room 14. It's on the third floor. I'm afraid there's no lift.'

Holt was surprised the caretaker had not asked for some ID but then realized he must have a photo of him on his computer monitor, and had anyway been expecting him.

He mounted the stairs to the third floor with measured steps so as not to arrive like a panting labrador, taking sideways looks at the paintings and etchings adorning the walls. Though it was a Saturday, sounds emanating from some of the rooms indicated activity inside. What activity?

The doors all had digital locks with touchpads. That and the CCTV cameras probably explained why no one had accompanied him. Also, it was a Saturday, and maybe on weekdays they had someone more mobile than the caretaker to take visitors up the stairs. Overall, it was a spooky place. Possibly inhabited by spooks.

He paused for half a minute to gather his wits before knocking twice on the door to Room 14, making sure the knocks were sharp enough to suggest he was a confident young thing.

Instead of the expected 'Come in,' there was the sound of footsteps. The door opened.

18

'Jeremy Holt?'

'Yes.'

'I'm Major Bell. Glad you decided to drop in and have a word.'

The major had put him at his ease right away; perhaps too much at ease.

The sizable room had light streaming in through two large sash windows to create a very relaxing atmosphere. The high ceiling added to the feeling of traditional elegance.

The first thing that struck Holt about his interviewer was how well turned out he was, with a well-cut suit in a material that hung comfortably on his large frame. He looked fit, though his face showed he obviously managed to enjoy the good things in life. Holt guessed he was in his late forties.

In keeping with his relaxed style, the major said in a strong but gentle voice, 'Do sit down,' indicating a comfortable chair in front of a large wooden desk, behind which he went to sit, with his back to the window.

Holt tried to move into as comfortable a position as possible and adjust his jacket, which had ridden up. The green treetops visible behind the major for some reason reassured him.

'We told you this would be an exploratory interview, and so it shall be,' said the major on looking at Holt with an X-ray gaze, 'but to start with, I am afraid I shall be doing all the exploring. It will be recorded so that those for whom you might possibly be working, not to mention the security people – who have their noses everywhere these days – will be able to judge for themselves.'

He pressed a button on his desk.

'Interview with Holt, started at 10.10...'

Holt cleared his throat and thought he should at least say something.

'I don't know what I might be letting myself in for.'

'It is early days. You haven't let yourself in for anything yet. No point in worrying about the home stretch before getting to the first fence. We have to start by sussing you out, to use a phrase my children have recently latched on to. Are you ready?'

'I'm ready as I ever shall be.'

'Sorry, I forgot. Would you like a coffee or tea?'

'No, thanks, but I wouldn't mind a glass of water.'

The major pressed a button on his phone and asked for it to be brought. They chatted amiably until a middle-aged woman came in with a tall crystal glass and placed it, with a beermat underneath, on the desk just to Holt's left, as if already aware he was left-handed. Maybe she had simply checked the documents he had submitted and there was nothing sinister. The major did not speak until she had closed the door quietly behind her.

'I'll get straight to the point, Holt. The reason a certain department is interested in you is that your profile combines three talents: firstly, creativity, demonstrated by the practical jokes and so on you liked to play at school and university – don't let me ever hear you call it uni! Secondly, technical know-how. And thirdly, lateral thinking. And, of course, you have an extremely high IQ.'

'I see,' replied Holt, none too sure what it was that he could see.

'In a nutshell, how would you sum yourself up? How do you feel about yourself?'

Holt had not been expecting something so direct, knowing that job interviews sometimes start with the interviewer asking what it was about their organization that made the interviewee want to join, but of course in this case he did not even know what the organization was. He would have to be frank, even immodest. To hell with it – he had to say something.

'I lost much of my love for life when my parents died, and could not focus on anything in particular and decide on a career. I missed opportunities to do something serious on the science side. The trouble is, if you do not use your intelligence, you switch off and end up demotivated and lose it.

'Sometimes I think I would like to get away from it all, like a Swiss guy I met once on one of those small-size cargo ships that take a dozen or so passengers. One night there was a film show, and afterwards I casually asked him what he thought of it, and he came up with an unbelievably insightful analysis worthy of

20

Sigmund Freud. Found out he used his brilliant mind and knowledge of geology to help oil companies find oil but preferred the easy life on the boats, going from one place to another with no responsibilities. I felt a bit like him – too clever by half, as they say – and wondered whether I should do the same. No grief.'

'But whiling away your time on a boat is not really you, is it?'

'No.'

'We have heard about the pranks you played in your schooldays and were aware that your parents were tragically both killed in that terrible car crash, which might be a plus, as you will not have them prying into your affairs, though the psychiatrists might wonder whether that makes you damaged goods and make a meal of that.'

'I think I have fully recovered from their demise.'

'I would not be so sure. These things have a long-term effect. I know from having lost comrades in action. Anyway, psychiatry is not my domain, I'm glad to say. First, tell me about school. Anything that suggests you have initiative other than as regards playing practical jokes.'

'I can't think of anything special.'

'It does not have to be miraculous. Just think of something – I've got to have some nitty-gritty. Oh, sorry. I've been told by the PC brigade not to keep using that word. Fortunately, most of my work is covered by the Official Secrets Act, which means I cannot be taken to public tribunals by anyone pretending to have been offended. Anyway, forget I said it. Try to put some flesh on the bones of your submission – that actually sounds worse to me. You know what I mean. Tell me something that shows initiative. Imagination.'

'There is one thing that might be relevant. My holidays always got off to a bad start because end-of-term school reports were in alphabetical order, with art first, and art was my weakest subject. I might as well tell you, I can't draw for toffee and can't dance for nuts; can't play any musical instrument either. To get back to the point I was making, at the end of one term the art master wrote,

"Crude misery not worthy of further comment" on my report, sending my father up the wall.'

'If I had been your father, I would have thought it amusing,' commented the major. 'I was no good at art either, though for a military career I at least had to be able to draw plans of battlefields and so on.'

'Anyway, I realized I had to do something. I knew the master was not really interested in the untalented like me and based his reports on coursework. I therefore bribed the most talented boy in the class to draw – or rather, paint – a picture of a yacht in my art book. Yachts fascinated me at the time, and it would at least enable me to dream about them in class.

'While not quite a Turner, my friend's oeuvre was something of a masterpiece. My father was incredulous when he saw the first page of my next school report, though subsequent art reports became less and less complimentary, as I defaced the yacht by daubing vulgar colours on it in class while pretending to paint.'

'Does show initiative. Actually, someone told us about that too.'

'The whole class knew about it. I wonder which of them told you.'

'Need not have been one of them. They might have mentioned it at home in the presence of their parents, or even in the presence of a brother or sister, don't you think? Maybe the art master was not as naïve as you thought. In this business, you should never jump to the most obvious conclusions.'

'Yes, I see your point.'

'Anything else school-wise that I can put down in my notes?'

Well, my father's mania for academic perfection meant that any spelling or grammatical mistakes in my letters home were seized upon. I solved that problem when much younger in a very similar way.'

'How's that?'

'With some help from a kindly master, I created a perfect template letter along the lines "Thank you for the cake/biscuits. The weather is cold/hot/rainy/inclement. I am slightly indisposed but expect to be better soon. Hope you are well despite both of you being so busy."

'By busy, I was really thinking they were too busy for me. Failing to find a mistake, my father would become quite irritated, asking whether I might deign to send some real news. I overcame that problem quite simply by saying the letters were censored. One could not be too careful, I said.'

'Not bad, not bad at all. Again, shows initiative. What about girlfriends? No one has suggested you were gay – admittedly, that is not meant to be an impediment nowadays, as one can no longer be blackmailed for that, and in some people's eyes it is something of which to be proud. What are your relations with women? How do you get on with them?'

'To be honest, I am a bit shy – or rather, too hesitant. In my present IT work, I admit I give the more beautiful of the females more help with their computers than I do their homely colleagues, but I only tease them, without taking things further. I lack confidence, perhaps due to lack of experience. Girls were a mystery to me, never having had a sister.'

'Neither did I, but I managed to cope. I went out with the boys to look for complaisant girls. As we were tall, fit lads, they would swarm all over us.'

'I had no such luck. In my case, the best relationship I ever had was with a fantastic girl at university. It lasted only a week. Took me a long time to get over it – not that I ever did. Besides being unbelievably beautiful, she was too rich for me, moved in different circles. Even so, we remained friends. She was even willing to let me use her as a reference to submit to you people.'

'Actually, the young woman – we checked her out – was rather complimentary about you. Seems she still has a soft spot for you.'

Holt could not believe he was getting carried away, being so frank. The major seemed to be able to make one say things one would not even tell a best friend. Perhaps not even a psychiatrist. The major would pause, making you want to fill in the details. He should have been more careful.

'What's the situation now?'

'At the moment, I have an on-and-off girlfriend. More off than on, to tell the truth. Knowing that it will not go anywhere, I feel my hands are tied behind my back. How I envy Italian men, living for the moment and able to put everything they have got into a relationship as if truly in love, even though it might be just a fling. I think ahead too much, imagining it's over before it has even properly started.'

'You sound an honourable chap. Not many people like you.'

After further probing and exploration of other less sensitive pastures, with Holt able to give non-incriminating explanations for youthful indiscretions, the nature of the interview suddenly switched, indicating he had perhaps got over the first hurdle – or rather, fence.

'Have you ever thought you would like to work for the secret service?'

Holt did not answer immediately. In fact, he did not know quite what to say. While it seemed the major was asking about his present state of mind, he decided to answer as if the question concerned the past.

'Not seriously. Like all boys and perhaps some girls, I did dream of becoming an astronaut or airline pilot but knew my eyesight was not good enough. Of course, every time I came out of the cinema after watching a James Bond film I dreamt I was him, but the mental swagger only lasted about five minutes.'

'The secret world is not for everyone. Young people, especially females, cannot bear giving up gossiping with outsiders about their work and colleagues.'

More related questions were to follow.

The major then remained silent for a full couple of minutes, looking through his notes. Finally, he looked up and changed tack again.

'Have you any particular views regarding terrorist attacks?'

'It is difficult to generalise.'

'I mean 9/11, the IRA bombings, and the 7/7 bomb attacks on London's transport system, which resulted in fifty-five people dead and over a thousand injured, more or less seriously.'

Here at last was a subject about which Holt had long-held heartfelt views. Although not a wannabe terrorist, he felt on home ground.

'Apart from the terrorists responsible for 9/11 and a few other attacks, the perpetrators have usually been inept. I could have done much better myself were I so inclined. Sometimes I wonder what fun it would be outwitting the often stupid authorities. Sorry…I didn't—'

'So you think you could do better than the terrorists?'

'I mean, those are just thoughts, ramblings if you like, not things I would ever consider actually putting into action. I don't have a religious – or, for that matter, any other – axe to grind.'

Had he overstepped the mark and ruined his chances of being accepted for whatever the task was? Not that he was quite sure he wanted to be accepted.

'I think,' said the major, with his face breaking into a smile, 'we can wrap this up for now. We cannot go any further without an official nod. You'll be hearing from them in due course, though I should perhaps warn you that "due course" may mean quite a long time. Many things have to be checked, and we do have some other irons in the fire, though I must say I am impressed with you. But then I am not the arbiter. Meanwhile, keep all this under your hat.'

The major stood up to signify the exploratory interview was over, but instead of dismissing Holt there and then, he accompanied him down the stairs to the entrance to the building, where they shook hands as the old caretaker looked on approvingly. With that, a slightly shell-shocked Holt stepped out into the tree-filled square and took a deep breath, before heading for one of the pubs he had passed an hour earlier.

The interview had gone more easily than he had anticipated. True, it had been one-way, like dinner a couple of weeks earlier with that divorcee with two young children. Hunting for a partner with prospects that Holt could not pretend to match, she had been unwilling to give anything, and certainly not herself, away.

The major had not given anything away either, other than that the work had something to do with terrorists.

The time between Giraffe's first letter and the exploratory interview had been so short that the silence that ensued seemed interminable. With seven weeks having gone by with not a word, Holt was getting twitchy, notwithstanding the major's warning that the vetting would take time.

Another reason for his nervousness was that the longer he waited, the more doubtful he became about the whole enterprise. His profile might be just right for *them*, but would their profile be right for him? What did they want him to do? How would he fit into an environment with surely many constraints? Would it be exciting, or even dangerous? Added to that, he got the impression someone was watching him. Not all the time, but on odd occasions. Was he getting paranoid?

Chapter 4
Cut-Glass and Sir Charles

Needing a break and some fresh air, he decided to accept the brigadier's long-standing invitation to visit him at his new residence in Hampshire, where he had moved on retiring. He might even learn whether the security people had questioned him. The retired officer was the star reference on his list, and if anyone were to be interviewed it would be he.

The brigadier himself answered the phone and sounded delighted at the prospect of Holt's visit. Samantha, his daughter, was coming down for the weekend, and it would be good for her to have some younger company, and especially someone from the good old days. Holt had an odd feeling at the thought of the daughter being there. The goddess he worshipped from afar.

Not wanting to trouble his hosts and, more importantly, preferring to meet them for the first time in years in the comfort of their home rather than at a draughty railway station, he took a taxi. The quaint village where the brigadier and his wife lived, and the house itself for that matter, made him think of the oddly named *Midsomer Murders* TV series, though he was not expecting anything as dramatic as murder to happen during his visit. It was the old England – reassuring. Comfortable and comforting. Just what he needed. There was a wooden plaque on the brigadier's gate with the name 'Goose Green'. Holt knew from his parents that was where he won his DSO medal for gallantry in the Falklands War.

He pressed the doorbell, feeling he was stepping back in time, for this was the family he had frequented in his impressionable preteens and early teens, when his parents were still alive. The door opened to reveal Samantha, their daughter – she too had been a teenager then. Here she was, a woman, albeit a young one.

'Hello, Jeremy. Great to see you,' she said, holding Holt's hand longer than perhaps necessary.

'Mum, Dad, he's here!' she called out in a loud voice.

Mother and father arrived from different directions and welcomed him effusively, with Emma, the mother, giving him a hugging kiss. Holt had not seen them for some eight years and thought they looked considerably older than he remembered. The brigadier still looked imposing, a tall figure with a square jaw – Holt had read how an analysis of graduation photos of cadets at West Point, the US military academy, showed that the ones with the squarest jaws tended to become the generals.

Emma, whose strong and engaging personality had doubtless been a great help to her husband in his army career, showed Holt around the house, and although he was not staying for the night, indicated a bedroom with an en suite bathroom he could use.

The house consisted of two semidetached thatched bungalows fused into one, with three low-ceilinged bedrooms squeezed on to the second floor. Thus it was elongated, with views onto the large garden from almost every room. It certainly was a very comfy place, though Holt would have preferred larger windows.

Looking out, he commented on the size of the lawn.

'Must be a lot of work to keep it looking so good. It's so large.'

'Don't tell me that! We had to buy a motor mower – one of those you sit on. My dear husband put a pennant on it so it would feel like he was driving an armoured vehicle into battle. You see how the lawn rises steeply at the bottom. One day he drove across right at the bottom there – the side slope was such that it toppled over. To think how silly it would be to survive a war and stupidly get killed like that. Luckily, the mower did not land right on top of him. Don't tell him I told you.'

Holt promised and went to his allotted room to spruce himself up, while she went down to the kitchen to join Samantha, already at work preparing the meal. After washing his face, Holt felt much better, even relaxed.

In the event, mother and daughter produced a great lunch, and, with the help of a couple of bottles of good wine on top of the pre-lunch whiskies, things were going swimmingly. Samantha, with the passage of time, seemed so much more mellow and approachable – not that she had ever put him down or purposely ignored his presence, like many girls of her age did. Their difference in age – a year – had seemed so much when he was a shy thirteen.

After the coffees in the drawing room, the brigadier took Holt's arm and led him out to the garden for a private chat.

'Thank you, sir, for letting me put your name forward as a reference,' said Holt, reverting to the way he spoke to the neighbour his parents called the 'brig' but insisted he be polite to and call 'sir'.

'Think nothing of it,' replied the brigadier.

'I had to provide five others as well, but I am sure yours carried the most weight. It may not come to anything. To tell the truth, I don't know anything much about the job yet.'

'It must be,' said the brigadier with a wry smile, 'something quite special to require so many references.'

The raising of the brigadier's eyebrows convinced Holt that he knew more than he was letting on. He was part of the establishment and, with medals for gallantry, could be relied on, which was more than could be said for some of the other characters Holt had asked to provide references. However, the brigadier did not allow him to pursue the matter.

'Let's get back and rejoin the ladies; not that I see my daughter as a lady. I am hoping she will eventually end up with a more suitable partner and become one. Pity you were much too young for her. You at least are a good egg, unlike that good-for-nothing she is drooling after.'

His wife was on the terrace, catching up with her daughter's latest news – impossible in the brigadier's presence, as he could not bear to hear the boyfriend's name or anything concerning life with him mentioned. How could his daughter, who had been daddy's girl, become beholden to someone like that scumbag?

With the return of the two men, the conversation immediately switched to the old days, when they were neighbours, before the fatal car crash. When the mother asked Holt about his plans for the future, Holt wondered whether the brigadier had let something slip, but before he could come up with some noncommittal answer, the brigadier stepped in.

'Jeremy has just told me he is applying for a new job in research but is not sure yet what is involved.'

This half-truth neatly forestalled further questions, and the conversation moved on to other topics. Holt was surprised how open they were, treating him as family, which was fortunate, for if he did join Giraffe, the brigadier might be the only confidant he could keep without raising suspicions.

After afternoon tea, Holt bade them farewell and gladly accepted Samantha's offer to drive him to the station, seven minutes away by car.

He wished it had been ten times as far but was compensated on arrival by her kissing him on the forehead and saying, 'It was nice having you as neighbour. I wish we had got to know each other better…I am not so uptight these days!'

Deeply touched by the kiss and a trifle saddened by the thought of her at a time when his parents were alive, Holt fought to regain his composure as he waved her goodbye. Again he realized too late that he should have made more of a relationship; not that it could ever have blossomed into anything serious, but he could have done with a friend like that at that difficult time.

All in all it had been a good day, and he returned to London quite refreshed, and, judging from the brigadier's reactions, wheels were in motion.

Indeed they were, for a few days later, on returning home he heard his landline phone ringing as he was standing at the front door, fumbling with his keys. Having got the door open, he dumped his stuff, dashed for the phone, and managed to answer it before the other party rang off.

'Mr Holt. Jeremy Holt?'

'Yes.'

A cut-glass female voice proceeded to ask him for private details, as if it were his bank or credit card company checking on his identity before imparting any information. Since the voice was far too superior for that, he assumed it was Giraffe but wanted to show he was streetwise.

'I am not in the habit, madam, of revealing personal details without first ascertaining the identity of the individual soliciting them. Might I ask whom I am addressing?'

'It's Giraffe.'

'Big Bird on the line. A chirpy evening to you.'

'Not funny, not funny at all.'

Made to feel rather silly, Holt apologized before furnishing the required details.

'You remember the major?'

'Of course...How could I not?'

'He opines that you need a decent suit and has graciously arranged for you to have one made at our tailor's. It will remain your property, even should you ultimately not...er, become one of us.'

Holt could feel the heightened disdain in her voice following his childish joke. She had seemed to choke at the very thought that he could become one of them.

'It wasn't *that* bad. The suit, I mean,' he replied, disappointed that his best suit had failed to 'cut the mustard', as the major might say.

'The major surprisingly took a shine to you and would be most hurt should you fail to take up his more than generous offer.'

'Yes, it would be churlish to decline. Tell him I'm most grateful and would be more than glad to accept,' said Holt, unconsciously parroting the woman's way of speaking and ending up sounding like an incongruous imitation of her, and with a male voice to boot.

Was this Giraffe's way of letting failed candidates down with no hard feelings? Was it all over even before the second fence and just as he was beginning to believe he was embarking on something exciting? His heart sank.

'Symes, our tailor, is located in Sackville Street. It's a quiet side street on the right as you walk from Piccadilly Circus along Piccadilly towards Bond Street. Just before you come to Fortnum & Mason on the other side. I presume you *have* heard of them?'

'I used to have high tea there with my grandmother once a month as a child.' It was a blatant lie, but stuck-up tight-arse needed taking down a peg.

The slight pause that followed indicated he had at last scored a point and perhaps gained a modicum of respect.

'Be that as it may,' she huffed, 'it's at number forty-five. Be there at six thirty tomorrow evening prompt. You cannot miss it. Have you got that?'

'Yes, number forty-five, Sackville Street. Symes, six thirty.'

'Correct. Allow plenty of time, as measuring you and choosing the material can be time-consuming. They may have to put you on the back burner if they have someone of importance there. I am sure you understand.'

Forced to grovel, Holt confirmed he fully understood.

Having thereby scored a final point, Cut-Glass rang off without asking whether the time was convenient. She had sounded like the headmaster's secretary calling him to his study for a telling off or worse.

Consequently, the following evening he arrived outside Symes much too early and to kill time ordered a coffee at the tiny delicatessen across the street. Sitting outside at one of the three tables, he watched the goings-on, or lack thereof, in the street, which was surprisingly quiet for one just off the main thoroughfare of Piccadilly, with its constant stream of buses, taxis, and other vehicles. Apart from the odd car, van, or taxi taking a short cut, there was the occasional pedestrian. Those looking lost were probably tourists seeking the Royal Academy, slightly further on along Piccadilly, where they were holding one of their special exhibitions.

The tailoring establishment looked just what it was purported to be and, judging by the amount of wear on the brass nameplate outside, had either been in existence for many years or had an overzealous polisher – probably both. Looking more closely, Holt could see an array of CCTV cameras covering not only the entrance but also the street. Realizing that one was pointing directly at him, he shifted uneasily in his seat, trying to adopt a suave, sophisticated air as he preened like he had seen actors do when savouring coffee in TV commercials.

Just before six thirty, a tall, smartly dressed gentleman came out from number 45 and stepped into the street. He clutched a fold-over bag for carrying suits as his long legs carried him elegantly towards Piccadilly.

At 6.31 precisely, Holt got up and, conscious of his relatively short legs, walked across the street with what he considered was a confident, nonchalant gait, for the benefit of the CCTV camera. For some reason, he found himself thinking how Britain's most accomplished official hangman, Albert Pierrepoint, who had executed at least four hundred people by the time he resigned in 1956, used to peep into the condemned man's or even woman's cell to assess the amount of rope required for optimum results. Was the tailor likewise covertly sizing up his subjects, or were the cameras for a more sinister purpose?

There were four bell pushes of a modern design out of keeping with the traditional brass nameplate. The top three had Christian names beside them – Jennifer, Tim, and Hugh – and it would have all seemed very innocent had it not been for the CCTV cameras. Holt pressed the bottom one, marked 'Symes'.

On hearing a loud click, he pushed open the heavier-than-expected door and stepped inside to find yet another door. He tried to open the second one but found that only became possible once the outer door had snapped shut behind him. Inside was a long, narrow hall with a straight staircase on the left, a long hallway going to the back alongside it to the right, and a door with a glass window marked 'Symes & Co.' in black letters on his immediate right.

Just as he was about to push the door, a hairy hand appeared on the other side and pulled it open for him. The hand belonged to a portly fiftyish man in shirtsleeves, who, from the tape measure slung round his neck, was obviously the tailor.

'Mr Holt? Welcome to Symes. We'll see what we can do for you. The major said you needed something snappy yet elegant.'

Evidently, he had learnt not to ask clients too many questions – indeed, no personal questions other than to confirm their name.

An assistant, possibly an apprentice, wearing a smart suit much too smart for someone barely twenty, stepped up to relieve Holt of his jacket with unmerited deference, considering the lowly object was the reason Holt was there in the first place.

Once measured in the usual places, one slightly embarrassing, Holt was escorted to the shelves along the right-hand wall of the establishment to choose the fabric. Taken aback by the wide choice, with some of the gaudier material more appropriate for pop stars, he was glad to follow the avuncular tailor's advice to go for one of the high-class ones with a woollen feel, favoured by the major. The tailor picked up a bolt of darkish blue cloth with a few highlights.

'This one would be ideal. It is informal enough for trendy receptions yet would not be out of place at a cabinet meeting.'

'I'm sure that would be fine – though I don't expect I will ever attend a cabinet meeting.'

'One never knows. If it's not a cabinet meeting, it might be a reception in the presence of the Her Majesty or the president of the United States – that is to say, in a professional capacity, with no food or alcohol, with only your suit to make you feel you are worth something!'

As soon as the words were out of his mouth, the tailor looked embarrassed, as if he had said too much and had better stick to tailoring.

'Of course, I was only joking. We'll let you know when to come back for a fitting – say in about ten days. We have your number.'

Having been reunited with his own jacket, of which he was beginning to feel extremely ashamed, Holt was gravitating towards the exit at the front of the shop when the young assistant grabbed his arm.

'No. It's this way!'

He was redirected back to the rear of the shop, where a tall woman with ramrod legs and a generous bottom ensconced in a tight skirt had suddenly appeared. Her haute couture ensemble followed her contours without revealing too much, yet just enough.

From her voice, Holt knew she was Cut-Glass, the uptight dragon he had fallen out with on the phone. In the flesh, she made him feel even more insignificant as she looked him up and down, her eyes settling on his suit, the sight of which made her raise her eyebrows at the tailor's assistant as if it, and the person wearing it, were something the cat had dragged in. She was the mistress of put-downs.

She led the deflated Holt out of the rear door and up the carpeted stairs, past the first floor, and then up again to the second, where the ceilings were much lower. She knocked on the door of the first room, pushed it open, and stood back to allow him to go in, saying, 'Major Bell would like a few words with you.'

The major was standing in the middle of the room, smiling.

'Hello, Holt. Glad you made it to the home straight. Don't feel committed. It's your life. Your future.'

'Thanks for the advice. I'll keep it in mind.'

'Hope you will be happy with the suit.'

'I'm sure I shall, Major. It's most kind of you.'

'Don't thank me. It was a good excuse to get you here without a lot of palaver and should come in handy if you come to work for our lot. A great suit gives one a lift – like travelling first class or, these days, business class. Of course, a military uniform with several pips would be even better, but we cannot go that far yet, can we, Jeremy?'

'I hope I can live up to it.'

'I'm sure you shall. It has been a pleasure making your acquaintance. Since I may never see you again, I wanted to take this opportunity to wish you all the best, whatever becomes of you.'

The idea of never being seen again was troubling, but before Holt could give it any further thought, Cut-Glass reappeared and indicated that he should proceed in front of her down the stairs to the lower landing.

'Wait here,' she ordered brusquely, before knocking at a door marked 'Private'. A sharp-looking man in a dark suit opened it, and they exchanged a few whispered words, whereupon she led him to another door, at the end of the passage.

'Wait in there. It's all we have free at the moment. I'm afraid it's not very comfortable.'

That was an understatement.

Virtually a broom cupboard, probably not unlike the one at nearby Nobu, the Japanese restaurant where tennis great Boris Becker had a brief fling with a young woman that cost him a fortune in child maintenance. Holt smiled to himself, thinking that unlike Becker he was being softened up. Unfortunately, all the secrecy meant it was a joke he would never be able to tell. It was only much later that Holt learnt that Becker's tryst had been in a stairwell and not a broom cupboard.

As if that were not enough, Cut-Glass soon returned to soften him up even further with yet another of her put-downs.

'A VIP was here. It was better they were not seen by commoners.'

Deflated, he allowed her to lead him back to the door to which they had earlier been refused entry. The man in the dark suit was this time seated inside at a desk at right angles to another door.

'Go straight on in,' he said with a nod.

Cut-Glass nevertheless gave a quick knock to announce their entry and introduced Holt to a tall, wiry man standing beside a large desk.

'Sir Charles, this is Jeremy Holt.'

'Ah yes. Good. Bring him in.'

'We had to *paaark* him in the boxroom until X vacated the building.'

'Thank you, Sandra.'

'Cut-Glass withdrew discreetly, leaving him in the presence of the person she had called Sir Charles, who had the style and class – not to mention the cool steeliness – of those who rise to the top of the civil service and judiciary. He seemed to be quizzically sizing Holt up.

'Holt. Not a bad name. Short, like Bond, but are you aware that Holt was the name of an attractive boy associated with the notorious Kray twins, who terrorized East London? The boy – or rather, young man – used to visit the late Lord Boothby's flat in Eaton Square, offering sexual services. There were security implications, as a certain Tom Driberg was associating with them. He almost certainly passed on information to the Russians.'

'No, I didn't know that. There must be some good Holts.'

'You're right. I believe the sportswriter for one of our popular daily papers is called Holt. He writes well, by the way, so do not let the Kray association get you down.'

'I'll google my name when I get back home…'

'Do that. One day you yourself may come up in a search, though in our business we prefer it not to come up at all, unless it is a cover role, such as a second secretary at an embassy.'

'Yes…but…'

'You must be wondering what this is all about, though you must have some inkling, in view of the questions the major posed, to which, by the way, you furnished highly satisfactory answers.'

'I hope I did not give the impression that I was a potential terrorist.'

'If you were, you would not have been so outspoken.'

Holt merely nodded. He wanted to avoid making some trite remark that would lower him in the great man's esteem.

'Sorry for having to confine you in the boxroom. My PA can be somewhat daunting on first acquaintance, but I can assure you she is quite accommodating underneath – that is, when you get to know her properly.'

Not sure how to take that remark and wondering whether he was still being tested, Holt chose the safe middle ground.

'I doubt whether I shall ever have the pleasure of finding out what's underneath.'

The astute answer apparently reassured Sir Charles that he was dealing with someone with his wits about him, for he immediately got down to business.

'Ever since 7/7 we have tried to find ways to prevent such events from reoccurring in Britain, and particularly here in London. We have used the services of various expensive consultants in addition to our own people at Five, which is what we call MI5, and at Six – that's MI6 – Special Branch, and in the other departments, but we still feel vulnerable. One well-known consultant maintains we will always be behind the curve, as we are always reacting to the last incident.'

'I can see that,' interjected Holt inanely. He had to at least say something.

'After 9/11, the accent was on flying schools. After the shoe-bomber incident, everyone was having their shoes checked. After the plot to make bombs by mixing seemingly innocuous liquids actually on the aircraft, everyone had their toothpaste confiscated if it was more than 100 cc. All this, the expert said, was ridiculous, as terrorists would always think of something else. Anyway, replicating 9/11 should be impossible now passengers know they risk becoming flying bombs and would not comply with terrorists' instructions, so why waste so much time on scenarios like that, he had said?'

Sir Charles paused and looked at Holt intently, before continuing: 'This special unit, Giraffe, was set up by me as a wild card operation to think outside the box. Of course, the departments I have just mentioned are all working on the problem and coming up with suggestions. However, they all have vested interests – by that I mean that their routine work and formal links tend to make them fixate on certain types of scenario. On the other hand, we who are in a way halfway between Five and Six – and that hopefully includes you – are free from those hang-ups.'

Was Sir Charles taking him for granted, or was it a well-honed technique to make him feel committed by letting him participate in the discussion as if he might already be one of them?

'We think you are a rare bird and want you to put yourself in the terrorists' shoes, thinking up outlandish scenarios they might use. You would be operating independently, with support from us, and reporting directly to me, though you would have a nominal boss with whom you would deal on a daily basis.

'We have special authority allowing us to seek the necessary cooperation from the other security departments. Even so, we must maintain Chinese walls. You could be a great asset.'

'Possibly,' replied Holt, glad that he was not expected to do anything particularly dangerous.

'How do you feel about it?'

'That type of work,' replied Holt, 'requires freedom coupled with the stimulus from others. One might be looking for merely a couple of great ideas. Thousands of people must already be doing likewise. How would I be any different?'

'You, Holt, would be different because of who you are, the great degree of independence you will be afforded, the resources at your disposal, and, not least, the conducive environment we will provide. Think of yourself as being part of an elite team and yet working as an individual, at times independently.'

'What would it mean in practice?'

Here in London, you would be working out of Giraffe's Farringdon bureau, though of course you would spend much of your time on your own outside, sometimes just wandering the streets and visiting notable places. Admittedly, it would be difficult to better – to use an unfortunate word – 9/11. The Twin Towers were the perfect target, and there are not so many like that.'

Not knowing why he chose that moment, Holt asked a question that had been nagging him right from the outset.

'Giraffe is an odd name. Why...?'

'I ostensibly chose the name Giraffe to convey the idea that we could see over the walls that bounded the more formal departments and agencies. In reality, it was to make them subconsciously feel inferior by virtue of having to look up to us and, incidentally, make our people feel superior by virtue of looking down on them. Don't quote me on that. If you do, your life won't be worth living.'

Here, for the first time in his life, was someone for whom Holt felt he could happily work. Sir Charles had sensed this, for he continued without using the conditional, as if Holt's commitment to Giraffe were a done deal, which in turn meant Holt began falling under his spell; as a father figure, he outclassed his late father, who was no slouch.

Sir Charles quickly brought him back to reality.

'Some basic training is required to ensure you are physically fit and able to cope with difficult situations – not that we expect you to encounter any in your back-office role. Might come in useful, though, if someone tries to mug you for your mobile phone! Actually, the real point of it is to help you think on your feet. Reactions do not always have to be physical, but physical fitness helps one cope mentally.'

'It sounds reasonable to me.'

'Let me make one thing clear: while I do not want you to withhold anything you think terrorists might come up with, I want you to concentrate on dramatic scenarios, ranging from large-scale ones, like 9/11, to small-scale ones, since the impact on the public can be great in either case. The recent beheadings are an unfortunate example of the latter.'

'What about the lone gunman trying to shoot the prime minister or the Queen on some special occasion, like Lee Harvey Oswald at Dallas?'

'Other departments' special units, such as the SAS and the SRR – that's the even more secretive Special Reconnaissance Regiment – with actual theatre experience in Iraq and Afghanistan are already dealing with attacks such as might occur on great national occasions, royal weddings, state funerals, or coronations. Not that we expect a coronation anytime soon.'

'I understand, but what about biological or nuclear threats?'

'Pre-empting them through good intelligence, detection equipment at ports, and so on is how we try and deal with that. We have people specializing in that. Handling any incidents that do occur is essential as well.'

'Put yourself in the bad people's shoes. Be an angry young man. Think like you did at school when you came up with those silly jokes.'

'But they were just for fun.'

'It's fun for some of those people.'

Sir Charles, like the major, then went through the ritual of warning Holt about the negatives involved in working in the secret world. He would no longer be able to be frank with people, not even with his closest friends, family, or partners, and so on and so on.

'It can produce a feeling of isolation and even exacerbate latent psychological problems. We do have our house psychiatrist, but the time he can allot to each individual is limited, especially as he has to prepare officers for physically dangerous, rather than technical, missions like yours. For your job, we need a neurotic with hang-ups. We put a lot of effort into finding you. I am not sure Blackwell, the in-house psychiatrist, will take to someone of your ilk!'

'I am not sure I will take to him either, by the sound of it. I have heard some bad stories about psychiatrists.'

'Then I suggest you steer clear of him, though he has to interview everyone for the record. A kind of health and safety thing – he's a general practitioner as well as a psychiatrist.'

'Thanks for warning me. Sounds as if you think I might well be joining Giraffe.'

'I very much hope you do, but only if your heart is in it. You won't be much use otherwise. Do you really want to join us? Though I have stressed the negatives, there would be many pluses.'

From having repeatedly watched *The Caine Mutiny*, the film where the young ensign on his first posting has to choose between staying on his clapped-out minesweeper or accepting an easy ride on the admiral's staff on a battleship or aircraft carrier, Holt knew that a good officer should be able to make major decisions under pressure. Asking Sir Charles for time to consider would risk falling in his esteem. He decided to take the bull by the horns.

'It sounds,' he said unhesitatingly, 'as though I might finally have found a way to use my talents productively. Yes, I would very much like to join Giraffe. I think I could make a worthwhile contribution.'

'Good. I expected you would ask for time to think it over but am impressed to see you can think on your feet. Congratulations. Welcome to Giraffe!'

Sir Charles got up from behind his desk, walked round to Holt, and shook his hand, smiling broadly.

Holt felt a page in his life had, for better or worse, been turned.

'What's the next step?' he asked.

'You will nominally be in the hands of Peter at our Farringdon operating unit. Don't ask him for personal details, his family name, or whether he's married with children. Do not ask any of them, or me, personal questions. Besides security, that policy has some incidental advantages, not least eliminating time-wasting gossip, though our female agents don't see it in that light. Some valuable women leave the service for that reason alone.'

He pressed a button on his desk, and within a couple of minutes there was a knock at the door, and Cut-Glass came in with a sheaf of papers.

'Sandra, Jeremy is to become one of us.'

Hardly disguising the effort required, Cut-Glass proffered her congratulations, without demeaning herself by adding a platitude about how great it would be working together.

She handed him the documents. The Official Secrets Act was on top.

Chapter 5
Not so Black and White

Someone must have had had a word in his employer's ear, for Holt was not required to give the usual one month's notice. Admittedly, in brokerages and the like it was customary for anyone leaving to drop tools immediately and be escorted from the building to prevent them taking valuable information, such as client lists, with them.

Even though it was short notice, the company arranged a farewell party for him, at which a number of the female employees, young and not so young, said they would sorely miss him, and Holt knew he would feel likewise, realizing he had crassly missed some open goals. Truth be told, he hadn't scored at all and had made only a few attempts at goal, whereupon others had headed in the ball.

The drawback so many had mentioned of working for the service immediately became apparent when he realized he could only give his erstwhile colleagues the vaguest idea of what he would be doing. 'I've been told it's what I make of it,' was a good way to halt speculation. Anyway, he was glad to be leaving with the thought that some would miss him. That said, not a few had reason to be grateful for his discretion, as working in IT, he knew many of their secrets.

Holt only had the weekend before assuming his new position. He would have liked to have asked for a week off to shoot off to some sunny place to recharge his batteries but had not dared ask.

Farringdon, not far from the City, was not a part of London that he usually frequented, other than going to the odd restaurant, and as he made his way to Giraffe from the station he was surprised at the number of architects' and interior designers' offices he passed. The Giraffe bureau looked like just another one, which was particularly good cover, as no one would be surprised to see models of central London used to study potential terrorist attacks.

Quite unlike Cut-Glass back at Sackville Street, the receptionist was in her mid-thirties and oozed smiles. Even before Holt had slithered to a halt on the shiny white flooring befitting a trendy architect's office, she had already spouted 'Jeremy to see Peter. Am I correct?'

'Yes, that's right. I think Peter is expecting me.'

'I'll let him know. Please wait over there,' she said, pointing in the direction of a row of uncomfortable trendy sofas off to her right.

He was still taking stock of his surroundings when the lift doors opened and out came a slim man with deep-set eyes. He must have been in his late forties, but he looked somewhat worn.

'I'm Peter. I'm afraid I'm in the middle of a meeting right now, so I'll just show you to your office, where you can relax. We'll leave the introductions for later. Something big has just come up. Not in the James Bond sense unfortunately, so I'll have to get right back and stuck in.'

'Sounds exciting.'

'I wish it were. To be truthful, this business is something like being an airline pilot – looks glamorous but actually involves days of routine and then the occasional mad crisis.'

He showed Holt to his allotted office, which would, on Sir Charles's orders, be his inviolable domain, except when the security people visited.

'You're a lucky man, Jeremy. Sir Charles insisted you have your own room. Most of us here have to make do with shared facilities. Some will be envious, so assuage their feelings by saying you have special confidential documents that must always be at your fingertips.'

'I'll do my best.'

'Acquaint yourself with the computer, which should be easy considering your IT background. I should be through in an hour, and we'll go for lunch. Dial one-nine-nine on the phone if you need a pee.'

Holt held out until they got to the pub, for having someone, possibly female, show him the way and standing outside would have been just too embarrassing.

Lunch was a typical one for a London pub – neither good nor bad. Conversation, limited to generalities unconnected with work, was pleasant enough. On their way back to Giraffe, with other people out of earshot, Peter opened up a little and talked about the office in general terms. He could have been describing any London office, so he was not giving anything away. He would be introducing Holt to the others. His meeting with Celia, who would be his partner when needed, would have to wait until the next day, as she was accompanying a VIP to some function.

'Sir Charles and I recruited her not only for her intelligence and probity but also for her what can only be described as guileless, virginal looks. When necessary, she will facilitate your reconnoitring by slipping into the role of girlfriend and, should circumstances demand, blushing bride.'

'You're having me on.'

'Quite the contrary. She will be useful even in the UK, to stop you getting picked up by the plods when taking photos. Of course, we can always get you released from police custody with a phone call from on high, but the less we have to do with the regular force, the better.'

'I can't believe my luck having a girl like that by my side.'

'Let me make one thing clear. There will be no hanky-panky, you understand?'

Made to feel like a schoolboy by the father whose daughter he is taking to the cinema for the first time, Holt promised he would behave honourably.

Once back at the bureau, Peter introduced Holt to the rest of the staff, with a brief explanation regarding their various specialities, such as firearms, explosives, dirty bombs, profiling, interrogation, and so on.

With all the introductions apart from those to Celia and the in-house doctor-cum-psychiatrist completed, Peter left Holt in the company of two colleagues, who would brief him on their side of the work and show him some of the special features of the office. Laid-back types, they made Holt feel at home. When he said he could not wait to see his female partner after hearing so much about her, they raised their eyebrows and said she belonged to the office as a whole, and her occasional assignment to him should not be misconstrued.

'We call her Miss Innocent, and some of us – the men – are placing bets on when she will lose her virginity.'

'How will you know when she does?' asked Holt.

'It will be written all over that angelic face of hers. She'll have a glow about her and look fulfilled, if you know what I mean – more at one with herself. One can sense these things,' continued Mike, the taller one of the two, with the other nodding knowledgeably and adding, 'You cannot put it into words, but you know.'

Were they all, including even Peter, having him on? She was probably nothing special, and this was simply a trick they played on all new boys. Her all-too-convenient absence was probably part of the con – the type of prank Holt himself would think up.

'She's probably,' said Mike, 'accompanying a randy old cabinet minister at some garden party to prevent him getting into trouble and being blackmailed.'

'Apart from Celia,' replied Holt, 'the only person I have not met is the psychiatrist. *B* something. What's he like?'

The two of them scowled.

'Name's Blackwell. Tricky bastard,' replied Mike.

'Sticks his nose in everyone's business – especially where sex is concerned,' added the other. 'Gets you to reveal your sex life or that of colleagues. He exploits the info while finding it titillating. Watch out. No one has succeeded in scoring a point over him, and anyone who did would probably live to regret it. We call him the Snake. Maybe you should try being the mongoose, though I don't give much for your chances.'

Holt returned to his tiny apartment that night feeling the future looked bright. His qualms about working in the secret world had been assuaged by his colleagues having trusted him enough to confide in him about the Snake. All was not so black and white.

Chapter 6
Miss Innocent and Dr Blackwell

The next morning dragged, and it was not until eleven thirty that Peter finally called him to his office

'Celia's here with me now, Jeremy. Come right away. She came back for a few minutes specially to see you. She's still on a job, so don't dawdle.'

Holt was at his boss's door along the corridor in moments. He knocked and, on being told to come in, opened the door and stepped inside with a poker face, steeling himself so as not to hurt the poor woman by looking disappointed.

'Celia, Jeremy. Jeremy, Celia,' said Peter as the two of them stepped towards each other to shake hands. They could hardly embrace in an office setting, though Holt would have liked to have done so, for never had he met a grown woman with such angelic features. One so pure.

In the face of such innocence, playing at goody-goody brother and sister or chaste couple would not be difficult. Surely, the famous saying by Benjamin Franklin that innocence is its own defence would be particularly apt in her case.

He returned to his office in almost a state of shock and sat at his desk thinking of what might lie ahead until it was time to go for his session with the house psychiatrist-cum-doctor.

The warnings from his two colleagues were not the sole reason for his disquiet as he sat in the psychiatrist's office. A French friend who claimed he had unjustly been accused of date rape had told him how he had been obliged to attend sessions with a shrink who showed scant interest in him personally but would spring to life invariably at some point, saying, 'Let's go through the "rape" again, step by step. Describe her reactions. Say how you felt, and above all, describe how you think she felt. Her twitches, her orgasms, if any.'

Holt knew that as a qualified general medical practitioner, Blackwell was empowered to perform physical exams as well as psychiatric ones, so he was not at all surprised when the doctor started his session by saying he would pose some questions to pigeonhole him before physically examining him.

'Do you pigeonhole everyone?' asked Holt, wondering whether he could brag later that he had indeed played the mongoose and outmanoeuvred the Snake.

'Invariably. I'm pretty good at it.'

'I see,' was all Holt could think of saying.

The next question, designed to throw recruits and especially females off balance, was one of Blackwell's favourites.

'When *did* you lose it – your virginity, I mean?'

'How,' parried Holt, 'is that relevant?'

Blackwell had his well-prepared excuse for posing the question.

'American intelligence officers triaging defeated Germans at the end of World War II found the earlier a man lost his virginity, the more likely he would prove to be democratic as opposed to fascist. Besides giving me a lead in to the person's political views on the democratic–fascist axis, I find that question opens up a Pandora's box.'

'I would think that in today's society, where sexual relations at a young age are in some sections of society more or less de rigueur, such criteria are meaningless. The converse might well be true, for nowadays saving one's virginity would often be going against social norms, at least in the UK. Perhaps in your day, Herr Doctor, the US intelligence men's thesis may have been valid. When did you lose yours – that is, if you have?'

'I'm the one asking the questions.'

'Of course you are,' replied Holt, leaning forward to press his point, 'but I would have thought more cerebral Pandora's boxes would be more valuable. Sex is not the only thing in life – though it might seem like that to psychiatrists, who are reputed to enter the profession because of their own hang-ups, even shortcomings.'

No one had ever talked to the psychiatrist like that. But before he could object, Holt continued.

'I shall be reporting you. In fact, I think you should be on the sex offenders list, but then I suppose MI5 would protect you

48

because of the security implications. You probably know too much about key people, not only in Giraffe but also beyond.'

'You little creep. You'll be sorry.'

'You've just proved my point,' replied Holt. 'Blackmail.'

'Enough!'

'Sorry, I got carried away,' answered Holt.

'Seems your emotions get the better of you. I'll have to note that. Could be disastrous on a mission. You could put people working for us at risk.'

'I'm a backroom, back-office man. Not a frontline agent. I won't be dealing with dangerous situations, here or abroad.'

'Okay. Anyway, more to the point is, what made someone like *you* decide to join the service?'

'I didn't decide. I fell into it after being told I had something special to offer and that I might save many lives. You will understand I cannot say more than that for security reasons.'

'You can tell me anything.'

'I would have to confirm that with a higher authority. If they said it was okay, I would warn them it could be very dangerous having non-line personnel like you asking wide-ranging questions about what we do.'

Holt was playing the system against him, and Blackwell would have to trip him up on terrain where his background information would give him a definite advantage.

'I gather,' said Blackwell, 'from your files that you have something of an inferiority complex in so far as women are concerned. All this bravado may be to hide the fact that *you* are the one with the hang-ups.'

'Is sex the only thing you can think off?'

'You're evading the question.'

'Not at all. It's not inferiority, more a matter of unfamiliarity, never having had a sister and my mother dying. I have to admit I am gauche in my dealings with the opposite sex, perhaps as you yourself are – seeing how prurient you are.'

This insulting comment had obviously made Blackwell furious, leaving him cornered, for if he continued he would look even more prurient. He would seek his revenge later. He altered course, but only slightly.

'I see you are being partnered with our beautiful Celia. Seems totally out of order to me in view of what you have just said. We don't want any trouble. She is the Virgin Mary, at least for the likes of you.'

'I have been made well aware that I must handle her with kid gloves – or rather, not handle her at all. That said, I want it put on record that you referred to her as the Virgin Mary. I don't want to get blamed when she falls pregnant on her own.'

'Get...get out! You're too clever by half.'

'You are not the first person to say that. At least you got something right.'

Holt stood up and stalked out as ordered, glad to escape the physical exam. Had he been a young woman, it would surely not have been omitted.

He half slammed the door behind him, knowing he had foolishly made an implacable enemy. The Snake would inevitably seek his revenge in one form or another. The question was, would retribution be immediate, or was he one of those people who believed revenge was a dish best served cold?

Chapter 7
Terrorist Ways

One cannot go into detail regarding Holt's initial training and secondments to the various security-related departments. Far less exciting than one might imagine, most of it consisted of briefings on all aspects of terrorism. Disappointingly, it was more like being back at school than at university.

Celia accompanied him to some of the lectures. This was allegedly to make her a better sounding-board, though Holt did wonder whether it was to enable her to keep an eye on him and get him used to being in her presence in situations where he could not compromise her.

Briefings on particular terrorist incidents included videos and photos not deemed by the media to be suitable, other than for the occasional glimpse, for public consumption. Two of the worst incidents in that regard were at schools. The recent one in Pakistan, where seven Taliban came into a school at Peshawar and opened fire, killing 132 children and 145 people in all. And the Beslan school hostage crisis, in the Russian Federation in September 2004, which lasted three days and ended in a bloodbath, with 380-plus deaths as the school was stormed by security forces. More than 1,100 hostages had been taken, of whom 777 were children, with the rest mostly staff. The militants were threatening to blow them all up if their demands were not met or the authorities intervened.

Conditions became horrendous as temperatures soared inside the school, with many of the younger hostages taking off their clothes and sitting in their underclothes, if that. The exact order of events when the authorities did intervene after three days is disputed, with some alleging that the authorities tried to make it seem the militants started the explosions that prompted them to intervene, and hostages were incidentally killed by those who were ostensibly rescuing them.

While bombs were of constant concern, firearms scenarios such as the Mumbai siege of 2008, where the terrorists outgunned the police and SWAT teams led to the British authorities carrying out secret exercises throughout the country codenamed Operation Pride to ensure mobile response units had the necessary firepower and would not have to wait for the army to arrive from their barracks.

Then there were the lectures on how terrorists' minds were supposed to work and what made them, apart from their bombs, tick. What made them become terrorists and even suicide bombers in the first place. These and the reading material that accompanied them were fascinating.

Holt was told time and time again that though terrorists could mostly be pigeonholed according to type, there were always the dangerous exceptions. From the perspective of Holt's mission, they really told him there were no simple answers. Terrorists came in all shapes and sizes. Even the under-tens could be a threat.

Halfway through the course, Sir Charles called him in to review his role.

'Remember, your job is to think up techniques and modi operandi before the terrorists think of them. While the lectures covering the way their minds work may help you do that, it is not your job to go looking for them. Leave that to the established departments. So far, Five, Special Branch, Six, and GCHQ have done a great job thwarting attacks year after year, but we cannot expect them to pre-empt every one, so any possible scenarios you come up with could be invaluable.'

Chapter 8
The Loughty

In preparation for their overseas trip, Holt and Celia were scheduled to spend a night together at a hotel called The Loughty as a dry run. 'Dry' was the operative word, though luckily that did not apply to alcoholic beverages. He would have to prove himself beyond reproach.

What they did not know was that the service had an ulterior motive, apart from facilitating the taking of photos, for pushing the honeymoon/happy-couple scenario. The country's glory days were over – in fact, the country's zenith had been around 1900 – and even its secret services, as well as diplomatic services, were short of money. Lavish receptions and entertaining were mostly things of the past, and travel expenses were being pared to the bone, with the result that agents were missing out on the little perks they once so much enjoyed, though these had hardly ever extended to 007's Dom Pérignon champagne.

By pretending to be on their honeymoon, agents could sometimes claw back some of the perks they enjoyed in the old days and, notably, hope to be granted upgrades in hotels. On their return to London, some would have dozens of complimentary condoms to give away, as some hotels seemed to believe half a dozen were required. The more brazen officers would then dole them out to secretaries, saying that while too small for them they should be ample for their partners.

Holt had heard the story of how, before Russia became an ally in World War II, the Russians placed an order for condoms of gigantic proportions to enrobe the tips of the guns on their tanks and prevent dirt getting in. The minister responsible for manufacturing told Churchill that the Russians' ulterior motive was to sap British workers' morale and wanted to refuse. Churchill allegedly told his minister the problem could be solved simply by having the workers put 'Small' on the packets.

Apart from saving money, having agents share rooms helped keep them out of trouble and away from temptation. It also made it more difficult for foreign services to contact individuals personally.

Peter had warned Holt that a mature understudy was waiting in the wings to take Celia's place should he fail the test at The Loughty.

'Don't worry,' joked jealous colleagues, 'with the understudy in question, you will have the commiseration of the hotel bellboys when you come down for breakfast after the big night. They might even propose something on the side to lift your spirits. By the way, Blackwell often briefs and debriefs the females going to The Loughty, ostensibly to ensure they handle their partners appropriately and are not importuned. You had better be careful.'

Such comments were making Holt apprehensive. The understudy sounded terrible, but then even someone with only slightly above average looks could never compare with Celia. More to the point, he did not like the thought that his nemesis, Blackwell, would be involved.

Colleagues who had been to The Loughty would not be drawn on what had happened to them personally there, other than to say it was a great experience, provided one did not make a fool of oneself. In fact, it was not a hotel at all but a training-cum-test establishment operated by the service to train operatives, who came increasingly from more humble backgrounds, in the ways of upper, if not high, society. As most could already handle a knife and fork, it was more a question of teaching them how to deal with sommeliers and not look ridiculous when faced with a menu written in French or Italian.

Arriving at the local station in the late afternoon, Holt and Celia climbed into the second of the five taxis waiting outside the station on the assumption that the leading one would most likely have been sent to test them.

'The Loughty is far too expensive for the likes of people coming here to visit us locals,' said the elderly driver, turning round to face them in the back seat when he should have been

54

concentrating on the road. 'Anyway,' he continued, turning back to see where they were going, 'it's always fully booked. You two were lucky to get a room.'

A converted country house set well back from the road, The Loughty was much more stylish than they had anticipated. A miserable agent, who had doubtless joined one of the services expecting to be engaged in something more glamorous, carried their bags up to their room and hovered for a tip – obviously to teach agents the usual protocol on arriving at a high-class establishment. Holt gave him a couple of pounds with a dismissive gesture to humble him even more and give the impression he was a habitué of such places.

Sharing a room did not mean sharing beds, for there were twin beds separated by a bedside table with the usual telephone.

Just as they were settling in, there was a knock at the door that was too sharp to be that of a room maid. Indeed, it proved to be the hotel manager, obviously a more senior agent who had had his cover blown or was otherwise deemed operationally ineffective. His crisp manner reminded Holt of the World War II Stalag Luft prison camp commandants he had seen in films.

'I have been briefed about your relationship – or rather, lack thereof – so have given you well-separated twin beds as requested. Actually, in the Far East many couples and especially married ones generally prefer them.' With an overlong look at Celia, he added, 'The beds can usually be pushed together, so one gets the best of both worlds.'

Dinner, he told them, would be the centrepiece of their stay. A table had been reserved for them at eight.

'Dress is smart casual.'

Having said somewhat ambiguously he was looking forward to seeing more of them, he left them to their own devices.

With time to spare before dinner, they went for a pleasant walk in the woods that formed part of the estate, returning at about seven thirty to spruce up for eight. Though Holt was well aware Celia was no longer a teenager, her nubile look and childish mannerisms made him feel like an uncle taking a pubescent niece out for a treat and having to share a room with her, albeit with her mother's permission.

The thought of the potentially embarrassing situation lying ahead was making him edgy, and just like many a young lady disappointed at her father's failure to measure up to her impossible hopes and expectations, Celia came up with the first of what were to be many put-downs of the evening.

'Get a grip, man! There's no need to worry about not rising to the occasion.'

What language and what cheek. What double entendre. It was a bit rich having someone so young and virginal lecturing him about not having to prove his prowess in the bedroom. He could only retort meekly that it was an unusual situation.

'I never had a sister. I wish I had. I would not feel so awkward.'

'We're not meant to discuss our private lives in the service. You know that, don't you?'

'You're right, as usual. You've been in the business longer than I.'

Continuing with her schoolgirl-on-a-day-out gush, she babbled on.

'Let's make the most of it. It's not every day one can feast oneself on the house like this. If you cannot get your head round the brother-and-sister act, just imagine we're twelve-year-olds on a sleepover who would never dream of doing anything really naughty.'

The 'really naughty' got Holt's imagination going. Not only did he lack a sister, he had never been on a sleepover either. The goody-two-shoes kids she was referring to must have been under ten years old to be that innocent.

Just as he was formulating a remark to try to take her down a peg, she interrupted his train of thought.

'Stop trying to make a big thing out of a little thing. All we have to do is to be natural – in other words, make the most of the goodies, including the champagne. I've heard from other agents that this place is fabulous in that respect. Anyway, I'm famished. Time we went down for din-dins.'

56

Holt presumed she was putting on this din-dins primary-school act to wind him up even further but guiltily found it appealing. Was she purposely being provocative?

In the words of the late bon viveur and restaurant critic Michael Winner, The Loughty dinner was truly 'historic', and had the establishment not been restricted to a special clientele it might well have earned a Michelin star.

During a holiday Holt had spent in France while a student, a French acquaintance taught him the secret of ordering quality French wines. Not only should one choose one that was *appellation contrôlée*, and preferably a top *appellation*, but also ensure it was château bottled (*mis en bouteille au château*), with a top château being a big plus. Finally, one should never buy any bottle with the label for the year separate from the main label, as such labels were easily falsified.

On reading the wine list, Holt had noticed two wines marked 'Appellation Margaux Contrôlée'. Both were château bottled, but the first and much more expensive one had the name of a château he had never heard of, while the cheaper one was a Château Margaux and one of the great wines, and usually very expensive. This illogical disparity in price was obviously a test to pick out the recruits who really knew something about wine. Holt naturally chose the latter and was quite surprised that Celia indicated her approval with a slightly ashamed look. Perhaps she had learnt much about wines in the course of accompanying VIPs.

The first bottle, brought to their table with great pomp and ceremony, was obviously corked, again to test them. Holt was quite proud of having detected this on raising his glass to his nose before even taking a sip, though it was not difficult, as the bottle had obviously already been used several times to test recruits. It was pretty far gone and truly reeked of vinegar.

The sommelier feigned an apology, to which Holt responded by saying that even the renowned La Tour d'Argent restaurant in Paris finds a third of their very oldest and expensive bottles to be corked. He added to the man's discomfort by saying, 'Of course, the sommelier at the Tour would have detected that by sniffing the cork even before proffering the bottle.'

What had the poor man done wrong in his secret service career to end up playing this inglorious role?

When a new bottle was brought and opened in their presence, Celia showed she could appreciate quality. Had recognizing a great wine featured in her training?

He noticed how her attitude to the hotel staff was that of a demure young woman, with no trace of the schoolgirl, which seemed to be purely for his consumption. Was she having him on?

Paying the bill was part of the test, and Holt added an extra tip in addition to the service charge. This seemed to unnerve the waiter, who said, 'That is not necessary, Monsieur.'

Holt nevertheless insisted, as if such petty largesse were nothing.

Having enjoyed their great meal, they made their way through the lounge towards the terrace, with Holt allowing Celia to go on ahead while he stopped off at the cloakroom.

On rejoining her in cool outside air, he found their coffees were already on the table, with a brandy just for him. The coffee was a disappointment; not up to the standard of the other fare but just about drinkable with the help of the velvety XO brandy. Celia seemed to be lost in thought as he sat silently in the semi-darkness, ruminating on what was or was not to follow up in the bedroom. Like the corked wine, the bitter coffee had possibly been a test. He would have to remember to note it on the guest comments form.

Thanking the disenfranchised spooks for their truly excellent service, they made their way back through the lounge, followed by some lascivious glances unbecoming of future agents of Her Majesty. Of course, had any of those eyeing her had the good looks and panache of a Sean Connery, Celia would have felt less uncomfortable.

Chapter 9
The Bare Cheek

The books they had brought to ease them through awkward moments in the bedroom proved unnecessary, as there was plenty of interest to them on the television. To make it feel like a real hotel, the secret service had even made pay-to-view porn channels available for aficionados or perhaps recruits on their own, which certainly did not apply to them. When at last the dreaded time for bed arrived, Celia simplified matters by indicating Holt should proceed first as she wanted to have a long relaxing shower.

'Jeremy. It *is* nice being here like this don't you think – even though we…shan't be…?'

Feeling too tired to worry about the 'even though we shan't be', Holt was more than happy to go to the bathroom first. Too much wine and brandy had made him weak at the knees.

Having changed into his pyjamas and the bathrobe supplied by the establishment, Holt came out of the bathroom to find Celia had divested herself of her dress. Wearing only her petticoat, she brushed past him without a glance on her way to take that long shower.

Climbing into the nearest of the twin beds, he stretched out his legs and snuggled into the soft pillow. A strange feeling had come over him. Here he was in the close company of a woman who made him the envy of all his colleagues, yet with no prospect of anything happening. Her intention was surely to drag out her time in the shower in the expectation he would be out cold on her return.

If so, she failed in that regard, for when he heard the click of the bathroom door being unlocked, he opened his eyes to see her emerge, enveloped in a bath towel. He had always wondered how real women ensured those towels stayed up, knowing that in the case of film stars they might even be glued on and that, anyway, there would be plenty on underneath.

This was certainly not true in Celia's case, for her contours were moulded by the towelling with no sign of anything underneath as she brushed past close to his face. A yard further on the towel slipped off by accident or design to reveal two pale, pert cheeks jutting out sharply below the concave of her back. Stark naked, she stood there, as if wondering what to do next, bent down to recover the towel and lobbed it casually onto the back of an armchair.

In the process she had left nothing to Holt's imagination. He was in a state of virtual shock, disbelief. He couldn't believe his eyes. Was more to come?

She ambled over to her overnight case, her left cheek and right cheek oscillating from side to side as each foot advanced, and fumbled amongst her things, seemingly untroubled by any thoughts that Holt might not be asleep. Having extracted a pair of knickers, she held them up for inspection as if unsure of her choice, stretched them wide open between her hands, and again bent down. Raising first one foot and then the other, she pulled them on over her ankles, hauled them upwards over the hump of her knees and then, with more difficulty, over her more ample thighs. Once they had arrived at their ultimate destination, she eased her fingers under the elastic to ensure they were comfortably in place. Being sensible, simple ones, they made her even more alluring than when completely naked.

Crikey, what kind of big sister behaved like that? A six-year-old with nothing to show might, but surely not a preteen or teen sister? Holt felt confused, in part because the spectacle had left him physically unmoved.

She turned round, and with her taut breasts in full view, came over to the foot of her bed, where she gathered up the linen nightdress she had laid out there beforehand. Slipping it on over her head, she wiggled her hips to allow it to slither down into place, covering her thighs but leaving her knees just visible.

Coming between their two beds, she sat down on hers, crossing her legs with some difficulty because of the confined space. According to books Holt had read as a teenager, crossed

60

legs when you invite a girl to dinner signalled that nothing would follow. This sudden prim routine seemed a trifle odd, as the prudish girls he knew would not only have been crossing their legs but surely wearing two, if not three, pairs of knickers in similar circumstances.

'You *are* awake, aren't you?'

'Yes, I guess so,' admitted Holt, trying to convey the impression that he had hardly been aware of what had been going on.

'Dr Blackwell put me up to this. I don't want you to get me wrong – I am not normally like that.'

'Really?'

'Blackwell assured me you would get a mental block if you saw me completely naked while not allowed to do anything. I was to act like an innocent child with no sense of shame. Above all, I should avoid being coy, as that would only wind you up.'

'You certainly weren't coy – at least, until a few seconds ago.'

'He assured me that if I did it right, you would no longer hanker after me.'

Had Blackwell actually said 'hanker', or was it a Freudian slip on Celia's part? Could it be that she was not the font of innocence she made herself out to be?

Having finished her lecture, she pulled aside the sheet and top blanket, drew up her long legs, swivelled, and slid between the sheets, taking care to grip the hem of the nightdress to ensure it did not ride up. Holt thought the hem-gripping precaution somewhat unnecessary in view of the earlier display, though it might just have been out of habit or simply to ensure she would be lying comfortably, with nothing ruffled underneath those sensitive thighs.

'Sleep tight, darling, sweet dreams,' she whispered.

'I expect I shall. I can't move. It must be all the wine and the brandy.'

He was not only paralysed, he didn't even want her, which meant game, set, and match to Blackwell. He had got his revenge and would have a good laugh when he debriefed her.

He woke up the next morning wondering whether it had it all been a teenager's dream. Dream or not, he was not even tempted to sneak a peek at Celia dressing nonchalantly in the middle of the room. It certainly boded well for their overseas missions together, though it left him feeling undermined as a man.

At breakfast he assured her that, loathe as he was to admit it, Blackwell's programming had worked so well she had nothing fear. Rather than seeming relieved, she looked at him with a guilty smile, which he attributed to the shame she must feel about the show she had put on for his and Blackwell's benefit.

After breakfast they went for a short walk in the garden. How nice it felt walking on the velvety grass in the fresh morning air. They would have happily spent another day at the establishment but knew they would be leaving that morning. On re-entering the 'hotel', they took care to wipe their feet on the mat so as not to risk losing a mark for that. As they passed reception on the way up to their room, the young lady behind the counter called them into the manager's office for a review of their sojourn.

'You,' said the manager, 'have both passed with flying colours.'

'I should think so,' replied Celia somewhat forcefully, to Holt's surprise.

'Off the record,' continued the manager, 'we have just had a request from a Dr Blackwell for the overnight video of you in the bedroom, but we told him it had been routinely erased. In normal circumstances – that is, if nothing untoward happens – we erase recordings of what goes on in the bedroom immediately. I say bedroom, because we only have one fitted up with cameras for special situations.'

'What do you mean by special situations – blackmail?' asked Holt.

'Could be anything. For you, it was in case the young lady claimed you had importuned her, even raped her, unlikely as it might seem. For your mutual protection.'

'Good idea,' said Celia. 'You never know.'

'Videos of what happens in the public spaces are kept for just long enough to show the guests what they are doing wrong, or as

62

evidence if they complain about the establishment or the service. If word got round that videos of what happens here in the bedrooms were being circulated to other departments, we would lose all credibility, and no one would ever come here.'

'Thank God for that,' exclaimed Celia.

The manager said he would put in his report that they had been a cut above the usual throughput, many of whom would have to come back for further training at the taxpayers' expense.

'By the way,' he added, 'we were a tad surprised the coffee served to you on the terrace last night was not quite up to par. We rather pride ourselves on our coffee. Maybe it got overheated by mistake, or the cup had not been properly rinsed and there were traces of detergent left on it. Anyway, sorry about that. Rest assured we will make sure it does not happen again.'

'I thought it might have been to test us, like the corked wine, which was so awful no one could ever drink it,' replied Holt.

'You're dead wrong there. The bottle you declined was shortly afterwards drunk by someone proclaiming it to be the greatest wine they had ever had, even on holiday in France.'

'Actually,' said Holt, 'it was a great wine. Perhaps a great wine turning to vinegar still has something special about it.'

'Anyway, all the best, whatever your mission. Hope it's not too dangerous and that your cover does not get blown as mine was. That's how I ended up here. Better than being dead, I suppose. But not much, after being active in the field in sunnier climes.'

'There's just one thing,' said Holt. 'We've been wondering why you call this place The Loughty.'

'Simple really. Quite a number of pretentious UK hostelries think having the letters o-u-g-h in their names makes them high class. We just added the letters l and ty as a joke, as our mission statement seemed to infer we turn louts into gentlemen. I would rather you kept that to yourselves, safe in the knowledge that it did not apply in your case and that by revealing it, you would make louts of yourselves.'

'Point taken. We won't tell anyone, will we, Celia?'

'Of course not, Jeremy. Would be nice, though, to find an excuse to come again.'

'I would love to see you again,' said the manager, looking at Celia. Had he seen her prancing around in her birthday suit? So what. She had been acting – it had not really been her.

With smiles all round, they bade him farewell, and after a twenty-minute wait boarded a minibus with other departing 'guests' to be taken to catch the mid-morning train back to London. With most of them looking like spotty schoolboys, they were glad they had been ordered not to fraternise on the train.

The following few days included yet more briefings, but nothing of note apart from having to go over the river to MI6 to collect their equipment from a Q (technical officer), just like James Bond. But unlike 007, they would not be issued with rocket-firing cigars and an Aston Martin – or nowadays, a BMW. Instead, they were only to be provided with a simple tourist-grade camera, a laptop with special communications software, and, to their incredulity, a 'honeymoon kit' with instructions as to the use thereof.

On their way to MI6's fort-like headquarters overlooking the Thames at Vauxhall, Holt and Celia discussed what might be in that honeymoon kit and concluded it must be party items, like confetti, to give the impression they were just married. Holt wondered whether it would include atropine to dilate the bride's pupils and make her look 'up for it', as well as serve as an antidote in the event of another nerve gas attack in Tokyo.

On arriving at MI6 and declaring the purpose of their visit, they were issued with their visitor badges with no name but apparently with an embedded chip. Q collected them at reception. Looking too young to explain the use of sophisticated equipment such as rocket-firing cigars, he was probably a junior in the dirty devices department. He looked somewhat immature to be explaining honeymoon equipment.

The first item was their camera, a Canon Power Shot S110, an inconspicuous camera able to take high-quality photos even in poor light, without using its flash. Junior Q hardly needed to remind them to take many innocent photos so the ones in which they were really interested would not be obvious.

The only special feature of the laptop computer was the encryption software enabling them to communicate securely. This would only be used in exceptional circumstances, say in the event of their being required to do something special. Otherwise, communication would be by phone between Celia and an ostensible woman friend in London, with innocuous-sounding code words used to convey instructions very much as al-Qaeda was wont to use. For example, mention of a death in the family was the signal that they should cut short their trip and return immediately. With neither of them being front-line field agents, this was most unlikely.

The boyish officer at last came to the item that had been occupying their thoughts, the honeymoon kit, which had been sitting on his desk in a small wooden box marked 'MI6 Honeymoon Kit' in bright pink letters.

As if he were the original Q in the James Bond films demonstrating some clever but lethal device, the officer extracted a tiny tube with a flourish.

'Whatever you do,' he said, his face lighting up, 'don't use too much of this!'

'Why's that?' they asked in unison, just as Bond would have done.

'I'll tell you why,' said the officer, pausing for effect.

'When we first developed it, one of our female agents was having a one-night stand in a foreign country with a diplomat and, having extracted the desired info in the course of pillow talk with the bait of the action to follow, could not resist subsequently deploying her new kit, smearing the dye from this red phial everywhere, even on the pillow. Early the following morning she left the hotel without waking her partner for the night.'

After pausing again to allow them to imagine the situation, he continued on.

'In his rush to get back to his embassy in time for work, the diplomat failed to noticed anything untoward, or if he did was congratulating himself on having deflowered a virgin. When the room maid came to do the room, the great amount of blood in unlikely places convinced her someone had been murdered, or at the very least badly injured, and she immediately alerted hotel security. They in turn called the police, who naturally went to question the embarrassed diplomat at his embassy. In the presence of the ambassador, he denied harming the woman but nevertheless claimed diplomatic immunity, which eventually proved unnecessary, as on analysis our blood proved to be fake.'

'He must have felt a fool,' interjected Holt.

'Yes, but that's not the end of the story, for his embassy concluded – wrongly as it happened – that he was the major leak they had long suspected. He was immediately recalled and shot, poor guy.'

'All that for a moment of pleasure,' remarked Celia.

'I cannot envisage a situation where we would need to use it,' added Holt. 'Using fake blood would make us look ridiculous. Celia would be like Fanny Hill keeping pig's blood hidden in the bedpost.'

'Quite the contrary. In some countries the use of such artifices increases the credibility of the honeymoon in the eyes of the authorities.'

'Really?' interjected Celia in disbelief.

'You see, it's not always used to deceive. Sometimes it's merely used as insurance. Ensures everything goes as expected, which as you yourself must know, young lady, is not always true in nature. Grooms may become suspicious at the lack of evidence...and in some countries, family members and even villagers will check the sheets. Thus the authorities are familiar with the various artifices a highly respected bride might resort to, to ensure her honour is not questioned, even though intact.'

Looking at Celia, who was nodding her head knowledgably, the officer explained that their kit, unlike Fanny Hill's, had the advantage of an almost infinite shelf life. As it was her side of the business, Holt let her take charge of the little box of tricks.

Chapter 10
Japan

With their flights booked and all their kit, they were ready to set off for Japan at the end of the week.

Furthermore, having survived that first night at The Loughty if not with flying colours at least with no major faux pas, Holt felt confident that he would be able to handle his relationship with his partner appropriately.

Prior to the horrendous sarin nerve gas attack on the Tokyo subway by members of the Aum religious cult, Japan had over the years experienced a series of pinprick attacks by domestic radical elements where simplicity and originality had been the hallmark. While only having limited impact, these capers were of great embarrassment to the authorities.

On one particular occasion, rockets launched mortar-like from cut-off drainpipes leaning against an apartment balcony balustrade facing the State Guest House landed in its grounds. As the guests had included President Mitterrand of France, the Japanese suffered great loss of face, though no one was even injured.

Subsequently, whenever foreign heads of state stayed there, the authorities would take over-the-top measures to forestall such action. These included welding shut manholes in the nearby streets and having the local plod, then more senior police, and finally a secret service agent, interview anyone living within drainpipe-mortar range. These and other measures taken by the Japanese police and security services proved largely successful.

Sir Charles, who himself had served in the Far East early in his career, therefore thought that that Japan might provide some useful lessons for Holt. Besides, an exotic overseas trip would be a good reward and help trigger his creativity after so many days passively listening to lectures and watching videos.

The good news was that it was confirmed Celia would accompany him; the bad news was that limited funds meant they would not be able to stop off en route. While the honeymoon routine was not strictly necessary in Japan, they would be sharing bedrooms to save money and to perhaps keep Holt out of temptation. Better than moping alone in their rooms.

Top people at Six – Sir Charles always had the ear of their top people, having been one himself – thought it best for them to deal directly with of one of their assets living in the country rather than with the embassy. In fact, an Englishman who had lived many years in Japan as a journalist working for a serious London newspaper and various US publications.

He had the double-barrelled name Smythe-Hewitt but preferred to be called SH. In the course of his work as a journalist, SH had followed terrorist incidents closely and built up good relations with a number of people high up in the food chain in the Japanese bureaucracy and even the police. He was not and never had been a full-time MI6 officer, more like a consultant on Japanese political and social matters. In fact, if he had been running agents he would have lost the confidence of the high officials, who, aware of his excellent contacts back in the home country, sometimes used him as a conduit to their counterparts in the UK, bypassing the embassy.

Now retired to a house perched on a hill overlooking the sea not far from Kamakura, with its famous giant Buddha, Smythe-Hewitt had a full-on view of Japan's iconic Mount Fuji. On visiting him there some years back, Sir Charles had been impressed by the privacy afforded by being perched on the steep slope of a mini-mountain with densely packed foliage.

Over a scrambled line, Sir Charles had briefed SH on the purpose of Holt's trip and found him more than happy to give the young man the benefit of his knowledge. He had reassured Sir Charles, saying that interfacing with some young blood after dealing mostly with very senior officers would be a welcome breath of fresh air. His trustworthy daughter, Sachiko, would be more than glad to be their guide.

He had suggested the two of them should spend a couple of days in Tokyo to get the feel of the city, with Sachiko showing them some of the locations about which he would be talking. They could then come down by train to the nearest mainline station for him to pick them up. They could spend a couple of nights at his place, which would give him time to brief Holt on Japan in a relaxed way. Sachiko could then take them to Kyoto and Nara to see something of the traditional Japan.

The three airlines flying nonstop to Japan – BA, JAL, and ANA – though not as exotic as regards on-board service as Singapore Airlines, all had decent reputations. Holt and Celia were told to be patriotic and if possible fly British Airways. After all, the taxpayer was paying.

BA had two flights a day to Tokyo, one to the relatively new airport at Narita, some fifty miles from the city, which had been the scene of pitched battles between police and local farmers supported by students and others opposing its construction. The other BA flight was to the recently expanded old Haneda Airport at the edge of the sea, close to the centre of town, and easily reached by monorail, taxi, or limousine bus. The trouble with the Haneda flight was that it left London around 9 a.m. and, worse still, landed at the ungodly hour of 4.30 a.m. They therefore opted for the Narita flight, departing from London around midday and arriving in Japan just after 9 a.m.

Someone they knew working for the airline had told them it was not worth trying the honeymoon ploy prior to boarding in the hope of getting an upgrade, as the check-in people were sick and tired of hearing all the reasons used to justify upgrades by undeserving tightwads. He doubted whether he could get them an operational upgrade (upgrade to shift people from seats in overbooked World Traveller or World Traveller Plus to vacant seats in business class) as it was school-holiday time, and the surplus business class seats would be taken up by airline staff and their families using their free travel or discounted travel perk.

Nevertheless, once onboard, it might be a good idea to acquaint the cabin crew of the fact they were on their honeymoon in an undemanding way. This they duly did, receiving special attention and goodies, such as a couple of glasses of champagne and superior wines from business class. Of course, Holt felt from time to time obliged to cosy up to Celia, hold her hand, and gaze lovingly into her eyes to prove they were truly enthralled with each other and merited these complimentary offerings.

'You're overdoing it,' grumbled Celia. 'Even genuine honeymoon couples don't have to be all over each other on the way out. These days, they've probably done it already,' she added, sounding like the know-all four-year-old little sister in the *The Power and the Glory* being held up to the keyhole by her ten-year-old brother to watch their sixteen-year-old sister in action.

Holt eased up on the pretend cuddling to let a fairly inebriated Celia drop off to sleep, and, having an aisle seat, he was able to get up and make his way to the rear of the extremely long Boeing 777 to thank the cabin crew, who were gossiping in the galley. They talked about this and that, and at one point he asked them who were the most difficult passengers and was quite surprised when told it was colleagues travelling in business class wanting all the free drink and attention they could garner.

As the aircraft was flying contrary to the direction of the sun, the night was short, and with the flight lasting around twelve hours and a time difference with the UK of eight hours, they would arrive at Tokyo's Narita International Airport after breakfast the following morning.

Holt had finally managed to grab a couple of hours' sleep but did not feel so good on waking for that breakfast. Looking around, he wondered why women always seemed to travel better. Maybe it was because they did not need to shave, or that a simple touch of make-up could transform them.

The only touch of excitement was when they were coming in to land. Almost at the last minute, the engines spooled up and they found themselves pushed hard backwards and downwards into their seats as the easy descent into Narita suddenly changed to a rapid climb out. A few moments later, the captain announced that they had had to perform a go-around manoeuvre, as the aircraft landing ahead of them had dithered on the runway. It was, he said, something that happened from time to time and was nothing to worry about. The air-traffic controller was being careful. In the most unlikely event that the aircraft on the runway did not get onto a slipway in time, there could be disastrous collision. The second landing attempt went smoothly, and even with the ten minutes lost on the go-around, BA007 landed virtually on schedule at 9.15.

As they disembarked, a Japanese flight attendant smiled at them, adding, 'I hope you had a good fright.' Holt wondered whether it was meant as a joke, as the Japanese girls he had met could nowadays differentiate between *r* and *l*, and this one had surely experienced quite a number of takeoffs and landings.

They were immediately struck by how clean and efficient the airport looked. Immigration went smoothly despite their having to queue for twenty minutes and have their fingerprints and photos taken. They were given their ninety-day tourist visas with hardly a question asked – they had already entered the name of their hotel and that they were tourists on their immigration form.

Back in the UK, the secret service officer briefing them on their e-ticket had told them that when dealing with immigration officers, one should keep things simple. One agent visiting Japan had added the information that the purpose of his visit was to learn a little Japanese, whereupon the immigration officer demanded the letter attesting his attendance at a language school.

On collecting their luggage, they were again struck by how well made and solid the luggage carts were compared with those in England. Even though there were green nothing-to-declare channels, each one was manned by a male or female customs officer asking a few questions after examining the customs declaration form people had filled in.

Their mention of the word 'honeymoon' elicited a wry smile, the first of many in Japan whenever the topic came up. Later at hotels, the young bellboys would be smiling from ear to ear as they came down to reception in the morning.

'Hope you good night,' they would say.

Japanese later explained to them that they should be careful how they interpreted these reactions, as Japanese tend to smile when embarrassed and are liable to grin with embarrassment when you tactlessly inform them one of your relatives has just passed away.

The customs officer was only interested in the duty-free alcohol and tobacco they had and looked pitifully at them for having only one bottle of cheap blended whisky between them on their honeymoon; they could have had six bottles, as the allowance was three bottles per person, which was perhaps not such a good idea, as many years before an Englishman had burnt down his central Tokyo hotel, drinking his duty-free while smoking in bed. The octogenarian hotel owner had skimped on money to repair the sprinklers, and there had been photos in the papers of guests dangling out of the windows at the ends of knotted bedsheets.

Since there was a direct limousine bus every hour or so right to their Tokyo Shinjuku hotel, eighty-one kilometres from the airport, Sachiko had said she would meet them at the hotel. A bus was leaving in twenty minutes, so they did not have to hang about for long; just time for a quick stand-up coffee before boarding.

As the bus approached Tokyo itself, the ricefields and independent houses gave way to apartment blocks and then office blocks, making them realize the sheer size of the city. It was a different world.

Sachiko had chosen the Keio Plaza Hotel at Shinjuku, a city within the city. One of the transport nodes on Tokyo's Yamanote, or Circle Line, it boasted Tokyo's city hall and many towering buildings, besides being a bustling area with many cafés and restaurants, as well as a Soho-type area with clip joints.

The Keio Plaza Hotel was on the other side of the tracks from the red-light district, called Kabuki-cho, with its host and hostess bars, clip joints, and love hotels, often under the control or 'protection' of gangsters – the traditional yakuza now being gradually replaced by Chinese gangsters with a harsher code.

The Keio was a good hotel just below the famous five-star ones that seldom give discounts. What was more, it was near some of the places Sachiko's father wanted her to show them.

Their bus stopped at several other Shinjuku hotels before reaching it. Sachiko was waiting for them as they alighted, identifying herself by carrying a large art book entitled *Van Gogh*.

The area of Shinjuku, called Nishi-Shinjuku, in which the hotel was situated was full of skyscrapers, a city within a city, somewhat like Paris's La Défense or London's Canary Wharf. The Keio Hotel, as one of the first, had a so-called tower but one that was not as high as the later ones. It was a modern complex, with many restaurants and reception rooms for weddings and the like in addition to many bedrooms.

Sachiko had already informed the hotel that they were on their honeymoon, and although they did not get an upgrade, they were pleased to find a hamper in their room with some nice items and a congratulatory message from the hotel management. Holt had almost certainly lost face by not opting for a deluxe room for his honeymoon, but with so many guests, that would not haunt them.

'I will leave you now,' said Sachiko, 'so you can have a rest. I'll come back tonight around six to take you for drinks at the Park Hyatt Hotel's New York Bar, not far from there. It was there that many of the scenes in the film *Lost in Translation* were filmed. It will give us a chance to talk about what you want to see and do. Then we can come back here for a light dinner at the Chinese restaurant on the ground floor.'

'Good idea. We are a bit shattered.'

The delightful Sachiko left them to their own devices, whereupon the two of them took the lift up to the 10th floor and walked down quite a long corridor to their room, which though not large was comfortable. After a nap and a shower, they were ready for action when Sachiko returned to pick them up at 5 p.m. – 9 a.m. UK time.

The Park Hyatt Hotel, some six minutes' walk from their lesser Keio Plaza Hotel, was on the 41st to 52nd floors of the Shinjuku Park Tower, one of the tallest buildings in Tokyo. They took the elevator up to the lobby on the 41st floor and noted how impressive the reception area was. Even from there, the view from the coffee shop was remarkable, and as they walked the fifty yards or so to the elevator to the top, they had a great view of Mount Fuji.

As they were arriving just when the New York Bar opened, at 5 p.m., they were able to get a table right by the window, facing out towards Shinjuku and the rest of Tokyo. They could even see the lights of aircraft landing one after the other at Tokyo's Haneda Airport.

'It's good,' said Sachiko, 'to come now. Not only can one get a good table but one also avoids the cover charge that applies from 8 p.m. onwards.'

'What a wonderful place,' remarked Celia.

Few words were said as they also drank in the view. Only when they were on their second round did Sachiko broach the main purpose of their visit.

'Dad told me the general purpose of your visit, but—'

'It's not,' interrupted Holt, 'a great secret. We just do not want to broadcast it or get noticed, as it could cause some friction, due to not going through the formal channels. After all, mine is just a training mission, not a high-powered visit.'

'I understand. I also know that you are not a real couple, even though you share rooms and claim to be on your honeymoon, which is a pity – you fit so well together.'

'We are not,' said Celia vehemently, 'fitting together.'

'I am sorry for my poor English. I didn't mean it in that special way.'

'I know, continued Celia, 'it must seem odd to you, but Jeremy here has been programmed by the psychiatrist so that we are like brother and sister.'

'In my humble experience big sisters are not too keen on sharing rooms with their brothers. I am sure you'll be glad to have your own room at our place – we've plenty of spare rooms. Also, when we go to Kyoto, let's share a room at the hotel. We can enjoy some girl time together. I don't get much chance for that nowadays.'

74

'I'd like that,' replied Celia, to Holt's dismay. 'Maybe we could do some shopping together.'

Holt had dreaded the word 'shopping' ever since his mother, an otherwise intelligent woman, had dragged him round London's Oxford Street department stores when five years old. It was not only the boredom that got to him but the memory of his difficulty in breathing when his nose and eyes were level with women's protruding bottoms, which sometimes poked him right in the face.

Realizing the sisterhood was making Holt feel uncomfortable, Sachiko tried to come up with something to tick his box.

'Do you know what a Narita Divorce is?'

'No,' they replied in unison.

'Well, many Japanese go abroad for their honeymoon – Japan is terribly expensive – and for some it is their first time; I mean, for going abroad as well as for the other thing. Anyway, the honeymoon abroad is sometimes so disastrous that as soon as the bride has her feet back safely on Japanese soil at Narita Airport, she declares her intention to divorce. That's why it's called a Narita Divorce.'

'Poor girls,' said Celia sympathetically.

'Why don't you say poor men?' interjected Holt. 'It takes two to tango.'

'Because you cannot imagine,' explained Sachiko, 'what some of us girls have to go through with these momma's boys, who have spent all their time swotting to get into a top university and then a job with a prestigious company or government department. There was one case where the groom phoned his mother back in Japan from Sydney to ask whether he should wear his pyjamas to bed with his bride!'

They all laughed, dissipating the tension that had built up.

'I'd heard about Japan's kamikaze taxis, but not that,' commented Holt.

'According to my dad, Japan's reputation for kamikaze taxis came about because a foreign journalist, having found nothing to write about, described a slightly scary ride to the airport in the hope his editor would sympathise. His editor published the article under the title "Japan's Kamikaze Taxis", and the myth of Japan's terrifying taxis was born. The article went all round the world.'

'We had heard about them and were a bit nervous,' commented Celia.

'In fact, Japanese taxi drivers would usually never even think of breaking the speed limit. Part of the reason may be that in Japan it is not the custom to give tips, though during the bubble, when the economy was booming, businessmen on expenses getting a taxi home late on a rainy Friday night from the Ginza would put up two or three fingers to show they would pay double or triple fare!'

'Point taken,' replied Holt. 'Sorry to have changed the subject. It must be the jet lag.'

'The fault is on my side. I am behaving like a tour guide when we have more important things to talk about.'

'Don't worry. We need to relax and have a bit of fun. Would be different if we were on a real honeymoon, wouldn't it, Celia?'

An awkward silence followed, before Sachiko continued.

'My dad...told me to show you some of the places he will be talking about when he sees you. The first is a toilet in an underground walkway not far from here. We have thousands such walkways here in Tokyo and other cities to avoid the heat, cold, and rain, and to make the most of the little space we have in Japan. Much of our country is mountainous, so the actual space where people can live is limited.'

'Why do you say "our" when you're half-English?'

'It's just that I was brought up here and got used to saying "our" and "we" when showing visitors from abroad around. I thought it sounded friendlier than saying "Japan" all the time.'

'I agree,' Celia said helpfully.

'Anyway, my dad's the one who knows the details. He said that apart from showing you one or two special places, I should just let you get the feel of the country. You and Dad will be able to talk at length. Reporting on the Red Army and terrorist incidents was once his speciality. I only hope he doesn't bore you. I have heard the same stories hundreds of times.'

76

'He sounds very interesting. I'm sure I won't be bored.'

With that, they went back to the Keio Plaza Hotel, and after dinner at the Nan-Yen Chinese restaurant in the basement, they said goodbye to Sachiko and returned to their room. The experience of the night at The Loughty and their proximity during the flight meant there was no sense of awkwardness as they prepared for bed, though aesthetically speaking, Holt would have appreciated another show. The time difference with the UK meant they did not feel sleepy, and they watched some local programmes on their TV, which seemed very strange, very different from those in the UK.

Again, because of the time difference, getting up the next morning was not so easy, but luckily they had arranged to meet Sachiko after lunch. She had suggested they go for a walk round on their own, saying too much hand holding would not be good for them. Despite being brought up in Japan, she was a very forthright young woman. So they lingered over breakfast, buffet-style, involving a lot of getting up and sitting down. There was a wide choice, both Western and Japanese.

The rest of the morning was spent wandering around. The first place they came across was a shop, or rather a complex of shops, called Yodobashi Camera, selling cameras and every imaginable item of electrical equipment, from computers to washing machines, at a discount. The choice was unbelievable. They then visited a department store, with the basement taken up with counters selling an enormous range of different foods, much of them destined to be gifts. The Japanese seemed obsessed with gift giving. They returned to the hotel quite shattered. How nice to have a room in which to recover.

Sachiko rejoined them as they were having a snack in the hotel coffee shop and said the first place they would be visiting would be the underground walkway where members of the Aum Cult had left a poison gas-generating device following their relatively unsuccessful sarin nerve gas attack on the Tokyo subway system in 1995.

Holt signed for their food and coffees, and they set off, with Sachiko leading the way, down into the labyrinth of underground walkways that she had been talking about, many of them with shops and restaurants on either side. As they passed under the Shinjuku National Railway station, they noticed the Marunouchi Line subway station on a lower level, with exits to their passageway at either end of the platform.

Sachiko stopped near the far exit before speaking. She explained that the police, fearing another nerve gas attack, had saturated the nation's railway stations and tourist spots, particularly Shinjuku, one of the busiest. A member of the public reported that something was burning in a bag in a toilet located off one of the walkways above the Shinjuku subway station. Staff quickly doused it with water, only to find that resulted in it beginning to emit acrid fumes. Finally, a specialized team from the fire brigade rendered it harmless.

On closer examination, it was found to be a crude device consisting of two condoms, the outside one containing sodium cyanide, and the inside one filled with concentrated sulphuric acid. It had been the concentrated sulphuric acid emitting the acrid fumes, giving the impression something was burning, which of course had given off even more fumes on coming into contact with the water sprayed on it. The intention had been that the sulphuric acid would eventually eat through the inner condom and react with the contents of the outer one to generate hydrogen cyanide gas, once used in death chambers in the US.

Placing the device in a location somewhat away from the subway station, where the police would be concentrating their efforts, was a clever move, as even there the gas could have killed over a thousand people once sucked into the ventilation system in the normal course of events.

'The layout,' said Sachiko, 'is now somewhat different from what it was then in that the location of the toilet has been changed, but that does not alter the fact that with it just here, many people could have been killed or injured. So many people, including myself, used to pass through this passage every day. It made me feel bad every time I walked along here.'

'Seems a very busy place,' said Holt.

'I used to come through here regularly to visit the Maruzen bookshop to read the English magazines for free. Did you know the Japanese have a special word for that? It's tachi-yomi. Literally translated it means "standing reading". Some people spend hours reading without buying anything. Some company people or academics note the details and buy the book through their organization or through Amazon. In no other country would shops allow people to do that. I think some people abuse it. I always try and buy something.'

They then went down onto the subway platform and took an underground train to Yotsuya station so that she could show them the Geihinkan, the State Guest House, where foreign dignitaries stay. Set in spacious grounds well back from the public thoroughfares, it seemed a safe enough place.

She then took them to a street a little back from the main road and pointed to a fairly low apartment building with balconies facing the guest house grounds.

'It was from there that they intended to launch the rockets from the drainpipes using timers. They were just primitive mortars, according to my dad.'

The following day they visited several other places mentioned by Sachiko in the New York Bar and came back to Shinjuku for a light tempura dinner at a well-known restaurant called Tenichi. Sachiko then went home, as they had to be up fairly early the following morning to take the train to her home.

A true Japanese, she was there right on time, and she took them to Shinjuku Station to board the so-called Odakyu Romance Car to Fujisawa.

'It's called the Romance Car, but that simply means it is a more luxurious train going to tourist places, such as Hakone, near Mount Fuji. The great thing is that you can reserve seats and not have to stand up, as on most commuter trains.'

'Call me Jim,' said her father on picking them up at Fujisawa Station. To Holt he seemed a delightful man and not the chinless wonder his name might suggest. No wonder he preferred to be called SH.

On the way to his house, they passed the giant Buddha statue at Kamakura. Truly impressive.

Her Japanese mother, Midori, was at the door to welcome them and ensure they removed their shoes before entering. She took Holt to his room, while Sachiko took Celia in hand to show her to hers.

'It used to be mine when I was at university.'

After sprucing up, Holt and Celia came down to join the others on the terrace.

They started talking about the old days in Japan when foreigners were a rarity. A time when the TV journalist Alan Wicker started out reporting on the Korean War, before working on his famous TV programme Wicker's World; a time when only the rich could travel afar, and flights from Europe took the southern route, stopping off in places like Karachi, Singapore, and Hong Kong.

SH explained that years later, with the introduction of longer-range jet aircraft, the route via the North Pole with a stopover at Anchorage opened up and much reduced the journey time, to something like eighteen hours. And then when the Cold War tensions eased, the much shorter trans-Siberian route opened up. At first, there were stopovers in Moscow, and then with the introduction of nonstop flights, there was always the possibility of diversion to an alternate airport in Russia because of technical trouble, with some at MI6 concerned that the KGB might pick them up en route. However, with the only alternative being the much longer southern route via the Middle East, many took the view 'If they nick me, we'll nick one of them.' Of course, those working on the Russian desk still would not risk it.

The return of the women cut short any further business talk, and they had less serious talk over drinks on the terrace, followed by a Japanese-style dinner. It was a family gathering with friends, and the primary object of the trip was far from Holt's mind.

'I read about Japan before coming,' said Holt, 'but it's still quite a surprise. Everything is different. Of course the people, but there is a different feel. I don't know what it is. I must say that Sachiko has looked after us so well we do not feel out of our element. We were, though, expecting kamikaze taxis, but she said you had told her it was only a rumour started by some journalist trying to think up some copy on the way to the airport.'

'There are a number of stories like that,' said Jim. 'I don't suppose she told you the one about why Japanese women came to wear knickers—'

'We're tired of hearing that old story,' interjected Midori.

'Dad, now you've started you might as well go on. It's funny really. I'm not sure it's true, though. It's something men like bringing up.'

'Well,' continued Jim, 'the story goes that Japanese women only started wearing knickers after Japan's first department store caught fire in the 1920s, and a number of employees preferred to die rather than shame themselves jumping from the windows with their kimonos billowing up.'

'They might have served as parachutes,' interjected Holt, adding to Sachiko's mother's displeasure, at which the conversation promptly changed to less sensitive topics.

Just before bed, Holt and Celia enjoyed – separately – a great feature of the house, a bathroom that was akin to a spa, before going to their separate rooms, much to Celia's delight, which was evident when Sachiko joined her for some more chat.

The next day, after a leisurely breakfast the women went out sightseeing and shopping, leaving Holt and Jim alone.

Jim ushered Holt into his study, its walls almost hidden by books, many of them about Japan, and some written by him.

He went straight to the point.

'I know you want to hear about terrorist incidents here in Japan. There have been quite a number over the years, but in general the home-grown terrorist phenomenon has wound down. Fifty years ago, students were demonstrating against the security treaty with the United States and the presence of many American troops here, notably in Okinawa. Now people see the presence of the Americans as a counterbalance to an increasingly assertive China.

'Problems related to the US presence do flare up, especially in Okinawa, say when one or two American servicemen raped a twelve-year-old schoolgirl, but things have calmed down now.'

'Funny,' said Holt, 'to think there are so many US military personnel around. I believe there are quite a number at Yokosuka naval base, not far from here.'

'Yes, years ago, apart from demonstrations against the Japan–US security treaty, the big news was the Red Army hijacking aircraft and seeking refuge in North Korea.'

'I read about that. Didn't one of them come back to Japan recently? He was homesick or something.'

'Yes, a year ago.'

'Hijacking,' said Holt, 'is not really my remit. Many people are covering that side. My job is to think up dramatic things opportunists or terrorists might do, other than 9/11-type hijackings.'

'Then the incidents like those that I told Sachiko to tell you about will interest you. Some are relatively low-tech. One group was able to discover where the cables linking the various radar installations used by air-traffic control in the Tokyo area passed and cut them. The ensuing flight delays left many red faces, as the backup had not been properly thought out or tested.'

'That's the type of thing I am interested in – simple yet dramatic in its way.'

'Perhaps most dramatic was the veranda-drainpipe incident that again I think Sachiko told you about and showed you where it was done. A group rented an apartment near the official guest house, which had a veranda facing it. They placed a number of drainpipes so that rockets fired from them using a timer would strike the guest house while world leaders were staying there. They were like mortars, with no need for a direct line of sight to the target.

82

'The rockets landed right in the grounds. Fortunately, no one was hurt. Again, there were a number of red faces in the police and the security agencies.'

'Anyone could set that up.'

'Yes, but they could not get away with it now. Prior to the arrival of any important personage, police and security people triple-check out residences and offices within range – first by the local plod, next the more-sophisticated police, and finally the security service. Furthermore, even the manholes for the drains are welded shut at sensitive locations.'

'Sachiko showed us the actual balconies – she said virtually all apartments have them for drying washing. We do not have those, or so many, in the UK. However, dissidents in Northern Ireland came up with a clever variation. In order to attack the central police station in Belfast, they took a van, removed the roof, and set up mortars on the floor inside it. As it would not have been easy to aim from within the van, the projectiles could well have landed in public areas, killing innocent civilians. Fortunately, police stopped the van en route. I think it was a random check, though it might have been reported as stolen, or there were other grounds for them to be suspicious.'

Jim went on to mention other attempts at disruption, and then their discussion was interrupted by Midori and Sachiko bringing coffee out to the terrace.

'Let's talk about the big one later,' said Jim.

Holt knew what 'the big one' was – the sarin nerve gas attack on the Tokyo Metro – but was glad to have a break before discussing something potentially so horrible. In one respect, the nerve gas attack was not so special or original, and not the creative thing he was meant to forestall. However, he had to learn about it if only to hold his own in meetings back in the UK.

Coffee was accompanied by some biscuits called RaisinWich, a Japanese abbreviation of Raisin Sandwich. These consisted of two biscuits with raisins, cream, and something alcoholic sandwiched between them, and were quite addictive.

'The man,' said Sachiko, 'who invented these not only had a clever idea for the name and the product but sold more by requiring that they be ordered in advance and making it appear they were in short supply. Consequently, people would order double the quantity they would have ordered otherwise.'

For the first time in what seemed a long time, Holt felt totally relaxed, and he noticed that Celia looked at ease too. Even though Blackwell had programmed him not to see Celia as a sexual object, there was always an underlying tension when they were alone together.

'The telling thing,' said Jim when the ladies departed, 'about the nerve gas attack was not the technique, which is really now widely known, but the way a sect can build itself up, exploit and control its members using very clever psychological means, and sometimes threaten society at large rather than simply exploit members for financial and often sexual reward.'

'Yes,' commented Holt, 'it is pretty scary, especially in the US, where it is not only sects but also extreme right-wing groups that see the US government as the enemy. They showed their teeth after Waco, and now, after Obama tried to introduce gun laws, they have increased tenfold.'

'At first sight, one could assume that Japan does not have a group of angry people, like in England, going abroad to learn how to make bombs and so on. However, there are many Koreans, some whose parents and grandparents were brought over as workers during the war, who owe their allegiance to North Korea. Also, there are many Chinese here officially and unofficially. These two groups blend into Japanese society, and it is not obvious from their appearance that they might have sympathies lying elsewhere.'

'In my briefings in London, I learnt that a number of the top people in the Aum Sect were highly educated, went to the best universities.'

'Yes, that's true, and that's partly why they were less troubled by the police than they might have been. Japanese society is hierarchical, and those leaders seemed so able. Almost looking down on the police after attending top universities.'

Jim explained to Holt that the Japanese system was special in that the ordinary people were very honest, but at the higher levels it was jobs for the boys, and how there was one corrupting tradition called *ama-kudari* ('coming down from heaven'), whereby senior government officials supervising industries are given plum jobs in those very same industries on retirement. This means they do not supervise those industries properly while in office. For example, not one of the ex-government officials responsible for the bad supervision of the nuclear power industry has been punished – they are still at their posts, in the *ama-kudari* tradition, in the electric power industry.

They went on to talk about possible terrorist scenarios, and it was not until dinner that talk turned to what was happening in England. Would Jim like to return? Not really. He had spent most of his life in Japan; besides, his wife was happier there.

'I was quite surprised,' said Jim, 'at how much England has changed with it becoming multicultural. America is changing too, and the Latinos will before long predominate in the electorate. Interestingly, here in the Far East immigration is limited, with countries trying to restrict it to talented people who will contribute to society. This is particularly true of Australia and Singapore. In the case of Singapore, the government unsuccessfully tried to bring in measures to persuade the more educated women to have more children.'

'What about Japan?'

'Same again. Here the problem is too many old people, but at least they do not have the benefits-dependency culture like the UK. Japan is one of the few advanced countries maintaining its identity. Immigration is very limited, but that raises problems, as there are not enough people for certain jobs. For instance, there is a shortage of pilots for the LCCs, the low-cost carriers that are spreading their wings. A lot of famous Japanese products are now produced largely in China.'

The conversation turned to other topics as they enjoyed their drinks in the warmth of the evening.

The next day, Jim and Midori took the two of them and Sachiko by car to Odawara Station to catch the bullet train to Kyoto. They would see something of the traditional Japan, and Celia would be able to do some shopping with Sachiko before their return to the UK.

Holt would be able to tell Sir Charles that the lessons learnt in Japan should serve him in good stead, but that the different environment meant that the incidents could not be exactly replicated in the UK.

Returning to London was something of a letdown after the novelty and excitement of the overseas trip. Japan, with 'terrorist' scenarios ranging from the absurdly simple and relatively innocuous to the deadly nerve gas attack on the Tokyo Metro, had really stimulated Holt's imagination. In Holt's view, none apart from the nerve gas attack – and that was already being covered by another department – were dramatic or novel enough to be worth discussing in detail with Sir Charles.

Holt sat at his desk at Farringdon thinking. His only conclusion was that his office needed a comfortable couch from which he could watch videos on his superb graphic designer monitor.

He missed Celia's constant presence at his side, though they did occasionally manage to arrange to be in the cafeteria at the same time. She had been allotted other work, often accompanying officials to meetings, ostensibly to take notes but more likely because the VIPs found her presence as congenial as he had. Of course, she would be keeping an eye on them and at the same time gaining intelligence on the people in the circles in which they moved.

Holt knew he could ask that she be assigned to accompany him as cover for taking photos but did not want to make his male colleagues jealous. The Japan trip had already raised far too many eyebrows, with smirking colleagues asking him whether he had had a good time.

Chapter 11
VIP for Half a Day

Luckily, the annual antiterrorist exercise in Scotland was coming up, and because of her work with him, Celia would be joining the party. The idea was that people from various sections of the government antiterrorist apparatus would network and, perhaps more importantly, suggest ways terrorists might perpetrate their attacks.

One problem with this concept, and especially from Holt's point of view, was that the bad guys might have a mole there picking up ideas. On the other hand, the powers-that-be thought that if al-Qaeda knew 'we knew they knew', they might not use a tactic suggested on the course.

Another problem was that the various government units, including Giraffe, were competing and keeping the best (or worst) ideas close to their chests so they could, in the event of such ideas materializing, show how well they were prepared.

The relatively junior people, like Holt and Celia, slept in huts, with the sexes of course separated. Celia had to share a hut with other young ladies and not-so-young ladies, since seniority was a question of rank rather than age with the older ones, apart from the lesbians, miffed at having to share with the mostly more attractive younger ones.

Running from Monday to Friday, and the first and last days taken up mainly by travelling and checking in and checking out, it was essentially only a three-day course. Most attendees regarded it as a holiday and a nice break from spouses or partners. The highlight was the formal dinner on the Thursday night, with a speech from the camp commandant, followed by dancing and much drinking.

Worried that Celia might latch on to someone new there, Holt reminded her how important it was to keep one's distance from other attendees, as some would certainly be handsome plants to sniff out anyone with too loose a tongue.

The Tuesday was spent attending replays, using models, of various incidents that were well-known and less well-known, including the Mumbai attack, where the terrorists arrived by water. The Wednesday consisted of representations and demonstrations of techniques terrorists might use, which was rather disappointing for the reasons already mentioned.

For his part, Holt threw in the idea that in parallel with an attack on London, terrorists could publicize a lecture with refreshments at the lecture hall on Parliament Square so that people wearing the burqa could discuss their problems. The police would not know what to do when confronted by hordes of women who might be men descending on central London. The idea served to raise Holt's profile but did not get much traction, as it was politically incorrect.

The evenings were rather more interesting, as they gave some opportunity for networking and allowed Holt to spend some time with Celia without raising the eyebrows of colleagues, though Peter always made his presence felt and joined them for dinner on the first night.

With only one full day to go and the party in the evening to look forward to, Holt was still asleep at six thirty on the Thursday morning when someone grabbed his shoulder and started shaking him.

'Mr Holt, wake up! You're wanted in the commandant's office ASAP. No need to shave or dress. Come in your dressing gown. The commandant is wearing his. I'll be waiting outside in the Land Rover.'

Holt sat on the side of the bed to gather his wits before going off to have a pee and splash some water on his face to wake himself up properly.

The commandant had obviously also been dragged out of bed, for unusually for him, he looked somewhat bedraggled. He did not waste any time.

'You're to go back to London immediately. Sir Charles wants to see you ASAP.'

'Have you any idea as to why?'

'No. All I know is that a special aircraft from RAF Northolt is on its way to pick you up. Must be something big. I suggest you grab a coffee and something to eat from the cooks. One never knows what they have onboard these special flights. There won't be anyone, and certainly not beautiful hostesses serving you champagne, that's for sure.'

'Anyway, good luck. Hope I will see you again. You were one of the more interesting characters.'

The 'hope I will see you again' was beginning to grate. It was if he were a member of SOE going to be dropped over occupied France in World War II.

'By the way,' said Holt as he stood up, 'I travelled up with a female colleague who partners me on some missions. She'll be wondering what happened to me. Could you give her a message? Just say I've had to go back to the office as something urgent came up – that is to say, reassure her that nothing terrible has happened. That no one has died.'

'It would be a pleasure. What's her name?'

'Celia Jones. She's Welsh.'

'I remember Celia. Quite a striking young filly, if I might say so.'

Thinking that well he might, Holt took his leave of the commandant and after a quick shower and shave went to get that coffee and a bite to eat.

Once Holt was onboard, the copilot, a flight lieutenant, pulled up the stairs and closed the cabin door. Without further ado, and with only Holt as payload, the twinjet lifted off easily from the camp's World War II runway and proceeded southwards.

When the aircraft came to a halt in front of the airport buildings at London's Northolt, the same flight lieutenant came back to open the door and lower the steps.

'Hope you had a good flight. I came back mid-flight to see how you were and have a powwow, but you were sleeping.'

'Thanks,' replied Holt, glad to have been asleep and not obliged to fend off questions.

With that, he clambered down the steps, at the foot of which were three very senior RAF officers waiting in line to salute him in the belief he must be extremely important. He not only had had a special flight for just himself, but also had a high-powered car with a motorcycle escort waiting to pick him up.

Caught unawares, Holt played out a scene similar to ones he had seen in films involving snobbish British officers and simply said, 'Um, carry on men' as he passed by them on his way to the sleek official car.

Left nonplussed and thinking that even Her Majesty the Queen would have deigned to acknowledge their presence with a few sympathetic empty words, the officers wondered who he might be. Would they one day be able to boast to their wives that they had met him?

Chapter 12
Mission Creep or Leap?

With the police motorcyclist clearing the way, the official car whisked Holt up to London's West End and, to avoid drawing attention, dropped him off as usual at the Reiss fashion store in Vigo Street, just at the top of Sackville Street.

He was thankful for the commandant's advice that he grab some breakfast. Even so, he was getting peckish, and in view of his sudden feeling of importance even felt emboldened to acquaint Cut-Glass of the fact. To his surprise and concern, she demonstrated none of her former disdain.

'Yes, Jeremy, I'd gladly go over the road and get you something. Anything you like.'

She had become protective, even motherly, showing the generous inner being Sir Charles had mentioned as being under that haughty exterior. But did her radical change of demeanour result from his having been chosen for some suicide mission? A jet down to London just for him, followed by an official car with a motorcycle escort clearing the way, as if he were a cabinet minister, and now respect from Cut-Glass herself. She surely knew something.

'Jeremy,' said Sir Charles, looking less self-assured than usual. 'Sorry to have dragged you out of bed at such an ungodly hour. However, this is a matter of the utmost urgency.'

'Sir Charles, it was quite something having those senior officers with all their stripes saluting me at Northolt as if I were James Bond. The only thing missing was 007's naval commander's uniform. I hope I am not being sent into the lion's mouth. I may not be as lucky as he would be.'

'I am afraid, Jeremy, the lion's mouth may not be so wide of the mark. What we have in mind for you could be dangerous, very dangerous. On the other hand, it could prove very pleasurable, if you are up to it.'

The pause before Sir Charles continued made Holt even more apprehensive.

'To cut to the chase, while you were in Japan another specialist section somewhat similar to ours came to us asking if we had someone on our staff or files with a particular profile that happened to be precisely yours. Not knowing what it was about, we admitted we did.'

'You mean, they wanted someone with exactly the profile I had to have to join Giraffe?'

'Precisely. They said it was highly unlikely anything would ever come of it, but a suspected terrorist organization was looking for someone with that profile, and they thought they might be able to infiltrate them via such an individual. As you were away in Japan and it was too delicate and complicated to discuss other than face to face, we somewhat reluctantly submitted an application in your name.'

'That's a bit much.'

'I know, but the fact of the matter was that we did not think they would be interested in you, as you would only be one of a large number of potential applicants, some, such as ex-IRA elements, with much more proven credentials in the field. Indeed, when there was no response we thought it really had come to nothing, and as the department concerned had insisted on absolute secrecy I did not mention it to you on your return.'

'That makes sense.'

'The trouble is, a couple of days ago, while you were playing tiddlywinks up in Scotland, we received a positive reply to your application, with a rendezvous fixed for tomorrow afternoon in Birmingham – hence the rush. We did not give your home address or details of where you work or worked, so they cannot be following you as yet.'

'That's something. But if they are still seeking experts like me, any action must be a long way off.'

'That's what we all thought, but SIGINT – that's GCHQ – has just found a tenuous link between people possibly related to them – they call themselves The Owl, by the way – and speculation in the money markets. Such concerted betting against the pound sterling suggests that some dramatic event is imminent.'

'What can I do? If what you say is true, there would no time for me to find out anything useful.'

'I know it's a long shot, but it's the only shot we have. Besides, information you might glean undercover could prove useful even after the event, whatever that might turn out to be. Their looking for someone talented like you suggests that whatever they are contemplating for now will only be an appetizer.'

'Which means?'

'You might have to remain undercover for some time, but hopefully not too many years. Anyway, we want you to go up to Birmingham and try and get accepted, and play it by ear. There will surely be a proving period before they accept you – that is, if they ever do. If you feel it is getting too hot for comfort, you can always tell them you have lost interest and pull out. Of course, you will have to do that before you learn any of their secrets, in which case there is no knowing what your fate might be. I am sorry to have to put it to you so bluntly but feel it only fair to be frank.'

'It would be just like when I applied to join you, except that you would have only used the Official Secrets Act to ensure I kept my mouth shut. They would surely have more definitive ways.'

He was seamlessly moving into the real cloak-and-dagger world without any special training or preparation. It was all moving too fast.

'I'm not sure I am cut out for that type of thing. I'm no James Bond.'

'That's what makes you so credible. That's your USP.'

'I've heard of mission creep; this is mission leap. Not at all what I signed up for, though of course I want to do my bit.'

'I think you should have a look at the questionnaire we completed online in your name, which is Jeremy Benet, by the way. You will be glad to know you offered your services as a technician, not a suicide bomber.'

'Nice of you!'

'Not necessarily. The reward for being a suicide bomber was pretty juicy – seventy-two virgins in heaven. Sorry to joke over something as serious as this, but you see we had to select a reward with sexual facets for you. After some discussion, we put you down for a trophy wife. Even Sandra thought that would be fitting. "Not bad going," she said, "for a young man like you needing experience".'

From the reference to his needing more experience, Holt surmised Cut-Glass had also read the transcript of his exploratory interview with the major.

'Run your eyes over it, Jeremy. Come back and tell me what you think. Whether you might see your way to helping us out. You could save very many lives. And remember, you can always pull out – well, at least initially.'

The old story – saving lives! Funny how the people telling you that never risked their own, except perhaps in the case of the major, who might well have done so while on active service.

Holt went back to the room where he had waited before. The downloaded application form that they had filled in on his behalf had no indication regarding the nature of what he was applying for – rather like the situation when he completed the application to join Giraffe, already a year before.

At least they had not portrayed him as some kind of messianic madman willing to sacrifice his life for the cause, and had presented him very much as he had presented himself to them. There was none of the chip-on-the-shoulder stuff, and perhaps that was his appeal.

Whoever had filled in his application had done a perfect job; not that it would have been so difficult with his application to join the service to hand. He could not really quibble.

Only when he reached the Rewards Menu on the last page did he understand Sir Charles's reference to virgins in heaven, which was one of the 'dishes' on offer. One could choose only one dish, be it a seemingly light hors d'oeuvres or a more substantial main course. One's options depended not only on one's role but also on one's age, and even being already in heaven.

94

Some options were self-explanatory, but for young Holt some were not. For instance, there was the Gandhi, for which one had to be over seventy years old. A footnote explained that Gandhi used to share his bed with young women, including his granddaughter, with the females naked and purporting to be virgins. This was allegedly so he could demonstrate he could resist temptation. Anyone opting for the Gandhi had to vouchsafe to keep his hands at least to himself. Also featured was Tossed Boys' Salad, with no explanatory footnote. Seemingly, the list had been drawn up by someone with a sense of humour, and perhaps all options were not intended to be taken seriously.

Not much could be wrong with the Trophy Wife option, though that too had a footnote, saying physical consummation was not guaranteed, but rendering other men intensely jealous was.

Holt found himself in an impossible position. He had come to regard Sir Charles as an idolized substitute for his father, making refusal even more difficult. Then there was the matter of saving many lives. The only plus for him personally was that taking such risks should elevate him in Celia's eyes – since their return from Japan, she had seemed tantalizingly distant – and possibly enable him to win her over. Finding the thought of living without her unbearable, he really had no choice.

In accepting what was quite possibly a suicide mission, he would insist that he be answerable only to Sir Charles and Giraffe, which of course was precisely what Sir Charles wanted, as it ensured he would be in a pivotal position.

'You will,' said Sir Charles when he returned to announce his acceptance, 'have to attend a crash course in undercover operations.'

'Not much time.'

'No. Such courses normally last six weeks and not the six hours available, but it's better than nothing.'

After they had discussed various aspects of the mission for another hour or so, Sir Charles summoned Cut-Glass.

'Sandra, as we hoped and you anticipated, our Jeremy has agreed to go undercover, at considerable risk to his person. He is going over to the Yard to see Inspector Holmes for some tips on how to survive. Please accompany him to Piccadilly and help him hail a taxi – something you are very good at.'

With no time for second thoughts, Holt found himself at the kerb on Piccadilly as Cut-Glass adeptly hailed a taxi before others standing nearby with the same intention could catch the driver's eye.

'Good luck, Jeremy!'

'Thanks, Sandra.'

He was going to need it, and the risk he had taken of calling her by her Christian name seemed trivial by comparison.

Inspector Holmes, a surprisingly kindly man in his fifties who had himself for many years worked undercover, was still in overall charge of several major operations. With his worn face bearing a couple of scars, he looked as though he had lived through some tricky situations.

Unlike many of the offices at the Yard, Holmes's afforded some privacy, which was fortunate, as the first thing the policeman did was to go over to a grey filing cabinet and take out a bottle of whisky and a couple of glasses and put them down on his desk, where there was already a bottle of sparking water. Holt was sitting in the chair placed sideways in front of the smallish steel desk.

'Working undercover,' said the inspector, returning to his rather more comfortable chair on the other side of the desk, 'you must avoid two things: getting emotionally involved – including falling in love, which is worst of all – and too much alcohol, so you had better have a drink now. You look as though you could do with one.'

With that Holmes poured them both a generous double shot and passed one of the glasses to Holt, commenting, 'I drink it neat, but put some water in if you like.'

'Thanks,' replied Holt, leaning over the table for the bottle of water and pouring a good measure into his glass.

'The secret,' continued Holmes, 'in undercover work is to blend in by being as far as possible oneself. Being oneself helps one avoid stupid mistakes and means one does not have to lie so much, which in itself is stressful and means one can easily get caught out.'

'I can see that.'

'In your case, you should obviously highlight the qualities – practical joking, and the idea that you think yourself to be superior intellectually and technically to the run-of-the-mill terrorist. Your reason for applying is purely boredom – you are not able to make use of your talents. You have no political or religious axe to grind. That forestalls tricky questions about political affiliations and relationships.'

'That's good, and true.'

'The greatest danger for you, Holt, will not be at the beginning but at the end, when you take the inevitable initiation test.'

'Initiation test? I wasn't expecting that.'

'Virtually all gangs, terrorist organizations – even secret services – use them after first assessing you to see whether you are worth the trouble.'

'What might it involve in my case?'

'Almost anything. Could mean shooting the prime minister, in which case we might very well end up shooting you ourselves. By the way, that's a joke.'

'I'm beginning to have my doubts. I don't want to kill anyone, friend or foe.'

'To avoid that eventuality, you should try to warn us beforehand, though I realize that might not be easy or even possible without blowing your cover.'

'I'm not sure I knew what I was letting myself in for.'

'Take it easy, boy! As you are claiming to be a technical guy rather than a religious fanatic, they are unlikely to order you to do something like that – unless of course they want to compromise you, have a hold over you, so you can never turn back. Never rejoin normal society. If they do order you to shoot someone and you cannot warn us so we can have the target wear a bulletproof jacket and simulate being seriously injured, aim to graze them.'

'One has to be a mighty good shot to just graze someone, and have the right weapon.'

'I am sorry. You will be out on a limb on this one. As a last resort, you can always refuse, but that has its risks too.'

Holt began to feel queasy. He could end up killing an innocent person by mistake. The only time he had used a gun before was when he fired an air rifle at some squirrels at a school friend's home in the country when he was thirteen or so.

'Good luck. You'll need it,' were the instructor's parting words, mirroring those of Cut-Glass.

Giraffe, the inspector had explained, could only establish his movements via the thousands of CCTV cameras scattered all over the country. Digital face-recognition technology would possibly identify him, and if for some reason he especially wanted Giraffe to know his whereabouts, he should look slightly upwards at the cameras when in the street, almost begging to be looked at. If he wanted them to make contact, he should do something that anyone following him would not notice, such as repeatedly touch his chin, which would still leave most of his face visible for identification purposes.

Should he give such a sign, Giraffe would most likely use Celia, as with her no 'handshake' (identity verification) would be necessary. Anyway, it was highly unlikely he would have to contact Giraffe at the beginning, as the target would be keeping him at arm's length until more sure of him.

He wished he had a woman waiting at home for him in whom he could confide – a ridiculous thought, as one could not confide in people outside the service, and the mission was too confidential to tell even Celia, who was anyway still up in Scotland. For once he was glad Peter would be up there keeping her out of any harm's way.

Chapter 11
Undercover

Holt slept fitfully that night. Sir Charles had suggested he see Blackwell, whose duties included preparing agents for overseas missions, to at least get some sleeping pills, but that was the last thing he wanted. Blackwell wanted him if not dead, at least sidelined. He would put in a report doubting his suitability for the mission, at the same time denigrating him to cover his back when in all likelihood it went bottom up. Sir Charles had not suggested he ask Blackwell for a suicide pill. Having one would have made him feel a lot better.

As per instructions, he arrived at London's Marylebone station in plenty of time to take the 10.20 train to Birmingham. How he envied the families and couples waiting on the concourse for their train's platform number to come up on the indicator board. Many would have been invited to spend the weekend outside London with family or friends, not to mention the young couples obviously looking forward to an uplifting weekend and all that entailed. Their carefree demeanour was depressing.

The kids were no solace either, for they reminded him that if he were exposed and killed, that would be it. No succession. He was being not only sucked in but possibly suckered in, having been put in a position where it would be psychologically difficult to say no.

It was already too late for second thoughts. Sir Charles was counting on him, and he could not have Celia knowing he had chickened out. The withering scorn of Cut-Glass would be unbearable after having finally gained her respect.

With eight minutes to go, the platform number still had not been announced. He was getting nervous as well as depressed. If he was not to miss his train, he had to concentrate.

With only three minutes left before the official departure time, the public address system came to life and announced the train to

Birmingham Snow Hill would be leaving from Platform 2. A small horde of people, Holt included, immediately rushed to the ticket barriers, fed their tickets into the slots and, on recovering them, made their way along the platform, looking for seats not occupied by the savvy travellers who had been waiting inside the wickets.

As instructed, Holt walked right to the front coach before boarding. Finding a window seat, he sat – again as instructed – facing rearwards, wearing the black tie he had been ordered to wear. He might have been going to a funeral, and in other circumstances would have caught the eye of friends and relatives of the deceased whom he might know. Was the black tie to psyche him out by making him think he was going to his own funeral?

Having waited to allow everyone to board, the train pulled out of the station a couple of minutes late, passed through a long tunnel almost right under Lord's cricket ground, and came out into the open air at a spot where underground lines ran parallel to it.

With two hours remaining before arrival at Birmingham, he snuggled down to try to catch up on the sleep he had missed during the night. His eyes had hardly closed when there was a sharp tap on his shoulder. Expecting it would be the ticket inspector, he looked up, only to have to look further down into the eyes of a young boy staring at him.

'Sir, sir, wake up! The bloke gave me this for you. Said I should give it to the man with the black tie called Beany in the front coach. Must be you. No one else around here has a black tie.'

'Actually, the name's Benet, but it must be me you want.'

Satisfied, the boy handed Holt the envelope he was clutching, then fished a mobile phone out of his pocket and took a photo of Holt holding it.

'Said he would give me five quid if I showed him the photo of you with it. My lucky day.'

Holt thanked the boy, who promptly scarpered off. No point in pursuing the matter further. Doing so would raise suspicions, and more than one person might well be involved, with one possibly sitting nearby, discreetly observing him. After all, they knew in which coach he would be sitting.

On opening the envelope, he found a message telling him that instead of the last station, Birmingham, he was to get off at the first, Gerrards Cross, though just in case the train stopped prematurely at another for a red signal, he was to check the station really was Gerrards Cross before alighting.

He was to wait at the front of the station by the telephone box for a white Mercedes driven by the 'Trophy Wife' to come and pick him up. If for some reason there were a last-minute change of plan, they would call the phone in the phone box just near there. If it rang, he should answer it to receive further instructions from the Owl.

It had been a wily move to give the impression he was heading many miles up north to Birmingham when in fact he would be just outside London. The people from Giraffe would find themselves wasting their time scouring video recordings from the cameras up in Birmingham. Also, use of the nonthreatening word 'owl' was something of a surprise, when organizations with evil intent would be more likely to choose something nasty, such as 'Spider', 'Snake', or 'Scorpion'. 'Owl' suggested wisdom.

He replaced the letter in the envelope and slipped it into his left pocket. The train, which had been travelling quite fast, was already slowing and pulling into a station. Having checked that it was well and truly Gerrards Cross, he alighted. The acceleration of events had given him no time to prepare himself mentally to meet his reward, and he was feeling tense.

Gerrards Cross was a simple station set away from the main road, with just the ticket office, a couple of ticket distributors, a taxi-service office, and the phone box he had been told about. There were one or two people about, but none hanging around. The wait was possibly intentional to ensure no one was following him.

Five minutes later, a white Mercedes came down the slope somewhat too quickly for the speed humps and stopped abruptly beside him. The side window wound down and the female driver leant over.

'You're Jeremy, I presume.'

'Yes, I am.'

'I'm to take you in hand. Get in!'

Although from outside Holt could not get a full view of her, it was immediately apparent she was a trophy, wife or not.

Having been told not to bring any luggage, he did not need to ask her to unlock the boot, and with nothing even to place on his lap, getting in would be easy. Stupidly, he hesitated.

'Either get in or pack it in. This is not a good place to linger. You decide. Makes no difference to me.'

Unable to chicken out, he opened the door and clambered in, pulling the heavy door shut with that dull clunk one associates with quality cars.

'We can't talk now. Just sit back and chill out.'

The car accelerated down the slope and did a U-turn to return to the main road. They were on their way. Holt did not dare ask to where.

He first concentrated on looking at the Trophy Wife's face, which exhibited a knowing yet reassuring smile on the rare occasions she glanced at him. When her gaze reverted to the road ahead, his would shift to her bare knees, remaining there longer than would have been polite had she been looking.

Telling himself to getting a grip, he turned his attention to the road ahead and tried to work out where they were going. She was a very adept driver, and despite her abrupt no-nonsense manner, the first part of his mission was proving not so bad after all. He even began to relax.

After about twenty minutes' driving, they arrived at a large house set back from the road and shielded from it by some trees. He noted that it was surrounded by the gravel so beloved by insurance companies, since it enables the occupants to hear intruders walking around outside. The car crunched to a stop a few yards from the front door.

Even though there was no one there, she stepped out with her knees close together, as though it was a well-practiced manoeuvre, and gestured that Holt should get out too. As she stood with her back to him while she opened the oiled oak front door, then hurried inside, no doubt to enter the code into the burglar alarm, Holt could see she had a generous figure that filled out her shift dress, with no hint of the vulgarity flaunted by some footballers' trophy wives and the like. Apart from her beauty and perfection, she was a normal person with natural-seeming breasts.

Appearing back in the doorway, she beckoned to him to come in, but before he had gone a yard and a half down the hall, an alarm went off.

'I'm sorry. I'll have to search you. But first give me your passport – the chip might have set off the alarm. You did bring it as instructed, didn't you?'

Holt said, 'Of course,' as he handed over the document.

'You won't be needing those clothes either. We have a whole wardrobe of clothes tailor-made for you in the closet in your room. You'll find both man-about-the-country and man-about-town, not to mention man-on-the-Côte-d'Azur. There is even a dinner jacket, so we can go anywhere, except perhaps to the races at Ascot. Strip down to your briefs so I can check you out. Then you can go upstairs to put on something decent.'

Holt again hesitated.

'If you want to pull out, I can take you straight back to the station. It's your choice.'

'You mean take off my clothes right here?'

'On second thoughts, it would be easier and nicer in the drawing room; there's more room. Let's go in there. Besides, it's warmer. My name's Consuela, by the way.'

Holt wondered whether the alarm had been set to go off anyway, just to show that there was a hard edge to all this gentility. As he had been told to come with no luggage, not even shaving things or a toothbrush, and only his passport, there was not much, other than his keys and coins, to set the alarm off.

Feeling intimidated standing there in only his boxer shorts, he nevertheless took in the fact that the trophy wife surveying him had assumed the detached professional air one associates with nurses, doctors, and no doubt prison wardens. Turning away, she picked up an object somewhat like a Geiger counter and proceeded to scan his hair and then the part of his body obscured by what little clothing he retained. The diverse buzzing noises emanating from the device made her frown for a moment, adjust the calibration, and recheck his more private parts, until she finally seemed satisfied and broke into what he thought was a wistful half smile.

'Sorry about that. It would have been easier without underpants, but we are not familiar enough with each other for that.'

'I hope you're satisfied.'

'I *should* say so. I'll show you your room.'

The room was large, bright, and airy, but pretty stark, though it did have an en suite bathroom. He presumed, from the lack of clutter, that it was rented accommodation. There was, however, a television. Would he be spending his nights there watching it alone, thinking of her also all alone in the room along the landing?

She had that air about her that fashion models often exude, indicating they are to be admired but not touched. Sexually she seemed an iceberg. He consoled himself with the thought that three-fifths of an iceberg is hidden underwater and slowly melting.

'After you have had a shower and put on some fresh clothes, we can have some drinks. Your new clothes are in that closet. They should fit. That is, if you filled in the application correctly. When I came here, I stupidly lied and could not get into the designer jeans they supplied.'

At last, she sounded human, as if she had been enrolled in the organization after undergoing a similar process to the one he was undergoing. Perhaps given time the iceberg would thaw, but how much time did he have?

He had a quick shower and slipped on the corduroy slacks and a smart woollen pullover, which of course fitted perfectly thanks to the precise measurements provided by the tailor at Sackville Street. Making his way down the stairs trying to look as suave as possible, he indeed looked the perfect man-about-the-country.

'Feel better now?'

'Much better.'

'You certainly look better too.'

'Where did you get the clothes?'

'I didn't. They were delivered by courier.'

'Funny thing about clothes,' replied Holt. 'People keep on telling me how important they are, but in my IT work they did not seem to matter. In fact, one dressed down so as not to get people's backs up.'

'Some people can look good in anything and better in something simple,' replied Consuela with a smile.

'That would apply to you!'

'Thanks for the compliment. I get a lot, but no woman ever has enough, I'm told. Let's have our champagne and caviar on the terrace.'

'Wow!'

'I might as well tell you right away. The Owl promised you a trophy wife – though not one to fornicate with. I am a real trophy wife in that my darling of a husband is a billionaire over in the States. By the way, I don't like keeping on saying "husband". If we ever to refer him again, let's just call him H.'

'Okay, H. Should I call you C?'

'No. Consuela will do nicely. Now you know, let's forget about H. I've put out the glasses and titbits. Can you do the honours, as all this secrecy means I do not have any staff here? Normally, I have a butler and a maid.'

Holt opened the bottle of champagne none too expertly and just about managed to pour it into the glasses before it spewed all over the place.

'I can,' said Consuela, 'see I shall have to give you some lessons. How are you with cocktails?'

'Not too good either, I'm afraid. To be honest, I do not get much practice. In fact, have hardly ever made one – at least, not a proper one.'

'One of these days, let's have a cocktail session. Sometimes getting the cocktails right can make all the difference to a party or reception, even with close friends. By selecting the right combination of cocktails, one can draw people out. Even the shyest.'

'Cocktails are, I suppose, more of an American thing. You say cocktails are good for drawing even shy people out, but isn't that what you're doing here with me with the champagne? A somewhat unusual role for a trophy wife. I mean, with you having such a great life with your H over there.'

'I am only doing this as a one-off for some excitement – horrible word. I was getting bored, despite all the receptions, jetting off in one of H's private jets to exotic places, and dinners with movers and shakers. I wanted to do something independently, even if it meant slumming it.'

'I wouldn't call this slumming.'

'I would.'

'Really?'

'I'm partly joking. I can, and have, taken the rough with the smooth.'

Holt did not want to be too inquisitive when he should be the one under examination. He therefore purposely avoided following up on her remarks and said nothing. There was always the possibility that all this honesty was to make him drop his guard.

'You must,' continued Consuela without any prompting, 'be wondering why the Owl took me on. You see, I studied psychology at Harvard but never used it professionally, as I was soon to marry an unbelievably rich man.'

'I see,' replied Holt, not exactly sure of what he could see but feeling he had to say something without being too nosy.

'Anyway, my involvement with the Owl was a tap-on-the-shoulder type of thing, where someone H knew asked whether I would care for an adventure assessing candidates for some people

106

I did not need to know about that might greatly benefit the country, indeed the world.'

'I'm surprised you're telling me all this,' replied Holt, trying not to let his own guard down.

'I have nothing to hide. To tell the truth, I did not even receive much training for this, other than how to defend myself in the event of unwanted attention – so watch out!'

'I'll try and be careful,' said Holt, thinking that he too had been given similar training, though not to fend off someone with amorous intentions.

'Anyway, I have been told I am to have ten days to assess you and that I must take you to certain functions, receptions, garden parties, and so on. I have a schedule. We're going to be pretty busy, so we won't be spending all day here looking at each other, thank heaven.'

Holt did not like her stressing how glad she was they would not be spending too much time alone together but had to admit that she would have turned him off had she been too forward. She had provided him with an opening, which he decided to follow up.

'You might be taking a bigger risk than you realize. What does H think about all this? Does he even know what you are doing?'

'He's cool about it. He said he had taken a lot of risks in his time to get where he is now, and that if I thought it was worthwhile and would get my desire to do something special for my country and the world out of my system, it was okay with him. He had three wives, not to mention numerous dalliances, before me, so is not too possessive. I suppose at his age the jealous looks of the young studs we come across when in public are satisfaction enough.'

'I think I understand,' said Holt, realizing that he could not safely pursue that line of questioning.

'All I know,' continued Consuela, 'is that the Owl is a very important or rich person or high official in the CIA or something like that, and that he might even be present at one of these events and talk with us without either of us realizing it.'

'It's going to be a bit creepy wondering every time we meet someone whether it is him.'

'Yes, it will be for sure.'

'Could the Owl be more than one person?'

'In a way, he already is. I have had phone calls purporting to be from the Owl, with the voice sounding different each time. Once it was a woman's voice; once it was even a child's voice. I presume people in his organization speak in his name.'

In his undercover briefing, Inspector Holmes had told Holt they would keep him at arm's length until they had confidence in him. In the present case, the arm – namely Consuela – did not know the body to which it was connected. Also, the situation was quite the opposite of what he and Sir Charles had envisaged in that he would be moving around quite openly.

'In addition to that,' continued Consuela, 'my role is to get to know you. I might as well tell you, the Owl said nothing about you other than that you were male. He said that would make it easier for me to judge for myself.'

'Really?'

'Within limits, we can proceed gradually. No need to rush things. You will inevitably at some point open up and reveal yourself, like a clam caught unawares. I am an excellent judge of character, thanks in part to my background in psychology. After all, that is why they decided to use me. Of course, my ability to socialise played a part.'

'I hope you don't find anything bad.'

'As Lieutenant Cable said in the movie *South Pacific* about the French planter who had moved to the Pacific islands after murdering a nasty piece of work back in France, something bad, as you call it, might make you "a useful person to have around". So do not hold back. Tell me like it is. I don't think they are looking for a saint.'

There was a pause with neither of them saying anything. Again, it was broken by Consuela.

'I should warn you that I am the easy part. After your session with me, I am told you will undergo some form of initiation test, in which I will play no part. On submitting my report, I will return to the US and sever what little connection I ever had with the Owl and his organization.'

'Didn't you have to take an initiation test?'

'There was no need, as I never sought to become a full-fledged member. I was to merely be a one-off consultant. I know nothing about the Owl or his organization, other than that its purpose is, I believe, benign. I am telling you all this to avoid you wasting my time pumping me for information I do not have.'

It could all be a trick to make him reveal all. Of course, as a mature woman of apparently great experience, she was not innocent in the way Celia made herself out to be. She appeared very genuine – perhaps too genuine. Funnily enough, he was not quite sure about Celia. Sometimes he felt it was all an act.

'Watch television, listen to some music, do some reading while I prepare the meal. Before I start cooking, I have to report that you are installed in your quarters, that all is going smoothly and, most importantly, confirm I should be able to put up with you for the next ten days or so.'

How did she make contact with the Owl? With the internet and disposable mobile phones, there were so many ways it could be done without GCHQ knowing. Back at Giraffe, they were probably still scrutinising the CCTV footage for Birmingham.

He had to admire the Owl for the way he operated at a distance, using people who could not give anything away or reveal his identity. Even the boy on the train and having him wear the black tie was a smart move.

Who was the Owl? The only thing he knew for certain was that he must be someone moving in high-society, finance, governmental, or diplomatic circles. He could even be in the service. Still, all that might be a pretence, with Consuela being duped as much as he.

While waiting for Consuela to submit her report and prepare the meal, he opted for the television but in a limbo could not concentrate on the news. The *CSI: Crime Scene Investigation* programme seemed all he could stomach. Besides, its US ambience might put him in the right frame of mind for dealing with a woman who had, it seemed, been mostly brought up there.

At dinner, he realized she truly merited her title of Trophy Wife, and not only for her looks, which would make any man turn his head, but also for her cooking. The meal was simple, with a divine ratatouille and a joint of lamb.

'Did you know,' remarked Consuela on presenting it, 'that in France, when you invite guests to your home and want to honour them, you serve lobster or langouste followed by a joint of roast lamb?'

'No, I didn't.'

'H and I visited some French friends in Paris, and they served lamb cooked to perfection, which then for me was nothing special. It was only afterwards that I learnt that they had been trying to do us proud.'

'Of course, the way the French and I cook lamb – almost rare – is quite different from the way most English people do it, overcooking it and compensating by serving it up with mint sauce. Let's have some of that wine. It should be a good one.'

It certainly was – a Petrus costing goodness knows how much a bottle. Even Holt knew it was one of the greats – Peter Ustinov's favourite, according to an article he had read.

'Is the Owl paying for all this?' he asked.

'For the food, yes. I, or rather H, paid for the wine, as I was not sure the Owl would go quite that far. Not that he seems short of funds. It is just that he might have thought it somewhat extravagant.'

'What's H like?'

'He's kind. And as I said, much older – I'm only thirty-two.'

Consuela paused as if reflecting on her own situation.

'I suppose one day he will die, leaving me with the wherewithal to continue, as the lawyers say, in the style to which I am accustomed. I must seem a money digger, but that was not the reason I married him.'

'What was it then?'

'He rescued me from an abusive relationship.'

'Really?'

'Yes. You would think that with my education, my study of psychology, I would not fall into such a trap. Actually, it was the psychology that did me in – I thought a poor jerk needed help. But once I helped him, he would not let go.'

'Why didn't you cut him loose?'

'I did. But he kept on stalking me. Threatened to kill me, throw acid in my face, and the like. You know the routine.'

'Couldn't you move somewhere else? Go to the police?'

'The police could not protect me. Besides, he had friends in the mafia with informers in the police, and he would find me wherever I was.'

'Why didn't you try what that woman did in *Sleeping with the Enemy*, where she faked her own death to stop her husband looking for her?'

'Because in the movie the fiend found her in the end, and I can identify with the fear she felt when she went into the bathroom in the villa where she was hiding and saw the towels were perfectly arranged in threes in just the way he had always insisted, and then on descending to the kitchen finding everything in the cupboards had been lined up perfectly. By that, she knew he was in the house. The man was a control freak, and a perfectionist to boot.'

'I saw that film. It was really scary.'

'I was a bit like Princess Diana or Jacqueline Kennedy in that I could only escape and be free with the help of someone with real money, yachts, gated properties, not to mention bodyguards. H helped me, without seeking any special favours.'

'What happened to the fiend in the end? Is he still around? Could he find you – us – here?'

'No. No. Not long after H took me under his wing, my nightmare ended, with my nemesis dying in a road accident. It seems he was driving under the influence of alcohol and drugs. Came off at a bend on a mountain road without even braking – there were no skid marks. His auto tumbled down the hillside and caught fire.'

Had it really been an accident? Holt thought it wise to avoid asking the obvious.

'How did you feel when you heard he was dead?' he asked instead.

'Relief. To be honest, reborn. For even with the bodyguards and all that, I knew he would get me in the end and was just biding his time, waiting for his chance. For absolute security, I would have had to have been the president of the United States, and even then...'

'You didn't feel sorry for him?'

'Funnily enough, once I knew he could no longer harm me, there were flashbacks to the time when we first met, when I believed in him. I was only a child then in a way.'

'Why did you stay with H and even marry him when there was no longer any danger?'

'Partly out of gratitude for having protected me in my time of need, but more perhaps because I had gotten so used to the good life with very few strings, and the freedom that money provides. He's so satisfied with what he is doing, he does not need to control me. Quite the opposite of the other one. He lets me do almost whatever I want, so long as we cooperate and keep up appearances. Then there is the simple fact that with his intelligence and great sense of humour, he is wonderful to be with. Then there are all the fascinating people he knows.'

'I suppose it was partly because you were on the rebound.'

'Yes, there's that too, but what people cannot understand is that being too attractive is a lonely business. The nice guys are afraid to make a move, and the bad guys have no compunction, like the creep I was talking about. You see what I mean?'

'I think so.'

'Being married to a powerful person means fewer people trouble me – not that I allow them to get near me. You are first person I have talked frankly to for a long time, and I'm not letting you get too near either. You understand?'

Holt did understand. Being in her presence was reward enough. Her revelations had made him really relax. Besides, he was already getting used to the good life, and this was merely a foretaste of what lay in store in the days ahead. That is, until the dreaded initiation test.

The meal over, he helped her clear the table and arranged the dishes in the dishwasher while she busied herself making coffee.

As they sat side by side on the sofa with brandies on the coffee table before them, Consuela let out a sigh, which he took as a sure sign she felt at ease in his presence. He had felt like this with Celia on the terrace at The Loughty, replete after a great meal, but this time there had been nothing wrong with the coffee, which was truly excellent. The Loughty scenario had been Blackwell's doing. Somehow, he did not think that would be the Owl's style.

So as to be more comfortable and avoid his left hand pressing against Consuela's thigh, he raised that arm and placed it on the back of the sofa behind her shoulders. In so doing he moved closer to her, but not close enough for their bodies to more than sense each other. While she did not to seem to object or even notice, she did nothing to encourage further encroachments on her private space. He had to behave like one of those good guys afraid to make a move, which was in fact not far from the truth.

After watching a film on television and then the news, Consuela promptly declared it was time for bed.

'We are going to hit the ground running. Tomorrow we're off abroad. I booked the flight using the details on your passport. I hope you are not on any no-fly lists as a potential terrorist?'

'I see no reason why I should be. Where are we going? Pakistan?'

'No, no. Not nearly as far as that. You'll see when I give you your boarding pass. Don't worry. It'll be fun, great fun. It'll be something for you to remember for the rest of your life – at least, what remains of it.'

'You're winding me up.'

'That was only a joke and partly to prevent myself getting carried away, even getting attached to you. Besides, I want you slightly on edge so you reveal more of yourself when you eventually unwind. I have probably said too much about myself – there's something about your naïveté that makes me talk too

113

much. You're a breath of fresh air after the society people I frequent. I'm going up to my room. I've got to update my report on you; not that there is much to add as yet. Good night.'

With that she stood up, leant over towards him, and gave him a peck on the left cheek. Though the air kiss was probably one she had done hundreds of times as a society hostess at receptions, Holt wanted to believe there was more to it than that.

Later, in his own bed, alone, he had a feeling of nervous anticipation like a fifteen-year-old, even though it had been made clear that he should not expect anything physical and the way things were going that could well prove to be the case.

After a night sleeping fitfully, thinking of Consuela, he came downstairs to find her already in the kitchen. She was wearing a fetching cotton dressing gown.

'Sleep well?' she asked.

'Yes, thanks,' he lied.

'Good. We have a busy day ahead.'

'I'm intrigued.'

'We're having breakfast in the conservatory. Can you take these things in?' she said, giving him no chance to ask how she had slept.

He had never lived in a house with a conservatory, though many of his parents' friends had been adding them to theirs. Besides generating extra space, they enabled one to partly enjoy the outside life, despite the lousy English climate. It was bright and a nice place to be.

Breakfast was a simple continental affair with croissants and slightly toasted French bread. There was also fruit, including some quite exotic ones. Having made sure he had enough coffee and toast, Consuela again took the initiative.

'You have been very reticent about yourself. You have to give something away for me to assess you.'

'I don't know where to begin.'

'Begin by telling me about your family, whether you have any brothers or sisters. That sometimes provides good clues regarding a person's motivations – sibling rivalry and all that. Was

114

your mother forceful in making you do things, like making you read?'

'I'm an only child...'

'I thought as much.'

Realizing that she had obviously not been given any real details about him so that she could make her own assessment, he explained that his parents had died in a car crash when he was thirteen years old; that although clever, he just got by at school with the minimum of effort because he was bored and made up for it by playing practical jokes. His mother had tried to get him to learn the piano and had a grand piano that took up most of the living room in their tiny house.

'The music mistress at my school said, "Why learn the piano? There's only one in an orchestra as opposed to twenty or so violins. Learning the violin would give you a much greater chance of getting in." She seemed oblivious to the fact that my complete absence of talent meant no orchestra would want me, even to play the triangle.'

'Which parent influenced you most?'

'Neither. They left me to my own devices. They were too busy with their intellectual pursuits, though they did question the fact that I spent a lot of time with a guy about to get married who was into electronics and had all sorts of fascinating gadgets. They didn't realize it could have been the gate to a great future in Silicon Valley.'

He went on to proffer information very similar to that which he had provided at the exploratory interview for the service with the major. It was only when it came to his present work for Giraffe that he found himself in a quandary.

Sir Charles had told him to say something near the truth but not the whole truth. So he said he worked in a government think tank, thinking up scenarios for all sorts of situations, including what would happen were a hub airport to be built in such and such a place.

'I can't say more than that. All I can say is that I am an ideas man.'

'You must be doing something important for it to be so hush-hush.'

'Not really. I am just an ideas man, and brainstorming throws up scenarios in all sorts of domains, with some having security or military implications. I'm simply a backroom boy, supposedly able to think laterally. It's not as exciting as it sounds – that's why I am looking for something else, something that will stretch me a bit.'

'Do you have to travel – go on missions? I saw from the stamps in your passport that you recently went to Japan.'

On the principle that his undercover personage should be as close as possible to the truth, the service had copied his entry and exit stamps for Japan into his new passport under the name of Benet.

'I don't have to travel, though the people I work for think it is stimulating,' he said warily.

'You seem distant, withdrawn. As if you are hiding something from me, and I am wondering why.'

'Do I?'

'Are you sure you're not some kind of undercover cop?'

'Do I look like one?'

'No, but undercover cops never do. You can often tell one because they are too good to be true – more extremist than the people they are penetrating.'

Had he been, in the major's words, sussed out on day one? Was it so obvious?

Anyway, all was not lost. She could not prove it, and whatever his role, he could always claim he was bored and looking for greater challenges in keeping with his intelligence. Also, there was a chance that Consuela might come to like him and only mention the possibility he might be a plant. He would neither admit it nor deny it – leave her in suspense. If he denied it, she would not believe him anyway.

'Do I look like an extremist?'

'No, not in the least. It's difficult to work out what you are.'

Holt felt that he should do some serious explaining, including revealing truths that would make him more believable. After all,

116

the inspector had told him to present the real him, as far as possible.

'I am not sure who I am either, as when my parents were killed, I was at a loss, and turned off for a year or so, and did not latch on to anything. You see, my trouble is that I cannot find a job where my talents are made use of. I don't feel stretched, if you know what I mean. People say I'm too clever by half. I don't intend to get people's backs up when I say that. I don't want to get yours up.'

'Having a high IQ wouldn't get mine up. After all, H has an exceptionally high IQ. What's yours?'

'One hundred and fifty or sixty.'

Consuela raised her eyebrows and looked at him more intently than before, as if learning how intelligent he was made him of much greater interest.

Consuela parked in the car park at Heathrow's Terminal 5 – the new terminal dedicated to British Airways flights – and with a flourish handed Holt his boarding pass. Club Europe to Nice. They were certainly doing everything in style, for the extra cost for business class would be considerable.

'I've never been to the Côte d'Azur. Seen it in films, though. For instance, in *Dirty Rotten Scoundrels*, with Michael Caine and Steve Martin. Always dreamed of going there.'

'That,' retorted Consuela with a glint in her eye, 'was a really funny movie – especially the whipping scene, where Steve Martin has to retain a stupid smile, pretending he has no feeling in his legs while Michael Caine is slashing at them with a cane. Of course, the fact that I've been there many times made the movie all the more enjoyable. The Côte d'Azur is too crowded in the high season, unless of course you have a yacht or the use of a great villa with views over the sea, like Cliff Richard, not to mention many other friends of ours.'

'Isn't it the high season now?'

'Yes, but rest assured we have a motor yacht at our disposal, albeit a smallish one. It belongs to a couple of my best friends. In fact my best friends.'

As they made their way through immigration and the maddening security check and then on to the Executive Club lounge, Holt looked up at various security cameras so he would be identified. At one point he even gave a thumbs-up sign. He was sure Giraffe would know which flight he was on, as his name and passport number would have been given when Consuela made the booking. He did it more to reassure them and make them less likely to tail him – something that could lead to his downfall, as the Owl would soon find out. At least they would know where he was going and that he was still okay.

Although the Club Class on European flights was not nearly as luxurious as that on the long-haul ones with flat beds, it did mean that one had three seats for two people, with the middle seat left vacant, and less likelihood of being seated next to someone totally unpleasant. Also, one was served drinks and proper food as soon as the 'Fasten Seat Belt' signs were off. Nominally a two-hour flight, the journey seemed to be over in no time, and in fact they arrived early.

Chapter 12
Hotel du Cap-Eden-Roc

Terminal 1 at Nice, handling BA and only a few other airlines, had a very relaxed ambiance even though Nice was said to be France's third busiest airport after the two in Paris. They were through passport control in five minutes and as a result their checked-in baggage seemed to be taking a long time to arrive, although it was in fact not so long, and they were out on the public concourse within twenty minutes of landing.

As they stepped out of the baggage retrieval area onto the concourse, a young man in an elegant dark brown shirt with buttons down the front, offset by smart off-white trousers, came up to them with a measured stride.

'Madam Consuela?'

'Yes.'

'I'm William, the new captain, and dogsbody. The car is over there.'

They walked the few yards to the Peugeot and got into the back seat while William put what little luggage they had in the boot.

'Where are we going?' Holt asked Consuela.

'To Antibes, where we will board my friends' high-speed motor yacht to take us to the Hotel du Cap-Eden-Roc. That's where movie stars like Leonardo DiCaprio stay during the Cannes Film Festival. We will spend just a couple of nights relaxing there before going to a reception-cum-seminar on a mega-yacht moored at Villefranche-sur-Mer – a beautiful deepwater bay just beyond Nice on the way to Monaco. The hotel featured in *Dirty Rotten Scoundrels* is at Beaulieu-sur-Mer, just over the headland on the far side of the bay.'

Was the seminar to be a clever way of winkling out his political views? He had better watch out. What at the outset had seemed to be a holiday was not to be pure holiday.

119

The car left the confines of the airport and after a lot of twists and turns joined the A8 highway, running along the coast all the way from the Italian border through Monaco, Nice, Cannes, and then on to Aix-en-Provence. They were heading westwards, leaving the outskirts of Nice behind.

'You cannot,' said Consuela, 'see much from the autoroute, but soon you will see Haut-de-Cagnes on top of a hill on the right. It's one of those picture-postcard places. Actually, there are number of similar medieval towns and villages perched on top of what are virtually mountains, designed to repel attackers. The most well-known is Saint-Paul de Vence. Yves Montand and Simone Signoret and famous artists such as Marc Chagal lived there. Pity we haven't time to travel around. What attracted all those artists was the light.'

Holt got a glimpse of Haut-de-Cagnes, a medieval village dominated by a fort, itself on top of a hill. Soon after that they left the A8 and struck south to cross the busy Route Nationale and join the minor road along the coast. They passed near some striking apartment buildings Holt had seen from the plane as it came in to land over the sea.

'Those crescent-shaped apartments,' said Consuela, 'border a marina – nowhere as large as the one we are going to at Antibes, but it does have a spa, which is quite nice as you can come by boat.'

Holt, having only seen the Côte d'Azur in films, was surprised that much of it looked so ordinary. However, when the road began hugging the sea, with the railway line on the right and the Route Nationale running parallel beyond that, he began to feel different. It was the colour of the sea that did it – truly the Côte d'Azur. There were people bathing and many more sunbathing, with a few topless. After ten minutes or so, they deviated from the beach to skirt a hill with a square castle on top, which Holt learnt afterwards was called Le Fort Carré – the Square Fort.

'We're almost there,' announced Consuela.

Indeed, beyond the fort was the marina. Holt was staggered by the scale of it – one of the largest, if not the largest marina on the Mediterranean – and by the number and sizes of boats, ranging

120

from small yachts with sails to mega-yachts like mini ocean liners crammed into it.

'I can't believe the size of some of these vessels,' said Holt.

'Paul Allen, the cofounder of Microsoft, brings his yacht here in the summer. He once invited H and me onboard. It was unbelievable, with two pads for helicopters – one right at the bow, the other at the stern – and a couple of mini-submarines. In addition, there were several stations for launching various small craft, such as those for Jet Skiers. The accommodation was out of this world too. There was, of course, a cinema and the usual swimming pools.'

As they drove into the car park encompassing the marina, Holt noticed most of the boats were moored so that their sterns backed onto the piers. This meant more could be crammed in and also made it more difficult for undesirables to gain access, especially as most of the boats had electrically operated gangways that would extend themselves to the quay when commanded by remote control, very much like some garage doors. Each mooring had its own stanchion supplying water and electricity.

Many of the more luxurious vessels were registered in tax havens, including the Isle of Man and Jersey.

'I'm beginning to feel quite poor,' he said to Consuela with a wry smile.

'You see that long, rampart-like harbour wall and the spot two-thirds along with the roof where the windsock is? That's for helicopters, for people with craft without a landing pad.'

'My…!'

'We're going on one of those sleek medium-size motor yachts. They can do up to thirty knots, whereas the massive ones, although impressive, only do ten or twelve, unless the owner is fabulously rich and able to have turbines like those on a warship.'

'How do you know all this?'

'I used to come here every year with these friends. When the Owl said I was to take you to see some people on a yacht near Monte Carlo, I came up with this idea of a side trip, ostensibly to better get to know you. Amanda and Jonathan are great friends from way back – I can always trust them not to spread rumours about whom I'm with, or even what I do…or more likely, do not do with them.'

The car finally stopped at the stern of a sleek silver motor yacht some twenty metres long, with the narrow gangway already extended. The driver gave a discreet toot on the horn to announce their arrival but not loud enough to disturb those on nearby boats.

A few instants later, a fiftyish-looking man appeared from below, followed by a woman about ten years younger.

'Wonderful to see you, Consuela!' said the man. 'We do not see much of you these days, other than in the society magazines. Come on up!'

The narrow gangway with just a flimsy line slung between supports on one side was quite tricky to negotiate, but no doubt easy to do so if practised. On stepping down from the gangway onto the afterdeck, Consuela was hugged warmly and showered with kisses. She returned them almost as avidly and then introduced Holt, explaining her relationship to them but not hers to Holt, other than saying that he was a friend.

'This is Jeremy, my English friend. Jeremy, my best friends, Amanda and her husband, Jonathan. We used to spend a lot of time together down here, even before Jonathan had his big break.'

Holt too was showered with kisses, but fortunately not so profusely as Consuela.

'I like your new toy, Jonathan,' said Consuela. 'Somewhat more luxurious and sleeker than the previous one, though there was nothing wrong with that. We had a lot of fun on her.'

'We've only had this one a couple of years. It's comfortable, fast, and it's got a stabilizer that works even when at a standstill.'

'Follow me,' said Amanda. 'I'll show you your cabin.'

Descending quite a number of steps, they went forward through a narrow passage until they were under the bridge, though 'bridge' might again be too grandiose a word for the helmsman's place on a vessel of that relatively small size. Opening the door at the end, Amanda showed them into a cabin with an open space in the middle and a bunk along each wall.

122

On either side of the entrance through which they had entered there was a door. The one on the left – facing towards the stern – led to an en suite shower and toilet, while the one on the right led to a small cabin with merely a single bunk and washbasin.

Noting their surprise, Amanda explained that the boat had been designed for a family with two children plus an au pair; the son and daughter slept on either side against the walls well away from each other, while the au pair had the tiny adjoining cabin. The kids could play in the middle, where in normal circumstances the double bed for guests would be.

'We could now put a bed in the middle, but the friends we sometimes let use the boat – with William in charge – very much like this setup. They sleep in the master cabin with the big bed, and the children here.'

'What a great arrangement,' commented Holt.

'With kids on a boat,' continued Amanda, 'a constant worry is that they will run wild and fall overboard. If this cabin door is locked, the only way out is via the au pair's cabin. Of course, when they get older things will probably get more complicated.'

'Like the boy getting a crush on the au pair,' remarked Consuela with a smile, and then adding, 'Of course these days I hear it may be the other way round.'

'We unfortunately or fortunately never had children. I'll leave you two to freshen up. See you topside, say in ten minutes. I'm sure Jeremy would like to watch as we make our way out of the marina, past the billionaires' yachts, which of course your husband, Consuela, could well afford.'

'He says he's too busy and doesn't have the time to waste on toys for other people's benefit.'

Amanda left them, and Consuela went into the washroom to change.

Profiting from her absence, Holt changed clothes as well. When she returned, they went up to join Amanda and Jonathan, who explained that they only had two crew members: William, who they called 'captain', and a young girl, Veronica, who helped with the cooking and cleaning.

'I can handle the boat all by myself,' said Jonathan, 'so we only need the one man, though we are training Veronica as a backup. It's not very arduous, as once out at sea you just have to enter the route into the computer and the boat sails itself. Of course you have to keep a lookout for other boats, but even then the radar tracks them and issues an alert if there is any risk of collision. The biggest danger is hitting some kids in a small rubber boat that might not show up on the radar.'

'Sounds easy,' commented Holt.

'Usually is, but not always. We can control the boat from two places – from the bridge at the front of the enclosed main cabin, which is suitable for all weathers, and from the front of this upper, relatively open deck, which has similar but less sophisticated controls but in good weather is nicer and has better visibility.'

With the 'captain' controlling the boat from the main wheelhouse and the four of them on the upper deck, they eased their way out of the crowded marina, passing small yachts, cruisers, and finally some gigantic ones, like mini ocean liners, near the end of the mile-long quay.

'What are those domes for?' said Holt, pointing to the couple of plastic domes not only on the superstructure of their own craft but also on virtually all the large yachts.

'Though they make them look like spy ships, they are usually to protect the rotating antennae, which automatically track the satellites for TV. You just key in the code, and the antenna tracks the satellite automatically. Some of the smaller pods are for antennae tracking communications satellites – some people run their businesses from their boats. Keeps them out of the arms of the taxman.'

'I suppose people onboard have a lot of spare time to watch TV and videos,' said Holt, wondering whether he would find it boring after a time.

'We'll soon be there,' announced Consuela. 'The hotel is the height of luxury and tranquillity, and will be the ideal place to talk. I need some juicy details for my report.'

'I see,' commented Holt, slightly unsure of what juicy material he could think up.

'Don't worry! It won't be all talk. There is an infinity pool blasted out of the rock with a view over the Mediterranean. Tomorrow afternoon Jonathan and Amanda will come and pick us up to take us off to La Garoupe Beach, where we will have a barbeque onboard, like in the old days. Afterwards, they will take us back to the hotel, and they will come back early the following morning to take us to Villefranche for the reception, followed by a lecture by some Russian expert.'

'What on?'

'The Owl didn't say. Anyway, over there you can see La Garoupe Beach, where Amanda and I, and sometimes Jonathan, used to go some years ago. That is before he sold his software company. The water is very warm and the beach faces east, so you have the sun behind you and not in your eyes from midday onwards. Some people come by boat and moor offshore. Those that do not have their own launch can phone the restaurant or hotel and ask to be fetched by pedalo. We'll come back here tomorrow evening for old times' sake.'

Holt was only half listening, for he was taking in how great Consuela looked. It was not only her looks that were remarkable, but her gaze – the way she looked at you with those bright eyes as if for a moment she were entranced by what you were saying. Perhaps the look was not reserved for him and was turned on at the numerous receptions she held and attended, and was the asset H appreciated most. He was still lost in those thoughts when she turned to address him.

'Jeremy?'

'Yes,' he replied, finding an excuse to feast his eyes on her directly.

'I am sorry. I should have warned you. The hotel we are going to is one of the most exclusive hotels in the world, and this is the high season. They only had one room available. In fact, we only got it because someone cancelled and we – that is, H and I – know the manager.

That means we shall have to share the room and, I'm afraid, the bed. It won't be too horrendous, as the bed will be enormous and the bathrooms all have two washbasins, which is normal for people like us. We women like to have our own basin with essentials at hand, and above all, everything kept spotless, something real men seem incapable of.'

The boat eased alongside the Hotel du Cap jetty, allowing Holt and Consuela to jump off onto the close-set wooden planks. With staff from the hotel arriving to greet them, Holt wondered then and later whether an essential part of their role was ensuring undesirables did not importune the well-healed guests.

The bellboy took them up to their *Superior Room* in the main building. It was elegant in a traditional style, with a view of the Mediterranean and the park surrounding the hotel, with its graceful pine trees. It was an oasis of calm, cut off from the rough and tumble of the normal world. Truly a place for film stars and those able to pay for graceful tranquillity.

'As I said, look how large the bed is,' said Consuela before adding that Holt could sleep on the far side should he wish.

'I'm not sure...'

'You did sign up for a Trophy Wife.'

'Yes. But...'

'Let's play it by ear, though I am not sure that is quite the right expression in the circumstances.'

'You mean, play it by—'

'By how we feel when the situation arises. But remember what goes up always comes down in the end, as if it never went up. So don't worry. Let's forget about those little things for now. As soon as you are ready, we can go down and have a relaxed dinner on the terrace.'

Chapter 13
What Did You Expect?

The Grill and Lounge Bar, where Consuela had reserved a table right at the front, overlooking the sea towards Cannes, was a wonderful, relaxed locale, with the setting sun adding to the romantic feeling. They started with a cocktail recommended by Consuela. Holt ordered crab with Japanese wasabi dressing, followed by a superb roast from the trolley, while Consuela opted for a summer vegetable dish followed by turbot meunière with young leeks and caviar, amongst other things. All accompanied by fine red and white wines. They could not resist the great desserts brought to them on a trolley.

Though the service was impeccable, key to the whole setup was how relaxed, unpretentious, and laid-back everything was. Holt pointed this out to Consuela, who told him that in the highest circles, where everybody is somebody, there is no need for pretensions.

After some exceptional champagne in the Eden Roc Champagne Bar, overlooking the sea, they made their way to their bedroom, with Holt feeling very merry but not weak-kneed as he had been at The Loughty. Consuela was the first to go to the bathroom and to bed.

'It's your turn in the bathroom now. Don't take too long. I don't want to fall asleep waiting – for what, I am not sure.'

Holt did not take long – just a quick shower and so on and he was soon out, bedecked in the elegant bathrobe supplied by the hotel. Not knowing what to do, he stood hesitatingly at the side of the enormous bed, which seemed to have grown even larger, leaving ample room for him to sleep on his own. She had told him she was thirty-two, an age at which, according to some, women are reaching their prime.

'What are you waiting for?'

'Maybe I should take off my bathrobe.'

'That would be a start.'

'Right then,' replied Holt in a hesitant voice.

'This is beginning to sound like *The Graduate*, with you the eighteen-year-old virgin son of H's best friend rather than a twenty-four-year-old. This is not meant to be an initiation test. That's for later, and nothing to do with me.'

'You hit the nail on the head. To be honest I *am* worried about that initiation test. Will I have to parachute out of a plane – I can't stand heights – or worse still, harm someone?'

'Your only hope, Jeremy, is to keep me sweet so I put in a good report. Unfortunately, it won't be just what happens tonight. The people you will be meeting on the mega-yacht in two days' time may be reporting on you too. The Owl might even be there, who knows?'

'You're dead right.'

'Forget about him. We only live once. To tell you the truth, I really like you. You're a breath of fresh air, and I should thank the Owl for giving me the chance to meet someone like you, outside my normal circle yet intelligent. So get in before I have second thoughts and get bored with this Mrs Robinson routine.'

Feeling embarrassed, Holt divested himself of his bathrobe, slipped into the bed with his pyjama bottoms still on, took a deep breath, and moved over towards her.

'Hey, you've got nothing on.'

'What did you expect? I'm a recently married woman.'

Feeling more like a meek six-year-old boy climbing into his mother's bed after a bad dream – except his mother would surely have had her nightie on – he wondered whether Blackwell's stunt at The Loughty had not permanently emasculated him. So much so that like then, he remained transfixed as Consuela undid his pyjama bottoms and pulled them down and off. It should have been the other way round, with him doing the undressing using the secrets he had gleaned as a teenager from a book which said women liked order, and that if you managed to get one stocking off, she would take off the other one herself. Admittedly that book must have been written before the horrible invention of tights.

'I haven't taken any precautions,' he stuttered.

'Don't worry that big head of yours about that. I won't be seeking child support – you do not have that kind of money and never will.'

Holt felt the delicate touch of her hand in the place where at his medical the doctor had checked his reflexes by asking him to cough, but unlike then, desire started coursing through him. His feelings ran wild. Clutching her breasts, he rolled her over and ended up right on top. Pausing for a fraction of a second as if to savour the moment, he penetrated deep within her without any foreplay. Indeed, none was needed, as she was already as wet as could be.

'I was wondering,' gasped Consuela afterwards, 'whether you might even be a virgin. Evidently not – or rather, not quite.'

'I might just as well have been. I've never experienced anything like it. The way you...'

'It was a new experience for me – I suppose like being with a teenager, not that I have ever been with one.'

Holt took her hand and held it until it was time for another joust, with him bringing more to the party the second time.

Too tired after the flight from London for a third tryst, they fell asleep in each other's arms.

Holt woke up thinking of Michael Douglas's frenzy with the bunny-boiler in *Fatal Attraction*, though he was sure Consuela represented no danger in that respect. He had, though, a twinge of guilt regarding Celia but told himself that if pressed, he could tell her it had been for queen and country.

To his surprise, Consuela did not want to get up for breakfast and seemed to be content to just lie there propped up on the luxurious soft pillows. Perhaps she was accustomed to lying in and having breakfast brought to her. It would have been nice, though, to have breakfast on the terrace overlooking the sea where they had eaten the night before.

'I've booked a cabana,' Consuela announced as he came beside the bed.

'What's that?'

'A kind of fenced-off beach hut and private space amongst the trees beyond the swimming pool. The great thing about them is the privacy they afford. We need to talk a lot more if I am to write a proper report. Maybe it would be good if you knew more about me too. Everything is not always as it seems. From there we can go to the swimming pool from time to time. It's only a few yards away.'

As Consuela had said, the great feature of the cabanas was the seclusion they provided. Holt could well understand how a film star could languish there for much of the day and, on venturing to the pool, be protected from pesterers by the hotel staff; not that there would be many importuners at such an exclusive establishment. There was the gentlest of breezes. Ideal conditions for talking.

'I am not,' said Holt, 'used to such simple luxury, nor ostentatious luxury for that matter.

'Neither was I.'

'Really? I thought you were to the manor born.'

'What do you mean by that?'

'Something like being born with a golden spoon in your mouth.'

'Quite the opposite. I was adopted and brought up in the Deep South by a poor and very strict Baptist couple, who already had a boy much younger than I. They lived frugally out in the sticks, miles from anywhere. They were actually quite loving and nice people, except where discipline was concerned.'

'How do you mean?'

'If we seriously misbehaved, they ordered us to go and cut a switch. That meant undressing and going out to the yard in just our underpants, making sure to select a nasty enough one. Of course we would take our time removing the twigs and leaves to delay matters, but the wife did not seem to mind, for she reckoned touching the implement before it touched us helped us reflect on our misdeed and was a key part of the punishment.'

'How could they be so mean?'

'They claimed they were doing it in God's name.'

'Good excuse if you ask me.'

If they deemed the switch too flimsy, the culprit had to go and cut another and receive five extra licks.'

'Must have been terrible.'

'Yes, it was. Besides the pain there was the humiliation – being bent right over with panties pulled down below the knees, showing everything not only to them but also to the gawking brat.'

'But you watched him getting his comeuppance.'

'Yes, and thoroughly enjoyed it, I'm ashamed to say. That was when he had been nasty to me and I, being the oldest, I was not to be next. But it's different for a girl.'

Was Consuela making it all up to unearth what the French call the English vice? He would try not to sound too curious about her spankings, lest it gave the wrong impression.

'How long did that – the beatings – go on for?'

'Until I was fifteen or so. They stopped when I threatened to do the same to their dog if they did it again. As they loved the mongrel more than me, that put an end to it. Instead, I was grounded, which in many ways was far worse.'

'Why didn't you leave them?'

'Not so easy, for it seemed I would be jumping out of the frying pan into the fire, which is what I eventually did. They actually meant well, now I think back.'

Anyway, with the support of a counsellor who took to me at high school, I managed to get a scholarship to university and did psychology in the hope it would help me sort myself out and help others in similar predicaments. Being attractive meant the male, and even some female, students started coming on to me in what to the innocent me at the time seemed a vile way.'

'There must have been some that were okay.'

'Perhaps, but I was too scared to lower my defences. Finally, it was the psychology and my wanting to help people that was my undoing. I met the fiend I told you about. He got through my defences by getting me to take pity on him. He snared me by saying he had never been given a chance in life, but once he had taken my virginity he started to knock me around, saying it was for my own good. I suppose I put up with it at the beginning because he was punishing me for being bad, just like my step-parents did.'

Holt sensed she was being honest but still feared she was putting it all on so that he would eventually have to open up himself. He would have to play the game, whatever it was. He had better not try on the self-pitying card – she would see right through it.

Their conversation was interrupted by the hotel waiter, who had appeared at the entrance to their cabana plot, asking what they would like for lunch. Holt could hardly tell one member of staff from the other. They were all fit and trim and seemed in their thirties or early forties.

They ordered a couple of salads and some mineral water, and while waiting for it to arrive, went over to the infinity pool for a swim. There they found themselves in the presence of a famous American film star, to whom no one was paying any attention.

After lunch and a nap, it was his turn to reveal details about himself. He started with his upbringing, which in fact was the easy part, though he had to be wary of sounding as though he was to be pitied regarding the premature death of his parents. This was interspersed with the occasional swim following which they went for a walk around the grounds, enjoying the shade of the beautiful trees and the tread of the carefully tended paths.

On returning to their room, they readied themselves to go down to the landing stage to be picked up by Amanda and Jonathan, who arrived precisely on time, there being no traffic jams out to sea.

Consuela said she needed to spend some time on her own in the cabin, perhaps to send in a report to the Owl, so Holt stayed up topside with Jonathan.

'How was the hotel? Get a good night's sleep, Jeremy?'

'Yes, thanks, like a child.'

Jonathan would not have been duped by this understatement, particularly as Holt had a swaggering gait, suggesting the night at the Cap had given him a considerable lift. Also, he must have overheard Consuela the day before saying they would have to share that large bed.

'You were pasty-faced,' continued Jonathan, smiling, 'and somewhat downtrodden when you arrived, as if you had been under a lot of strain. I am sure this break will have done you good.'

'I feel a new man. The hotel was out of this world, but it's your boat and relaxing in your company that is the icing on the cake. You are making us so welcome. By the way, how did you get to know Consuela?'

'She's like our daughter. We don't have children, and have known her from way back – although, sadly, when she needed us most, we had temporarily lost touch, due to my being so wrapped up in the business. But in the end it was we who introduced her to her liberator, now her husband. That, in one way or another, solved a lot of her problems.'

'She did tell me how she had a hard time with her step-parents as a young girl, and later with some dreadful man.'

'Yes, but her success, if one can put it that way, was not only thanks to her looks but to her genuinely nice character. Beautiful women who have found themselves in the money through no merit of their own can be horrible – like that American hotel heiress who said taxes are only for the little people. Unfortunately, she was partly right. Just look at all these luxury yachts registered in tax havens. You can see Georgetown – that's the one in the Cayman Islands, not Malaysia or Washington DC – on many of the sterns.'

'I find Consuela such great company. She's so natural,' said Holt in reply.

'Although,' continued Jonathan, 'she can put on a very superior air to discourage overfamiliarity at the fundraisers and receptions she and her husband host, she's actually very unpretentious. The only thing she can't bear is stupid stuck-up people. She said you appeal to her because you are highly intelligent.'

'People think I am clever, but that does not mean I am satisfied with what I am doing. I want to find something meaningful before it's too late. I envy you.'

Although he was pretty sure Jonathan had nothing to do with the Owl and was simply a friend of Consuela from way back, he could not be sure and wanted to give the impression he really was on the lookout for something new.

'I can understand you feeling like that, though in my case I was lucky in that I was hooked on the idea that subsequently made my fortune – if you can call what I have a fortune compared with what these billionaire yacht owners have.'

'It's not really my business, and don't answer if you do not want to, but what's her husband like? She does not say much about him.'

'Driven. Ambitious but open-minded and generous. He does a lot for charity, as I said, and not only for the tax breaks. He's got a great sense of humour and gives Consuela a free rein, but that does not mean she sleeps around. Quite the contrary. She always seems to be giving pursuers their marching orders. She adores rather than loves her husband. They make a good couple. Neither can bear fools. He is very powerful. Not someone to be trifled with. I wouldn't like to get on the wrong side of him.'

This left Holt again wondering just how much chance had to do with Consuela's ex's fiery end in that car accident.

They were rounding another headland and dropping anchor off the beach that Consuela had pointed out the evening before.

'We're here,' called out Jonathan, even though Amanda and Consuela could hardly have failed to hear the clanking of the anchor being lowered.

'Let's go to the beach, Jeremy, darling,' said Consuela on coming up to join them.

'I'll get William to take you in the launch,' interjected Jonathan. 'As we're a big boat, we've had to drop anchor rather far out. To get to the beach, you would have to swim between the smaller craft further in and risk getting chopped up by one of their propellers. Not worth the risk, slight though it is.'

The tiny crane lifted the dinghy from the upper afterdeck and lowered it into the azure sea. The 'captain' jumped in, followed by the two of them. In a couple of minutes, they were through the pack of other boats further in.

Looking great, this time in her swimsuit, Consuela turned to Holt.

'Do you think you can make it to the beach from here?'

'Sure,' replied Holt, trying to look more confident than he really was.

With the buoyant salty water at such an agreeable temperature, it was finally no problem making it to the shore. Even so, they lay panting on the sand, as Consuela had swum very fast.

'Reminds me of when I was young,' she said excitedly. 'Had such a great time here. It was nice of them to let us come on our own, thinking we would prefer privacy. Your presence makes me feel young again. Let's go and have a pancake at the café over there, in the cheap place with the ordinary folk.'

The atmosphere at the unpretentious café was relaxing, though it did not have loungers, like the more sophisticated ones further along the beach. The sight of the children playing nearby in the water gave a greater holiday feeling than at the hotel. All too soon it was time to go back, and Consuela called Jonathan on the waterproof mobile phone he had lent her to ask him to send the dinghy to pick them up.

Back on the yacht, they went down to the cabin to change into something more suitable than bathing costumes for dinner, albeit in the open air under the awning.

Veronica in her uniform, consisting of a beige skirt and a white blouse hinting at her young breasts, busied herself at the specially designed barbeque that fitted neatly along the coaming. When she left, Holt remarked how nice she looked and asked Jonathan what it took to be a crew member.

'Everyone believes the men have to be tall, dark, and handsome, and the girls have to be blonde with legs up to their armpits. In fact, the people with enough money to have a decent boat are quite capable of finding their own beauties for entertaining to suit the occasion. What they are seeking for crew are people who present well, have a nice personality, and are willing to buckle down to almost any task without complaining. And above all, are trustworthy and discreet. No selling of titbits to the gossip columns.'

'I see. What about Veronica?'

'Actually, she's an exception. She's William's cousin, which makes everything easier all round, as we are like family. In the old days, everything on boats, even smallish ones like this, was very formal; now it's much more relaxed. As I said, the great thing is trust, and owners look for people with experience who can prove they are reliable. That makes it difficult for a young girl, or lad for that matter, to get started in the profession. Indeed, it is a profession, and early on crew will often work for a number of owners. Hard work, though, but it can be quite exciting.

The four of them were sitting around the table under the awning on the top deck, with William and Veronica beavering away below.

'We've,' said Jonathan, 'a small but fully equipped kitchen below, but up here we've hotplates and the mini barbeque set in the coaming. Means we can finish things off up here in private.'

'I've always wondered,' said Holt, 'why these boats, and the much bigger ones owned by Russian oligarchs, are called yachts when they don't have sails.'

'I wondered that myself,' said Jonathan, 'and actually looked it up in Wikipedia. It seems a yacht was originally a fast Dutch boat for catching pirates and smugglers in shallow waters. After Charles II of England used one to bring him to Britain from Holland for his restoration, the term came to be used to mean a vessel for conveying VIPs. Of course, in the old days all those boats used sails, and for a time the term "yacht" was synonymous with boats with sails. Nowadays, for people with money, it often means a motor yacht.'

'I see,' replied Holt.

'Interestingly, the great improvements made to motor yachts are now being applied to sailboats. The introduction of carbon-fibre-reinforced hulls has made a big difference. They are so strong and easy to maintain, though repairs in the event of serious damage can be expensive.'

136

'I would love a boat like this, Jonathan.'

'Be careful about for what you wish, my dear Jeremy. A boat is something you should only have if you have enough money left over after buying it to pay people to look after it, and if a large one, enough money to pay the crew. Wasn't it when being taken to task about the high cost of maintaining his yacht that J. P. Morgan famously said, "If you have to ask the price, you can't afford it"?'

'Yes, but can't one do a lot oneself?'

'That's the big mistake people make, for without adequate funds, the boat becomes your master and takes over your whole life. It was worse in the old days when the hulls were made of wood rather than carbon-reinforced plastic. An English guy I once knew bought a sailboat he could barely afford. He thought it was his dream come true, but with little money left, he had to spend every weekend scraping barnacles off the hull and painting it, leaving his wife sulking at home. Plus she hated boats.'

'I can understand her,' exclaimed Consuela. 'That is if the boat was in England with the bad weather. Here's different.'

'Nowadays,' continued Jonathan, 'you can remove the barnacles and foreign matter from the plastic hulls with a high-powered water jet, but even so there's a lot that needs to be done. You've only got to look around the marina at Antibes in the two or three months before the season to see the crews assiduously polishing and painting.'

'Jonathan, you yourself are lucky to be rich enough to do it in style.'

'It wasn't luck. I worked my arse off, but now I've finally got all this, I'm almost too old to enjoy it. My greatest satisfaction is seeing other people, like you and Consuela, enjoying it. Please make the most it.'

'I certainly am. By the way, what happened to that English guy with the boat?'

'Oh, his wife got fed up sitting at home alone, divorced him for half his money plus maintenance for the three kids, and married a young layabout who was always on hand to rub her down. My friend had to sell the boat and ended up with the dog, which at least had enjoyed the days spent watching him scraping away. But let's forget about that loser and have some more champagne.'

Veronica had come up with some nibbles – and what nibbles. So fresh and appetizing, made all the better by the dry champagne. Shortly afterwards, Amanda and Consuela joined them, and Holt took the opportunity to give Consuela a broad smile, which she returned, pretending to bite her lower lip for being such a naughty girl. Had she told bosom friend Amanda what they had been up to?

It was a lovely evening, with only a slight swell. The food and wine, the great company, plus being served by Veronica made it one of the best evenings Holt had ever spent. To cap it all, he had the night to look forward to. Were it not for thought of the initiation test that lay ahead, it would have been perfect.

As on the previous morning, Consuela remained in bed for breakfast. Having time to spare, they went for a last walk around the grounds with the freshness of the night still lingering under the trees.

Consuela signed the very substantial bill as if it were nothing, telling the receptionist to debit it from her husband's account. A member of staff took charge of their bags and accompanied them down to the jetty as Amanda and Jonathan's boat eased its way alongside.

They would cut right across to Villefranche-sur-Mer, where a tender from the *Vessos* would pick Holt and Consuela up. No need to moor.

After they had cast off, Jonathan pushed the throttle fully forward and the boat surged ahead. Soon they were hydroplaning at high speed with hardly any pitching, thanks to the stabilizer, and Holt commented on that.

'I should,' said Jonathan, 'have explained that there are basically two kinds of motor yacht: light ones with relatively powerful engines like this one, which rise out of the water and hydroplane at speeds up to thirty knots, and heavy ones, which sit in the water and travel relatively slowly.'

They were at the tip of Antibes Peninsula, with the long coast leading to Nice Airport well to their left, and were able to watch several aircraft make their approach over Antibes, descend over the water and land. They scanned the long beach at Nice through binoculars as they passed. Soon they were rounding the headland, jutting far out to sea beyond, and entering Villefranche bay. There they found themselves in a different world.

Encircled on three sides by high mountains, the bay had a tranquil atmosphere, quite different from the bustle of nearby Nice.

'It is actually,' said Jonathan, 'a very convenient spot for a gathering of important people. It's next to Nice, with its airport, and not far from Monaco, with its rich residents. Did you hear the story about one of them, the famous tennis star Boris Becker?'

'All I know is how he had an expensive fling in the broom cupboard at Nobu, the well-known Japanese restaurant in London.'

'Well, Becker, who claimed to be resident in Monaco, was allegedly caught out by the German tax authorities, partly because his accountant boasted to a man he happened to meet on a German train, who unknown to him was a tax inspector, about how clever he was helping Becker avoid tax, as they could not prove anything. However, the kicker was that Becker snubbed a fanatical fan by refusing to give him an autograph. Enraged, the man went to the German tax authorities with proof that Becker had not been in Monaco long enough to avoid German taxes – he had newspaper cuttings reporting everything Becker did and where.'

Down in their cabin to get ready, Consuela changed out of the somewhat formal attire she had worn to check out of the hotel into a striped fleece sweatshirt, tucked into white twill shorts. The contrast with the expensive-looking black leather belt drew attention to the shorts and her thighs. Had Holt not lain between them, he would not have been able to take his eyes off them.

He himself had what he thought was a trendy rich-guy-on-a-yacht number that Consuela had insisted on bringing. They were not quite film stars, but looked successful.

The *Vessos*'s tender arrived promptly and took them to the boarding steps. Holt had intended to mount them two at a time and request 'permission to come aboard', just like US Navy officers do in films, but with Consuela determined to precede him he was unable to do so. Instead, the more senior of the two officers waiting for them at the top was the first to speak, saying, 'Welcome to the *Vessos*,' to which Holt was obliged to reply lamely, 'Thank you.'

'Although,' continued the sarcastic and supercilious officer, 'we shall not be graced with your company overnight, you have been granted a stateroom so you can relax before the reception begins.'

' "Granted" is a very impolite way of putting it,' replied Consuela, none too happy with their implication they did not automatically merit one.

'My humble apologies. I am Greek and my English not so good. In Greek it means it is an honour.'

'Apologies accepted,' replied Consuela, unfazed.

'My colleague will show you the way. Many guests have yet to arrive, so we suggest you relax and come up to the afterdeck in an hour or so. If you don't appear, we'll send someone down to call you.'

As she didn't speak Greek, there was no way Consuela could verify his excuse, but she seemed happy at the prospect of their having some time alone in their stateroom, leaving Holt wondering whether they might even find time for a session.

They did, and when they arrived on the afterdeck they were flushed, as if they had just won a mixed-doubles tennis match. The two officers who had welcomed them aboard had noticed their sprightliness, with the elder one asking whether they had recharged their batteries, and the younger one unable to keep his eyes off Consuela's lithe legs.

'Yes, we really needed it,' replied Consuela with a broad smile and what seemed like a wink.

140

The officers, now showing due respect, proceeded to introduce them to their host, Zeon, a smooth elderly man who seemed to be the owner of the ship and master of ceremonies.

'Great to have you with us. We were told to look after you as you represent the future. As you can see, most of the people here are elderly and well established in their careers or whatever. I do not always agree with what they do or believe. In fact, I hold these reception-cum-seminars in the hope those attending will be more enlightened afterwards.'

'You know,' whispered Consuela into Holt's ear after Zeon had excused himself to welcome the prime minister of some resource-rich republic south-east of Russia with a name ending in "-stan", 'a luxury yacht is very different from an ocean liner. There is none of that infra dig competition to sit at the captain's table. The crew, including the captain, are here to serve every whim of the owner or charterer.'

'To judge from the abundance of beauties,' said Holt with a smile, 'a number of whims are being served, though none of them could equal you.'

Consuela seemed to appreciate the compliment, though flattery was hardly necessary in view of the admiring looks she was getting. Being rich or important, and assuming Holt was likewise financially well provided for, they knew how money and power attracted women and were not surprised at the disparity between Holt and Consuela. His Owl application form had been correct in guaranteeing the satisfaction of other men's envious looks, even though not promising he would be getting what they were thinking.

Zeon returned, having left X-stan's prime minister in the good company of one of those young women. The girls probably would be classed as entertainers rather than crew and invited onboard for the occasion, so the qualifications Jonathan ascribed to crew members, notably discretion, would still apply.

Zeon introduced them to one VIP after another. Sheik so and so, interior minister so and so, and so on. There were some fifty people altogether, and all were obviously rich and successful as heads of companies and hedge funds, and as government officials and politicos from various countries. Was the Owl of their number?

Having given time for people to circulate with their drinks and make acquaintances, the crew opened some sliding doors to reveal tables laid out with a sumptuous buffet. Caviar, lobster, hams, the works. There was none of the meanness of some in the country set in England, described by Kingsley Amis in *Take a Girl Like You*, who, to save money, would have an impressive giant ham which was never eaten, as it had toothpicks with cheap titbits stuck all over it, defending it like the spines on some giant hedgehog or porcupine.

While Holt felt he was living the high life, Consuela was looking disdainful, as if it was boring everyday fare for her. Again, having allowed his guests time to enjoy the food, Zeon banged on a table with an awl to draw attention.

'Ladies and gentlemen, we are very gratified that so many eminent and clever people are here with us today and hope you are enjoying the buffet designed to suit all tastes. In half an hour, the talk by Prof Toplinski will begin. Those of you with invitations to attend should make their way to the cinema on Deck 2 so as to be seated by 2.25, since proceedings start at 2.30. Meanwhile, make the most of the food and fine wines. Thank you!'

After finishing, Zeon came over to Holt and Consuela.

'Jeremy, I have been asked to ensure that you attend.'

'Am I included?' Consuela asked.

'There was no mention of you, Consuela. In fact, I am sure you will be happier with some interesting people with an interior design business you may soon meet again in New York. Let me introduce you.'

Zeon seemed very well briefed. What connection, if any, did he have with the Owl? He said there had been an intermediary, but there was no knowing whether it was true. For the first time in a week, Holt would find himself separated from Consuela, and with a mixed bunch of people, any one of whom might be reporting back to the Owl, if one was not the Owl himself.

142

Chapter 14
Rethinking Democracy

Zeon had already led Consuela away, leaving Holt to finish his drink alone before making his way down the couple of decks to the cinema. When he eventually reached it, he found it to be sizable but not so large as to lose a feeling of intimacy, making it just right for a lecture.

Others had already taken their seats, and Holt found himself sitting at the end of the third row next to a fit-looking fiftyish man, who, without naming the department, even introduced himself as a civil servant from the UK. For his part, Holt told him he worked for a think tank in the mother country without citing the name. Neither of them wanted to probe – or rather, be probed.

After being introduced by Zeon as a political analyst, Prof Toplinski began his talk on rethinking democracy.

Prime Minister, ladies and gentlemen.

Winston Churchill said something along the lines that democracy was not perfect but was the best system we have. Until recently, this perhaps seemed to be so, but raw democracy combined with the shift to favouring those according to need rather than merit, as in the UK, is having perverse results.

While Eisenhower with good reason warned of the dangers of the military-industrial complex, we now have the something-for-nothing complex supported and supporting local council members and human rights lawyers, where those not contributing to society have too much electoral sway.

What I am proposing is a society based on a vibrant, creative, intelligent yet humanistic core. One advantage would be that at a stroke, religious maniacs, and senile and nonproductive people would be on the back burner.

This would necessitate an electoral system with weighted voting, aiming to improve society. Thus, pensioners might get a lesser vote, and those not seriously seeking work might get no vote at all – even those without a vote would have a surfeit of do-gooders with votes batting for them.

I am not suggesting a crude system where the poor, less intelligent, and handicapped are victimized, but one where, say, the increasing number of pensioners do not skew the system as they are doing now. The aim would be, without being a Hitler, to improve society.

Some societies to some extent get over the problem of the 'wrong' people having too much electoral sway by having them run by the 'party' and setting certain qualifications for joining. However, this is open to abuse and corruption, and then there is the problem of the theocratic societies, like Saudi Arabia and their enemy, Iran...'

The lecture continued for a further thirty minutes, after which some of those attending, including Holt, asked questions – he thought it would make him look good in the eyes of anyone watching.

On rejoining Consuela, he merely told her it had been thought-provoking and that he would go into detail at another time. Ten minutes later, Zeon came over to them to announce one of the ship's tenders was waiting to ferry them to the pier, where a car was waiting to take them to the airport.

They were not back 'home' in England until almost midnight. Too tired for any serious action, they dropped off to sleep in each other's arms in Consuela's bed.

Chapter 15
US Ambassador's Reception

Of all the interesting things they did following their return to England – visiting museums; attending concerts, receptions, and garden parties – one event stood out above all others: the reception at Winfield House in London's Regent's Park, the official residence of the US ambassador.

It was a grand yet relaxed affair, graced by the presence of senior officials, diplomats, and genuine celebrities. Not only that. The ambassador, not a career diplomat but as often the case for the London and Paris embassies, a political appointee, was a close friend of Consuela's husband. In consequence, Consuela and Holt were sitting with the ambassador, his wife, and the elite at the top table.

'I don't expect you've met the French ambassador to the Court of St James's, as you Brits say,' said the ambassador as he introduced them to an elegant woman.

'I haven't had the pleasure, Your Excellency,' intoned Holt, pleased that he could conjure up some diplomatic protocol.

'*Enchanté*,' replied the Frenchwoman as if it dropped off her tongue hundreds of times a day. There followed a stream of dignitaries coming to the US ambassador and his wife to pay their respects – with Holt and Consuela discreetly whispering together beside them. Out of politeness, Holt and Consuela would look up to acknowledge the presence of those being presented.

As yet another VIP couple approached, Holt looked up to see a cabinet minister and, to his surprise and indeed shock, his beloved Celia accompanying him. The ambassador, noticing that Celia was paying more attention to Holt than had the other guests, turned towards him and introduced him to the minister and especially to her as a clever up-and-coming young man whose partner was Kentucky Derby royalty.

Of course, the ambassador had not questioned the nature of the relationship between the VIP and Celia, just as he had not questioned that between Holt and Consuela. Such relationships were nothing out of the ordinary in the circles in which he moved.

Celia had allowed herself to show a flicker of delight at seeing Holt, but her expression had immediately blanked out when he showed no sign of recognition in return. He could not risk trying to take her aside later for a few words for fear of blowing his cover, or at the very least upsetting Consuela; the Owl, or someone working for him, might well be present, as the reception had been on the list of those they had to attend.

As the evening progressed, Holt caught glimpses of Celia looking decidedly upset, her discomfiture no doubt aggravated by the fact that even though he was a poor dancer himself, Consuela's elegance and long limbs made them an outstanding couple on the dance floor, and they bathed in the admiration of those watching. Furthermore, Celia would surely be harbouring thoughts of the two of them in each other's arms later in the night.

He knew she would report having met him at the reception to Sir Charles – and at the top table with the ambassador to boot. While he would reassure her that he must have been there in the course of his work undercover, he was hardly likely to explain that it was he, the respectable Sir Charles, who had selected the trophy wife for Holt out of a number of questionable options, including Tossed Boy's Salad.

The ambassador seemed genuinely disappointed when Consuela told him, on bidding him farewell, that she would soon be returning to the States and was therefore unable to accept his invitation to join him on another occasion.

Apart from a few comments on people they had just seen, including a diplomat with a musty dinner jacket covered in dandruff, Consuela and Holt said little on the way back to the house. They seemed to have bonded, even saying little when they climbed into Consuela's bed, where they lingered the next morning, as they had nothing scheduled and plenty with which to occupy themselves.

Holt came down first and sat in the conservatory, appreciating the well-kempt garden. There had been a lot of rain, and the lawn was very green. He heard Consuela come down and go to the front door to see if there was any mail, though it was a trifle early for the postman.

She came in carrying an envelope and handed it to Holt. Surprised, he tore it open and read the single sheet.

> You have shown yourself to be staff officer material; now it is time for the initiation test.
>
> Tomorrow you will take the 15.10 train to London. Before you board, Consuela will give you further instructions to read during the journey.
>
> This is the last you will see of her other than in the media. Bear in mind that she is not part of our organization. If you care for her, do not compromise her vis-à-vis her husband, or anyone else for that matter, by trying to contact her ever again.
>
> Goodbye will be a final goodbye.
>
> The Owl

Not only had the dreaded moment of the initiation test arrived, it was to be their last twenty-four hours together. He had had on-off girlfriends, some more on than off, but he had never been in a relationship with sex on tap day and night. But that was not all. He had been able to tell Consuela little private things he would be too shy to admit to other women, notably Celia.

Consuela had said she loved him *e, m, p*, but not *h*.

'What does that mean?' he had asked.

'Emotionally, mentally, and physically, but not as a husband. You're not husband material. No way.'

The reference to 'material' made him sure it was she who had told the Owl he was staff officer material.

With no special programme for the day, they felt rather awkward and unable to make the most of it. Holt was worrying about what the initiation test would entail and admitted as much to Consuela, who could only say she could not help, as she had no idea herself.

They had sandwiches in a nearby wood for lunch, and then went for a long walk, saying little. Even so, time went by quickly and it was soon evening.

'I'll make a simple dinner, and let's just relax like married couples are supposed to do. You had better be careful not to drink too much. You do not want to do your thing – I mean, the initiation – with a hangover and perhaps miss the target, whoever that might be. Sorry, I'm joking, but even so, you should watch it. With a top wine you should be okay.'

Their last meal. The wine and food as usual were perfect, but there was something missing.

'You know,' said Consuela in a velvety voice, 'our relationship may prove to be more productive than you realize. One thing is for certain: it seems to have made a man of you.'

'I don't know about that, but I certainly feel different – more confident. I have had, as they say, the time of my life.'

After watching some television, they trooped up to bed around 10 p.m. The great finale that the supposedly confident Holt had anticipated was not to be, and even before he made a move he had found himself wondering whether anyone could enjoy their last meal before their execution, however sumptuous.

The combination of trying too hard and sadness that it was all ending had made him tense up and unsettled, so in more ways than one it was a letdown. Even when what there was of it was all over, there was nothing to talk about, as there was nothing to which to look forward. He lay there, unable to sleep, his future looking bleak.

After a slightly more successful bout the following morning, Consuela insisted, as on previous days, on just lying there lost in thought, leaving only time for a late brunch. A last walk in the woods, again with hardly a word exchanged, was a sorry end. He had the impression from the few words that Consuela did emit that she was concerned about his future.

'As you know,' she said, 'this is the end of the road for you and me. I cannot say how wonderful it has been to discover the innocent pleasures I never had in my youth. All I can say is that I wish you all the best and that I submitted glowing reports – perhaps too glowing – about you. Now it's up to you, and luck.'

The ride to the station felt so different from the one when she had collected him from there ten days earlier. A page had turned. It was over. One consolation was that it was a clean break, with neither party resentful.

To avoid dragging out the farewell, Consuela did not even seek out a parking space, merely stopping at the 'No Waiting' drop-off point at the entrance to the station, and, as he was about to alight, handed him another envelope.

'I'm sad,' she whispered. 'We were just getting going; you were just getting fully into it. It's nice to finish on a high, with no recriminations and no lawyers – one rarely can.'

'I am sorry. I was too stressed last night and even this morning,' Holt muttered.'

'Don't worry.'

'I suppose it was like the final at Wimbledon – trying too hard, I blew it.'

'It was really no big thing.'

'You might well say that,' replied Holt ruefully.

'I didn't mean it that way. Even with sex, as with gifts that disappoint, on some occasions it is the intention...the underlying relationship...that counts.'

A policeman was coming towards them and gesticulating to indicate Consuela should move on.

'That's it then,' said Holt as he closed the car door, overcome with emotion.

Taking a deep breath, he spluttered, 'Goodbye, my love. I'll never forget you. I only wish I had something to remember you by.'

'Hey, take this,' said Consuela, slipping a diamond-studded bracelet off her wrist and handing it to him. The expensive-looking item had on many occasions caught Holt's eye and seemed altogether too much to accept.

'But I haven't anything to give you in return.'

'No need. What you have given me is perhaps worth infinitely more.'

With the gesticulating policeman by then only a few paces away, Consuela raised the window to bring their relationship to its close. Not quite, though, for as she drove off she blew him a final kiss while mouthing the word *adieu*, French for goodbye when you are never to meet again.

Chapter 16
Shine It on Nelson's Chest

Like a deep-sea diver surfacing too rapidly from the depths, Holt felt numb as he looked out the train window at the countryside, and then the outskirts of London flitting by. More than the lovemaking, it was Consuela's emotional depth and empathy that had, for the first time since losing his parents, made him feel really alive and at one with himself. How he missed her.

Inspector Holmes had warned him that when working undercover, falling in love was an absolute no-no. Unless he got Consuela out of his mind, he would arrive in London with his instructions unread and mess everything up. He ripped open the envelope and noted that the language was not as polite as before, as if he already belonged to the Owl.

INSTRUCTIONS

At 3 a.m. tomorrow morning, we are launching a cruise missile to knock Lord Nelson off his pedestal on top of his column in Trafalgar Square, just like Saddam Hussein's statue was yanked off his.

You, Benet, will be the target designator.

A room at The Trafalgar hotel with an unobstructed view of the upper part of the column has been booked for you under the name Hawke, and you will find the credit card used to book it attached to the back of these instructions. (You nominally checked in three days ago, with someone going to the room every day to rough up the sheets and so to make it seem occupied. You should not have to use the card, as we will keep the room for another couple of nights to avoid suspicion, and someone else will settle the bill using an identical copy.)

You will find the target-designating laser, together with the operating instructions, in a silver case in your room. Do not drink too much beforehand – or afterwards, for that matter. You will need a steady hand.

When the train on which you are now riding arrives at Marylebone station, walk to Baker Street station, where you will take a Jubilee Line train to Westminster station. On exiting the ticket barrier at Westminster, you will take the Bridge Street exit, facing you as you exit at the ticket wickets, turn right, and walk the few yards before turning right again into Whitehall. Walk calmly towards Trafalgar Square, keeping to the right-hand side.

This will take you past the Cenotaph war memorial to those who so nobly gave their lives in the world wars only for their heroic work to be undone by successive governments, and continue until you reach Number 33, a pub called The Silver Cross, which is the last pub before Trafalgar Square. Have a drink there and leave for the hotel at 5 p.m., a time when the reception begins to get busy and you will be least noticed.

Detach the other card attached to the back of these instructions to open the door to Room 507, your room.

We hope you will prove yourself worthy to remain one of us on whatever basis might then seem appropriate. You will have the satisfaction of having done a good deed, for England no longer deserves its greatest hero.

The Owl

Relieved that he had not been asked to kill someone directly, Holt was still concerned at the prospect of people being injured or killed when the missile struck the statue and exploded. The specified route to the hotel along Whitehall, with its government ministries and prime minister's residence, was something of a godsend as it was covered by some of the most sophisticated CCTV camera monitoring systems in the country, and there was a good likelihood he would be identified and tracked.

Still trying to stop Consuela popping up in his thoughts, he eased back in his second-class seat as the train entered the long tunnel just before Marylebone. Normally on returning to London, he would be nonchalantly on his way to Giraffe or home. Today was to be different.

As instructed, he walked the five hundred yards from Marylebone to Baker Street, and on entering the station looked up at the CCTV cameras. With luck, Giraffe would know he was not only still alive but back in London and desperate to be contacted, since he was vigorously rubbing his chin.

The Jubilee Line train to Westminster only three stops away did not take long. He had never been to that station before and was surprised at how deep the Jubilee Line was there after passing under the Thames. There were three consecutive escalators to the top, and the bottom looked like a nuclear bomb shelter.

On exiting into Bridge Street, with Westminster Bridge on the left, he found the phallic presence of Big Ben for some reason reassuring. Like St Paul's Cathedral and Tower Bridge, the famous clock tower above the Houses of Parliament had miraculously survived the bombing during the Blitz in World War II largely unscathed. The giant hands showed twenty past four. Perfect timing. So far things were going well. Would he be able to say the same the following day?

He walked the twenty-five yards to Parliament Square and contrary to his instructions crossed over to the other side of Whitehall, before turning right into the avenue so named. He reasoned that there would be more cameras on that side next to the Foreign Office and Downing Street, with the prime minister's residence at No. 10, not to mention other key government offices. Years ago, Downing Street had been accessible to the public; now it was barricaded and guarded by police toting sub-machine guns. How terrorists in one form or another had changed things. His toppling Nelson would doubtless lead to such precautions becoming even more stringent.

Looking upwards and glancing from side to side to where cameras might be, he had a begging look on his face as he intermittently rubbed his chin remorselessly to emphasise he wanted to be contacted ASAP. If he had not already been picked up by the facial-recognition software at Baker Street and Westminster stations, he surely would be now.

Here in this sensitive area, with police in civilian clothes as well as in uniform, they might be able to get one to follow him – that is, if they could identify him in time.

Beyond the Cenotaph commemorating the fallen in wars, he could see the two Horse Guards standing imperturbably in their boxes as tourists sidled up to them to have their photos taken. He had read somewhere that it would be cheaper to have actors in that role rather than professional soldiers, though they might not be so long-suffering in the face of provocations from young tourists, including cute girls wanting their faces as close as possible to theirs. Holt too made a show of having a good gawp, so anyone following would think he had crossed over to the other side of Whitehall for that very purpose. It would also allow Giraffe more time for him to be tracked.

Turning away to continue on his way, he could see Nelson's Column, with the admiral perched confidently on top, directly ahead. He couldn't believe that in less than twelve hours he would be instrumental in knocking the man off the top. His time with Consuela had in fact been the enjoyable appetiser; this was the main dish – and big time – and with the reality dawning on him, he was getting jittery. Thankfully, The Silver Cross pub, where he could raise his spirits with a stiff drink, was now just over on the other side of the road. Rather than risk making his way through the moving traffic, he decided to cross at the traffic lights at the foot of Trafalgar Square, which were not far ahead anyway, and double back the eighty or so yards.

Altogether, his detour had taken an extra five minutes, as he had had to wait for the lights to change. The entrance to the pub was narrow, but once inside he found there was plenty of room, with the seating area going way back from the busy street. The clientele – a mix of regulars, passers-by, and tourists – would coalesce around anyone following him and make it impossible to identify them. Indeed, the Owl probably already had someone there to report on his progress.

154

He went to the far end of the bar and ordered a double whisky and soda. Being intelligent, he never asked for ice in a pub, knowing that it was usually full of microbes – people ordering drinks unintentionally spit in the ice-bucket behind the counter and bar staff dip their fingers into it as they scoop out the ice for drinks after handling dirty coins.

He sat down at a table right in the middle of the pub in full view and drank his whisky slowly. There was plenty of time and, fearing to order another, he wanted to make it last. As the hands on his watch moved to show five o'clock, he stood up and made his way through the crowd to the exit. On stepping out into the busy thoroughfare, he was surprised by the sound of a helicopter hovering almost overhead. Then, realizing and hoping that it might be for his benefit, he looked up and rubbed his chin but tried not to make it too obvious to anyone standing nearby.

To get to the hotel, he had to cross busy Whitehall itself at the lights where he had just crossed and then cross The Mall in front of Admiralty Arch. He could not continually look upwards for fear of being run over. Also, looking up at the helicopter would raise suspicions should the Owl be having him followed.

The Trafalgar, a 'boutique hotel' belonging to the Hilton Group, was discreet, so much so that one could easily miss the entrance were one not especially seeking it. As he had been told to expect, reception was busy, with people returning to the hotel from meetings or going out for an evening on the town.

As someone had already checked in several days before using his alias, he only had to nod in the direction of reception and move a few yards further on to take one of the lifts to the sixth floor. Unlike at a number of less well-managed hotels, he had no trouble opening the door to his room with his card. Though not up to the Hotel du Cap at Antibes standard, the room was quite spacious, and, with its view of Nelson's Column, would in different circumstances have been a great place to impress a woman by virtue of its great location, with the admiral, himself no stranger to trysts, looking on.

Having had a peek at Nelson from the window, he went to check the silver case on the baggage stand. The laser with telescopic sights was there, together with a digital alarm clock showing seconds as well as hours and minutes, and of course the envelope with instructions, not forgetting the mobile phone.

God, he felt nervous.

Though the Owl had warned him not to drink too much, he could not resist taking a cold beer from the minibar. After all, there was still plenty of time before the big moment.

Surely that hovering helicopter had been for his benefit. Knowing he was staying at the hotel would be enough. They could examine the hotel videos, identify him, and note from the hotel computer what room doors had been opened shortly after his arrival.

His room was almost certainly bugged, quite likely not only for audio but also video. His making a lot of noise to prevent anyone hearing what was being said or leaving a sheet of paper for someone to pick up would raise suspicions. The only solution was to have a note ready and pass it to the person Giraffe would send to contact him.

He went into the shower booth with a pen and a beermat he had kept as a souvenir from the Hotel du Cap, closed the frosted glass door, and wrote a short note for Giraffe, describing what he had been asked to do, making clear that unless ordered not to do so he would proceed. With the beermat high up in his right trouser pocket, he returned to the room and picked up the phone to order a club sandwich and a coffee.

Having been told it would take about thirty minutes, as they were very busy, he had time to read the instructions in the envelope and check the laser.

INSTRUCTIONS

1. When it gets dark, try out the target designator by switching on the laser power supply and waiting for it to power up (only takes about 30 seconds) indicated by the red lamp changing to green. Squeeze

the trigger to switch on the laser and then harder to lock it in the ON position.

2. Using the telescopic sight, confirm that the red spot from the laser is visible to you high up on the admiral's chest, before switching off the laser by pulling hard back on the trigger to unlock it.

3. Repeat the process to make sure it comes naturally to you. Power down the laser and replace it in its case. Check that the battery charge indicator shows it is well charged. If not, recharge it using the adapter connected to the mains supply. Whatever you do, DO NOT LEAVE THE LASER SWITCHED ON when not in use! If you do, you risk finding yourself powerless when the big moment comes.

4. At least ten minutes before the cruise missile is due (i.e. at 03.50 for 04.00) power up the laser as above and when ready, shine it on Nelson's chest for a moment to get your eye in again.

5. Switch the laser off as mentioned by pulling hard back on the trigger and releasing it, but keep it powered up and wait for the arrival of the missile. Shortly before its arrival, a harmless explosive device making a loud bang and a nasty-smelling cloud will detonate at the foot of the column to disperse any people congregated there.

6. On hearing the detonation, you will switch on the laser and shine it on Nelson's chest as instructed.

7. Once the cruise missile has hit the admiral and almost certainly knocked him off his perch, switch off the laser, and return it to its case. DO NOT DRAW ATTENTION TO YOURSELF BY SWITCHING ON THE TV OR RADIO TO LEARN THE RESULT OF YOUR HANDIWORK.

8. At 7.30 a.m. someone will come to your room to collect the case. You will only hand it over after they have given you the password, which is Nelson's flag signal to his fleet at the Battle of Trafalgar: 'England expects every man to do his duty.'

ENSURE YOU HAVE TAKEN OUT THE MOBILE PHONE, and have breakfast in your room. (Remember to order it for 8.00 a.m. from room service before retiring.)

9. Leave the hotel (with the mobile phone) at nine o'clock without checking out. Turn right and walk south to St James's Park. Cross The Mall and go 100 yards or so towards Buckingham Palace, until you reach the path to the bridge across the lake, which you will take. Once on the bridge, *switch on* the mobile phone for further instructions.

10. Before leaving your room, tear this sheet into small pieces and dispose of it down the toilet and flush it three times, allowing a pause between each flush.

The Owl

Holt replaced the instructions in the silver case and sat in the armchair, waiting for his club sandwich. The long wait might mean the person bringing it would be from Giraffe. So when it did finally arrive, Holt gave the boy a searching look that was misinterpreted. Seeing his discomfiture, Holt concluded he was genuine and neither from Giraffe nor the Owl. The way he hovered for his tip confirmed it.

Every noise in the corridor raised his hopes, only for them to be dashed as the sound of retreating footsteps got weaker and weaker. It seemed he would be unable to warn Giraffe, and the responsibility would rest entirely on his shoulders. Then he heard some knocks at the doors of adjoining rooms, followed by a sharp knock at his own. A female voice that he instantly recognized called out, 'Housekeeping.'

'Coming,' he answered as he hurriedly opened the door to find Celia standing there in a snappy hotel uniform with a white pinafore in front.

Expressionless and feigning not to know each other, they stood rooted to the ground for a moment.

'Would you like me to turn down the bed, sir?'

'If you insist. I would appreciate it, though it's not really necessary.'

She pushed her trolley with housekeeping materials in the doorway to prevent the door shutting.

'It's a rule at the hotel that we maids, even the older ones, keep the door ajar when doing the rooms – and especially when a male guest is present.'

'I quite understand. In your case, I am sure it is a particularly wise precaution.'

'You naughty man!'

Playing the part to the full, she came in and walked to the bedside, unnecessarily wiggling her behind under her tight skirt. Was she was winding him up on purpose, notwithstanding the gravity of the situation? Or perhaps she could not help it, having got into the habit of toying with her VIPs.

Just as she was about to bend over to fold over the bedcover, Holt came up beside her, with his right hip obscuring the view of her left thigh from behind – straight ahead there was only the window, where there could hardly be a hidden camera – and slipped the beermat with his message into her apron pocket, pushing hard against her upper thigh so she could not fail to realize what he was doing. He had never before pushed against her there and found it an agreeable sensation that he would have liked to have prolonged, but he quickly stepped away.

'Is there anything else, sir?'

'Nothing that I would dare ask you for. Thanks all the same. I don't want to end up like DSK.'

'Who?'

'Dominique Strauss-Kahn. You know, the French head of the International Monetary Fund. The man expected to become the next French president who threw it all away by allegedly importuning the maid who had come to service his New York hotel room, just as you are doing now.'

'I don't know whether I should be flattered or insulted. But thank you, sir. Have a good night, alone.'

And then she was gone. Had she lingered for longer, it could have raised suspicions. Holt had kept talking loudly so he would not be suspected of having whispered something in her ear.

Relieved at having been able to inform Giraffe about what he was about to do, Holt found the sight of Celia had made him take stock of his situation. How he wished he were back with her in the fold at Farringdon, doing what he had initially signed up to do.

Would Celia read what he had written, or would a motorcycle courier be standing by to take it straight to Sir Charles? Unlikely, as someone might be watching. Even if she did not read it, she would surely make the link after the toppling of Nelson and realize he had graduated to the big time. That would make her respect him, but not a lot of good that would do him if he were no longer of this world to exploit it.

Too late for second thoughts; he turned on the television and started on his club sandwich. It is said one can judge a hotel by its club sandwiches, and this one was not bad at all; not that he could enjoy it with all that was on his mind.

There were some news flashes saying that the BBC and other news organizations had received warnings that something was going to happen in London that night, but no loss of life was expected. Apparently the event was to be a wake-up call that would precede a number of events in the coming weeks to prompt the government to stop the rot – the country did not deserve its heroes.

He watched some more television, hoping it would help him relax, but could not concentrate. Giving up, he had a shower, then set the digital clock alarm for 3.15 a.m. and tried to get some sleep.

He lay in bed wondering what Sir Charles and the government would do. Would they have the cruise missile shot down? Would they try and make it deviate from its course and risk it detonating elsewhere in central London? At least Trafalgar Square would be a large, virtually empty space at that time of the night. His guess was that they would think the success of his mission so important that they would do nothing.

160

It took him some time to drop off to sleep, and when he eventually did it was again only fitfully, with him constantly checking to see how long remained before the alarm would go off.

When it finally did sound, he got up immediately and pulled back the curtains to have a look at Nelson, who if everything went according to plan would soon no longer be there. With so much light pollution over central London, he would have been able to see him without the dim floodlight always illuminating him, as he faced south almost straight down Whitehall.

From where Holt was looking, the right-hand side of the admiral's chest, where he was to aim, was in full view and presumably would be where the missile would hit.

As he could not see the foot of the column, he wondered whether there might be some hapless tourists sitting underneath. He was glad the detonation that the Owl had mentioned would scatter them. There was nothing he could do, and perhaps it was better he could not see them.

He made a coffee and on finishing it turned out the bedside light and waited, having checked the laser had ample charge. There was ten minutes to go.

A little sooner than necessary, he switched on the laser power supply and listened to the hum, which quietened when the green light showed it was fully powered up.

He already had the window open, and nothing but the cool night air separated him from the statue. He pulled on the trigger but not hard enough to lock it and shone the laser on the admiral for a few moments, surprised at how relaxed he was now the great moment had come. More to the point was his relief that he would be targeting an inanimate object rather than a living being.

Everything seemed perfectly in order; all he had to do was to wait. He eased back on the trigger and rested the laser – he did not want to be tired and shaky when the time came.

Big Ben in the distance was striking the hour, but no sign of the missile. His digital clock was now showing 4.01.10. Where on earth was it?

Even though he had been waiting for it, when it came, the loud bang from the square took him by surprise. Squeezing hard down on the laser trigger to lock it, he aimed at the admiral's chest. Though the red spot was very obvious to him when looking through the telescopic sight, he was sure it would be hardly noticeable to anyone in the square, whose attention would anyway have been drawn downwards towards the sound and, presumably, smoke generated at the foot of the column.

Holt had expected the cruise missile to come up Whitehall – the route he had taken on coming to the hotel – as it would have provided a clear run to Nelson straight ahead. Instead, the 500 mph missile came over Buckingham Palace and down The Mall, veering to the left 300 yards before the end to skim right over his head, where it locked on to the target he had designated. Only afterwards did he realize the Owl had avoided sending the missile along Whitehall, where it could have been shot down by the ground-to-air missiles one would expect to be defending key government buildings.

There was no flash or explosion. The missile's momentum alone had been enough.

Nelson was no longer there.

Chapter 17
Taken

Holt got up at seven and turned on the television, just as any normal guest would.

Virtually all the main channels had extensive coverage of the felling of Nelson. The TV stations and media organizations had received phone calls from someone calling himself the Owl, claiming responsibility for the action at Trafalgar Square – carried out because the country no longer merited such a hero. According to the Owl, the country had sunk to such a low that those attending the next Remembrance Day ceremony at the Cenotaph to commemorate those who gave their lives in the world wars should hang their heads in shame.

At exactly 7.30 there was a knock at his door, which Holt opened holding the silver case in his left hand. The woman in a room maid's uniform gave the password, and he handed over the case with the laser target-designator without further ado.

Closing the door, he felt very pleased with himself. Not only had he completed the initiation test without a hitch and without having to assassinate anyone, let alone the prime minister, he had also covered his official backside by forewarning Giraffe, and he had impressed Celia into the bargain.

With few hard facts, the early-morning TV news coverage was reduced to repeatedly showing clips of the sandstone statue of Lord Nelson lying shattered on the ground, just as it had repeatedly shown Saddam Hussein's toppled statue in Baghdad.

The newscasts said that just before the arrival of the cruise missile, someone had let off a loud percussion grenade at the foot of the column. This had emitted a nauseating smell, causing the five people sitting at its base to move well away. The newscasters were able to interview the individuals concerned, who considered themselves mighty lucky. One even said how considerate the terrorists had been to make them scatter before Nelson arrived on their heads.

The BBC's authoritative security correspondent, Frank Gardner, was saying the government had no idea as to who the Owl might be, and that the incident differed from almost all others in that great care had been taken to avoid loss of life – as evidenced by the detonation of a device at the foot of the column to cause anyone there to move away.

As the government had been forewarned, Holt knew they could have shot down the cruise missile or sent it off course. As he had surmised, the prime minister must have considered his mission so important that it was worth taking the flak from the press, who, as usual, not knowing the whole story, were already accusing the secret services of bungling.

Anyway, Holt had the satisfaction of proving himself to both parties.

None of the so-called experts trotted out on TV and the radio on such occasions knew what to make of it. Much of traditional England was in a state of shock, seeing their most famous hero toppled in such a dramatic manner. Holt could not help kicking himself for not having thought up the idea himself – it was just the sort of outlandish scenario Sir Charles would have admired and expected him to have come up with.

On the dot of 9 a.m., he walked out of the hotel, with no one paying much attention, as the staff were constantly nipping into the office or the breakfast room to see the TVs there and try and find out what had happened just outside their door during the night. However, as Holt exited the hotel, a policeman moved towards him as if about to question him, but before the officer had taken more than a couple of steps, a tall figure standing nearby quickly stepped in, showed an ID, and told him to back off. The service was protecting him, for if he were taken into custody even temporarily, he might be compromised and at the very least suspected of having revealed something.

He had not anticipated the amount of disruption his night's work would cause. Trafalgar Square was a traffic node, transited by many bus routes, not to mention other vehicles. With the square cordoned off as a crime scene, all this traffic had been diverted, causing total gridlock. Much of central London was at a standstill. No wonder he had been told to walk and catch an underground train outside the immediate area.

On exiting the hotel, he turned right and walked down Spring Gardens, past the life-size white horse sculpture outside the British Council building, with its often ignored notice telling people not to mount it, and crossed The Mall at the first spot with an island midway across. He walked a hundred yards to the right towards Buckingham Palace, then turned left onto the footpath leading to the bridge across the lake.

Someone must have been watching or tracking him via his mobile phone – which he had, as instructed, switched on as he had entered the park – for it rang when he was halfway across. A voice said, 'Go to St James's tube station and take an underground train to Bank station, and from there walk along Leadenhall Street to London Bridge. Cross the bridge on the left-hand side, during which time you will receive further orders.'

Holt began to feel a trifle uneasy. He had detected a change in tone in the communications. Prior to the initiation test, it had always been a matter of instructions; now it was curt orders. Was it because they considered him to already be part of their organization and were taking him for granted, or was there some other significance? Still, there was nothing he could do. He would have to wait and find out – somewhat like the waiting period before he had been accepted for the service.

The paralysis of road traffic in central London meant the underground was packed, and he had to wait for the third train before he was able to squeeze his way on, and then only with difficulty. He was glad to be getting off at Bank only a few stops distant. With such a crush, he had to be careful not to slip down into the wide gap between the curved platform and the train at that station.

In keeping with the station name, the imposing building of the Bank of England was just outside. Five minutes' walk along Leadenhall Street brought him to London Bridge. As instructed, he crossed over to the left-hand side. And again, when halfway across the bridge, his phone rang, with the voice saying, 'At the traffic lights at the end of the bridge, cross over to the other side of the first street, called Tooley Street, and turn left on the other side so you are walking parallel to the railway lines and the River Thames. Walk along Tooley Street for about three hundred metres, until you come to a road tunnel passing under the railway tracks. Turn right into the tunnel and walk straight ahead on the right-hand side, with the traffic coming towards you.'

The pavement on the other side of Tooley Street was crowded with people going to the underground and railway stations. Also, there were queues consisting mostly of families waiting to visit the London Dungeon for a scare. After weaving his way through the crowd, Holt finally reached the entrance to the tunnel under the railway lines and turned into it.

Dark, dank, and depressing, the tunnel was a long one, with the sheer volume of traffic of all sorts coming through towards him adding to his discomfort. Why choose such a god-awful place? To think a week before he had been on the sunny Côte d'Azur.

On reaching the halfway point, he could see the daylight at the exit beckoning him, but just then two ambulances, one behind the other with sirens blaring, screeched to a stop alongside him, leaving a gap between them which happened to be exactly abreast of him. As he was wondering why they should stop there, with no sign of anyone injured either in the road or on the pavement, he heard the nearside rear door of the leading ambulance behind him spring open 180 degrees. He could see it not only blocked his retreat but also would prevent anyone walking along the pavement behind him from seeing him. Likewise, the nearside door of the ambulance in front of him had sprung open, blocking the view of anyone ahead.

Two well-built men wearing balaclavas came out from nowhere to grab him. Taken by surprise, he put up no resistance as they bundled him into the back of the leading ambulance and held him still while a nurse with her face obscured by a surgical mask pressed a cloth soaked in chloroform over his mouth and

166

nose. Even before he had lost consciousness, the ambulance had begun to move.

The whole operation having only taken about twelve seconds, the ambulance was out of the tunnel so quickly that no one observing from above would have imagined anything untoward had happened in the interim.

On failing to see Holt exit the tunnel, anyone watching from a helicopter or later looking at satellite images would have been unable to determine in which of the many vehicles entering and exiting the tunnel he would have been. Also, from above it would have been impossible to note the registration number on their number plates. Anyway, they were probably waiting for him to walk out of the other end of the tunnel. As evidenced before, the Owl was certainly a clever operator.

Holt's memories of his subsequent interrogation were vague. He finally woke up to find himself in bed in a darkened room with wires linking him to a monitor, which must have triggered an alert, for a nurse soon came in and turned up the light.

As the nurse's face was obscured by a mask, like that of the one who had held the pad soaked in chloroform to his mouth in the ambulance, he could not tell whether it was the same one.

'How do we feel?' she asked as though it really mattered to her.

'My head hurts.'

'That's to be expected in view of what we have been through this last week, or couple of weeks, my dear. What would you like for breakfast?'

The 'my dear' and the royal 'we' made the nurse sound almost kindly. Was this some good-cop, bad-cop scenario? Or was she mimicking the nurses in Dr No's lair to psyche him out? He had been interrogated or kept unconscious for goodness knows how long surely to disorientate him time-wise.

'Coffee most of all,' he replied.

He had no idea what time of day it was. He did not even know what day of the week or of the month it was.

Could he have fallen by mistake into the hands of operatives of another government department, who did not realize he was one of them? He might have admitted toppling Nelson, thereby raising their suspicions. Everything was a blur.

He did not ask for much for breakfast, just juice, more coffee, and toast. When the nurse had cleared that away, she gave him his instructions.

'You must prepare yourself for your make-or-break meeting with His Wisdom. To start with, you need a shower and a shave. Also, you must clean your teeth and comb your hair and evacuate your bowels – I can give you an enema, if you like.'

'Thanks very much, but no thanks.'

'Always trying to help.'

'What do you mean, "His Wisdom"?'

'The Owl, of course. He will be watching you, though you will not actually be able to see him. Besides, you yourself will feel better if you are cleaned up and decent. To tell the truth, you look awful, my darling.'

'Thanks very much...love.'

'You can talk like that to me, but you must address the Owl as Your Wisdom.'

'Really?'

'Yes. It's no different from calling an ambassador Your Excellency or the Queen Your Majesty. After you've done it several times, it will roll off your tongue. Remember this is, as I just said, going to be your make-or-break session.'

Holt considered asking her what make or break meant, but finally thought better of it. She would not know much anyway, though the mention of the word 'make' implied a possible positive outcome, whatever that might be. All he knew about owls was that they could see into the far distance in dim light at night, rotate their head 270 degrees, and had wings that enabled them to descend noiselessly without alerting their prey, somewhat like fifth-generation stealth aircraft.

After the shower and shave in the en suite bathroom, he did indeed feel better. No need for help from the nurse, who meanwhile had been busying herself in his room.

Chapter 18
Make or Break

Seeing him reappear with a towel around his midriff, the nurse told him to put on the pair of convict's striped overalls lying on the bed and watch the TV until summoned. The drab outfit undid all the good the shower had done him. It seemed destined to add to his humiliation.

The television had a recording of *BBC Breakfast* for the morning Nelson had been knocked off his perch. The public would never know the role he had played, though he was glad Celia knew.

After about twenty minutes, the sound of the door being unlocked signalled the return of the nurse – he could tell it was the same one by her voice and a stain on her otherwise immaculate uniform. She led him out and along a passage, before ushering him into a large bare room with an expensive-looking chair set in the middle facing a large flat-screen monitor. After telling him to sit down and wait, the nurse left the room, gently closing the door behind her. It was only then that he realized there was no door handle on the inside.

Certain that the large mirror to the left of the screen was two-way and unsure of who might be observing him, he began to fidget. As far as he knew, he had carried out the initiation test as instructed and not put a foot wrong. Yet his subsequent treatment meant something had gone awry and that they knew he was not what he purported to be.

What was going to be his fate? 'Make or break', the nurse had said. Did her solicitude mean she knew his life might be almost over? After what seemed a full ten minutes but was in fact probably much less, a rustling sound emanated from the speakers inset in the wall on either side of the monitor.

Was this going to be another interrogation?

He felt bad that the combination of scopolamine and threats had made him confirm he worked for Giraffe so easily. He tried to console himself by telling himself that, not being a field agent, he had no training in resisting interrogation. What else had he revealed under the effect of the truth drug? Perhaps much more, but another consolation was that it was not like giving away the names of fellow agents, like many had done under torture by the Gestapo in World War II. He did not know their names and now realized the rule about not discussing personal matters with fellow agents was a wise one.

'Look at the monitor!'

The loud, distorted voice had caught Holt by surprise. He looked at the enormous screen, which was flickering into life, showing Whitehall, along which he had walked to The Trafalgar hotel. And coming into view was he himself. Worse still, the video footage taken from the front clearly showed him going through his supplication routine – designed to attract attention without it being noticed by anyone following behind him. Of course, viewed from the front, as shown on the monitor, it was only too obvious. His heart sank as the voice emanated from the speakers again.

'Holt, Jeremy Holt. That is your real name, isn't it?'

Holt had to reply in the affirmative; there was no point in denying it. Though he felt he was talking directly with the Owl, the latter's voice seemed to be passing through some form of scrambler, distorting it and adding superfluous stock words and phrases such as 'um' and 'come to think of it' to make it difficult to identify. [For clarity, these are omitted here – editor.]

'In World War II, when we – um, the British – captured German spies, we gave them the choice of either being shot or working for us as double agents. Fortunately for us, many opted for the latter, and thanks to them we were able to deceive the Germans in key areas, notably the quantity of fighters we could produce per week during the Battle of Britain and the location of the landings on D-Day. Helped us win the war.'

'Are you giving me that choice?' responded Holt with a shaky voice.

'Too early to say. You thought you could trick us?'

'Was it that video that made you suspicious?'

'No. We only came upon it a couple of days later, though your crossing over to the other side of Whitehall on the way to the hotel left us puzzled.'

'So when did you know?'

'When we learnt Charlie had informed the prime minister about our intentions. You, Holt, were the only person who could have revealed we intended to topple Nelson with a cruise missile. So we were onto you hours before. What we didn't know was how involved you were with Giraffe and, indeed, my chum Charlie-boy.'

'There's not much I can say.'

'You've already said more than enough, though with truth drugs one can never be sure how much is valid.'

Holt had to admire the Owl's choice of initiation test. Toppling Nelson was serious enough, publicity-wise, to ensure the security services would inform the prime minister if only to protect their backs. It was a simple way to test him and at the same time learn whether he was working undercover or in league with the security services.

'Under questioning,' continued the Owl, 'you begged us to lay off, bleating abjectly you were merely a backroom boy tasked with coming up with 9/11-type ideas, which indeed was what we wanted you for.'

'I was only a cog.'

'Cogs get their teeth sheared off when the driver makes a mistake. Charlie should be ashamed – sending a boy to do a man's job. You're not cut out to be a James Bond, though even 007 would have relished Consuela. Though I am not sure she would have indulged him to the extent that, for some reason, she did you.'

'I don't know what to say, Your Wisdom.'

'Aha, aha, I see our nurse briefed you correctly.'

'That's all she said, other than that this would be make or break, and very important.'

'We have checked up on what you were doing. Truth be told, there was little likelihood of someone even as intelligent as you imagining what we might do, but then we are not the typical al-Qaeda-type organization. Though it's a pity Charlie found you first; you would have been more valuable to the country, to the world, working for us.'

To try to save his skin, Holt immediately agreed that had the situation been reversed, things might well have been very different. He told himself he was not really letting down the service, since the Owl was so highly placed, or so well connected, he obviously already knew what Giraffe and Sir Charles did.

Being unable to see the face behind the mirror made replying difficult. It was quite possible no one apart from a technician was there and the Owl was miles away, even in the South of France on *Vessos* or a similar vessel. The next question came as something of a surprise.

'Don't you think you *owe* us something?'

'How do you mean?'

'In return for Consuela. In normal circumstances, someone as lowly as you would never come near, let alone handle, to use an unfortunate word, such a gem – literally a gem for billionaires.'

'It was not just the sex, though even just for that I'll be eternally grateful. She gave me my life back – or rather, what's left of it.'

'Not so fast there. She reported you had many qualities and that she took you in hand at first in a motherly way, and then in a more physical way, believing you were an innocent young boy, which in many ways she found you were.'

The phrase 'taking in hand' made Holt wonder just how much detail Consuela had revealed.

'I was not *that* innocent!'

'Admittedly, she did say you at least knew your basic geography, but now she is right out of the picture and resuming her matrimonial duties, it's your political views we are interested in. She gave me some inkling as to what they might be – not that they were very deeply thought out. It seems that overall we hold very similar ones, though we might differ regarding the means whereby those goals might be achieved. What did you think of the Rethinking Democracy seminar on *Vessos*?'

'I thought it was very interesting. Very stimulating and informative, though it was more a matter of hypothetical questions than definite proposals about what should be done. I quite liked the idea of reduced voting power for people not contributing to society to prevent them having too much sway. And that even pensioners should not be allowed to skew the system. Though there remains the problem of how to evaluate those who contribute to society and hold sensible views who are not remunerated monetarily.'

They continued discussing democracy and what needed to be done in England, including taxing food, with penalties for excessive amounts of salt and sugar. Many of the Owl's gripes seemed reasonable to Holt, as he made clear, though he could not see how they could be achieved in the face of vested interests and lobbyists.

'I reckon,' said the voice, 'we can still make use of you, but in a way totally different from that originally envisaged.'

'What do you mean?'

'In the operation on which we are now embarking and future ones, you could be the conduit, not directly to His Pomposity the prime minister, but to Sir Charles, who will be able to understand our point of view and present it properly to the powers that unfortunately be.'

'Will His Pomposity, as you call him, go along with that?'

'He will have to.'

'How will we know it is you?'

'Neither you nor anyone else will be talking to me again in real time. We shall use the name the Owl, with it referring either to me or someone representing our organization. It could even be just an intelligent computer. We will give you a special phone, which we shall call the OwlPhone. Will you do it?'

'Seems quite reasonable to me, personally. Do I have any choice?'

'In reality, no. You know too much for us to just let you go. While we might not flush your brain and turn you into a zombie, we might have to lock you away somewhere for years. Wouldn't be much fun for you, though we might throw in a woman in a similar predicament as yourself. She wouldn't be a trophy wife, that's for sure. Could be a grandmother even. Won't be much of a life sharing a cell with a grandmother, will it?'

'Then the answer must be yes. Could even be exciting.'

'Don't count on that. Not everyone in government and the services will like you being the intermediary. They will play mean tricks to undermine you, and Charlie who they can never forgive for having outmanoeuvred them.'

'Better than the grandmother.'

'Okay then. You will tell Charlie that he – via you and the OwlPhone – will be the link between us and the government. You understand?'

'Yes, perfectly.'

'Before we part, let's talk some more about the situation in England. The sorry situation in which our country finds itself...'

The Owl went into a long discourse, covering many topics and pet hates. How, having lost Australia, we should now use the Falklands as a penal colony. Politicians and politically correct do-gooders, who over the years have wrecked the country, should be sent there, together with rapists, paedophiles, and mothers who allow their daughters to be circumcised – along with the doctors who cover it up, and illegal immigrants who have physically attacked people but cannot be deported due to their exploitation of human rights legislation, not forgetting benefits cheats and tax evaders.

'There won't be room for all that lot,' said Holt.

'I know. I'm getting carried away and partly joking, as I know we cannot have a perfect world. However, there are little things that many might agree with, such as taxing mobile phone calls, text messages and even emails with a double rate if they are in a foreign language, or fifty per cent more if one party uses an unintelligible dialect. Any form of encryption would be subject to a high penalty tax. We could make gossiping expensive, punishing those not working with time on their hands.

'The unbelievable thing,' went on the Owl, 'is that the French can do it, but we can't. They have a law making rip-off credit card processing charges like those imposed by the airlines illegal, a maximum unit charge for phone calls from hotels, and, long before the UK did anything, introduced serious measures to stop FGM. They also keep religion and the manifestations thereof out of their state schools.'

The Owl ended by saying, 'I hope you will appreciate the events that will unfold in the near future are merely a wake-up call, and items requiring action will be added subsequently. Should action not be taken, the country could expect a repeat of a different nature. We might then even have to target individual officials for incompetence or lack of action. I hope you understand this is for the good of the country.'

'I can see that. What's going to happen now?'

'You will be put to sleep again so no one can work out when we held this conversation and thereby identify me. When you wake up, you will have the OwlPhone beside you. It will be a bricklike device like mobile phones used to be, because it contains multiple SIM cards and other communications circuits, including Wi-Fi, and of course some C4 plastic explosive to deter any attempt to open it or subject it to rays, X or otherwise. Attempting to do so will result in it self-destructing and the loss of the handler's life and that of anyone else in the immediate vicinity. Also, interfering with it will render communication with us more difficult. You have been warned.'

'I understand.'

'That's all for now. I will leave you in the capable hands of your nurse. Good luck. The next stage of our operation should be even more fun than toppling Nelson, as well as being for the good of the country. I must warn you it is multifaceted and designed to make government fools look even more foolish. Goodbye.'

'Goodbye,' answered Holt somewhat sheepishly.

A couple or so minutes later, the door opened and in came the nurse with a pill and a glass of water.

'Don't worry,' she said, 'It's not fast-acting. You'll be conscious long enough to get back to your room and go to the toilet. I'm so glad it won't be the "break" routine. You seem such a nice young man, though somewhat naïve.'

Holt wondered what she looked like under her surgical mask – could she have taken a liking to him.

Chapter 19
Return to the Fold

Waking up under a tree at the edge of a wood, Holt had, as certainly intended, lost all sense of time. He remembered being woken up several times, given a little food, made to exercise, going to the toilet, and being given another pill to put him back to sleep. They could have gone through this routine several times each day to give him the impression more time had elapsed than had in reality. It was impossible to know.

There was a canvas sheet under him, no doubt to protect his clothes, since he was dressed in the clothes he had been wearing when abducted. His shirt and underclothes had evidently been washed, and his suit pressed.

He could not have been lying there for long, for he was conscious of recently having had people bustling around him. His arm ached a little from what had evidently been a wake-up shot. Next to him was a glass of water, a liquid that he sorely needed, as his throat was parched due to the drugs he had imbibed over possibly a period of many days. Also there was satchel attached to his belt; inside was the OwlPhone.

A tray with a sandwich and Thermos flask marked 'Strong Coffee' was also at hand on a low camping table. How thoughtful and considerate! After eagerly consuming the sandwich and drinking the coffee, he felt fit enough to stand up and look around. The first thing that caught his attention was a wooden pole with a sign saying 'Railway Station 5 miles'. He would not have to buy a railway ticket, as there was one pinned to the Thermos flask containing the coffee. The date on the ticket, which included travel by tube within London, showed almost a month had elapsed since his abduction.

Perhaps because of the reaction to the strong coffee, the first thing he did was to have a pee against the trunk of a nearby tree. Then, starting off somewhat unsteadily, he walked through the woods and fields before coming to some big houses and a hotel, where he asked for further directions, to be told the station was a mile further on. It was Gerrards Cross, where Consuela had picked him up at the beginning of his undercover mission. Small world.

Though people at Giraffe must have been wondering what had happened to him and whether he was still alive, he thought it better to wait until he arrived at London's Marylebone station before giving them a call. The phone at the local station might be bugged; not that he would be saying anything other than that he was still alive and relatively well and on his way to Farringdon.

The train was virtually empty, and he had no trouble finding a seat with no one nearby. While trying to take stock of his situation and check how much money he had, he checked his pockets and was surprised to find the expensive-looking bracelet Consuela had given him was still there. He took it out and looked at it wistfully. He would keep it for memories' sake. Not tell anyone.

On arriving at Marylebone, he made a very brief phone call to the receptionist at Giraffe, who was clearly surprised and overjoyed to hear his voice. Walking as instructed to Baker Street station, he caught a District Line underground train straight to Farringdon. With so many other things to think about, he found it odd to find he had time to muse over the fact that at one time trains on that section of the line had been drawn by steam engines. It was nice to be back in the real world again, however grimy.

Considering he had always worked independently and his interactions with the staff at Giraffe had mostly been intermittent ones in the canteen, he was touched and surprised so many turned out to welcome him back. To his disappointment, Celia was not of their number, but then he noticed her hovering outside the pack. Even though they had never had a physical relationship, she evidently feared being unable to hold back an excessive display of emotion on greeting him that would start the office rumour mill rolling.

Peter cut short the congratulations, saying Sir Charles wanted to see him right away, but first Blackwell would have to check him over to confirm he was physically okay.

'I have told Blackwell you are not allowed to give any details other than that you were interrogated after being softened up by a woman who cannot be named. To stop him getting too interested, I gave the impression she was an unattractive monster like Rosa Klebb in *From Russia with Love*. Above all, do not mention your role in the toppling of Nelson or the word "owl".'

'Blackwell's the last person I want to see after all I've been through.'

'I understand, but in this case regulations stipulate you be looked over physically – a kind of health and safety thing so you cannot sue us. Just keep shtum.'

So it proved. Blackwell wanted the details of what he had done with the woman rather than undercover in general. However, thanks to Peter he was able to stonewall him. As a result, Blackwell had to make do with reporting Holt was in such good condition he must have had an easy time of it, a holiday almost, which in fact had been true initially.

If Holt had described how intensive and stressful the subsequent interrogation part had been, that would have given Blackwell a pretext for saying he was damaged goods, suffering from post-traumatic stress disorder and therefore a liability.

It fell to Peter to recognize his fragile mental state and insist that Celia accompany him on the journey to Sackville Street in case a reaction set in. For Holt, this was a bittersweet choice of minder, for though pleased to see her, he felt guilty about his intense sessions with Consuela, for whom he still had lingering feelings and yearnings. He felt he had cheated on Miss Innocent, even though they were not in a formal relationship.

As the black cab sped through the midday traffic towards the West End, Celia inevitably questioned him about the 'hoity-toity' woman she had seen him with at the US ambassador's reception.

'You seemed very close, even though she was somewhat older than you. Did anything happen?'

'We were not together long enough for it to be meaningful. I was only with her up until the initiation test, which of course you know about. Most of my time undercover was spent drugged out of my mind or being interrogated.'

Their arrival at Vigo Street at the top of Sackville Street fortunately, or so he thought at the time, prevented Celia from asking him to define 'meaningful'. Relieved, he got out, slammed the door shut, and stood at the kerb watching her taxi disappear into the distance before walking down the street to number 45.

As on previous occasions, he rang the bell and pushed open the first door and then the second after the first had clicked shut. Cut-Glass was standing at the top of the first flight of stairs, and – surprise, surprise – seemed genuinely delighted to see him.

'Come on up, Jeremy. Sir Charles is waiting impatiently. So glad to see you made it safely back. We were all getting concerned about you when you disappeared into thin air after the Nelson thing. We guessed you had been rumbled and feared the worst.'

'I was rumbled, but not due to any mistake on my part.'

The door to Sir Charles's room was ajar, and on seeing Holt and Cut-Glass, he beckoned them to come in. Usually so calm and poised, he looked tired and strained as he walked over to shake Holt's hand.

'Welcome back, Jeremy, and let me say how much we all appreciate what you did for the country at great risk to your person.'

Holt put his fingers to his lips, walked to the far side of the large room, and put the OwlPhone under a cushion on the sofa. He walked back to Sir Charles and spoke in his ear.

'We must speak in a low voice.'

'Understood,' whispered Sir Charles, bringing a chair up to one Holt was sitting on and sitting down. Holt then proceeded to brief him on all that had happened.

'Sir Charles, before going into detail I must warn you that they have someone or even several people on the inside who tipped them off that the PM knew about the plan to topple Nelson beforehand. As only I could have revealed their intention, my cover was blown even before they launched the missile. That's why they abducted and interrogated me. I am sorry to say I must have given away some information when drugged and pressured.'

'What did you tell them?'

'I can't remember exactly, but according to their boss, called the Owl, as you are aware, and who seems to know you personally, even claiming you are a chum, I admitted that I worked for you. In fact, he knew all about Giraffe and you being in charge, so I was not giving much away – not like giving a list of secret agents – and anyway, I don't know the real names of the people working for you. I am sorry all the same.'

'Don't worry. You're lucky they let you go. It was your call. We couldn't help you.'

'There's much more to it than that. He wants me, and you – the two of us – to be intermediaries between his organization and the government. As you thought before I undertook the mission, something big *is* definitely about to happen in London, but I have no idea what it is.'

'Why do you think the Owl knew me personally?'

'He talked as if you had been chums at school – in very familiar terms. He even knew your nickname.'

'Anybody could have found that out.'

'He said you, like he, could have been prime minister had you so wanted.'

'He has quite an imagination, but it sounds as though all that may be a red herring to throw us off the scent.'

Sir Charles, evidently pleased at the back-handed compliment about him being a potential prime minister, knew it might all be a bluff, and that the Owl's main intention might simply be to make money speculating against the pound.

'Before I give you the details of what happened to me undercover and during my interrogation, I must tell you about the special phone I put over there just now. He calls it the OwlPhone, and its main purpose is for us to be able to communicate with him. I put it under the cushion because I suspect he could use it to listen in to our conversations.'

'We can easily check that,' commented Sir Charles. 'But possibly he would only activate it – the listening in – at certain times.'

Holt went over to the sofa and collected the OwlPhone to show it to Sir Charles.

'It is rather large,' explained Holt, talking in a normal voice, 'because it has multiple SIM cards and communication modes, which switch automatically, making it impossible to track the origin of the communications, not forgetting a self-destruct charge that will go off it is tampered with. His Wisdom says I should keep it with me at all times and not allow anyone to X-ray it or subject it to any form of radiation or strong electromagnetic force. It contains C4, by the way, so he could blow us up anytime. He is going to call us on it at 2 p.m. on Monday.'

Holt picked up a pen and a piece of paper from Sir Charles's desk and wrote, 'Tell Sandra to put this in the broom cupboard and not to speak,' on a piece of paper, which he handed to Sir Charles, who then called Cut-Glass and gave her the sheet of paper and then the phone, which she clutched somewhat nervously.

Holt proceeded to fill in the details of what had happened undercover, only leaving out the specifics of the amorous sessions with Trophy Wife. He explained Consuela was not part of the Owl's organization, knew nothing about it, and had in fact worked for them on a one-off basis for a bit of adventure, believing they were a US secret agency like the CIA. He was glad Sir Charles was not interested in her and only in the Owl himself and his organization.

'Who do you think the Owl could be? Maybe it's a she.'

'I don't think so, as the nurse kept on referring to the Owl as he. The only concrete information is that the Owl learnt that the government had been tipped off about the toppling of Lord Nelson. This means that either the Owl's statement that he has sympathizers at the highest levels of government is true, or that he himself is a cabinet minister, high official, political adviser, or someone in the security services. The great lengths the Owl went to in order to make it impossible to determine the exact moment our meeting took place and the use of his underlings in future dealings suggest he is someone operating in the centre of things, but of what things?'

Sir Charles asked Holt whether he had been able to gauge what type of person the Owl was.

'I hesitate to say it, but at times it seemed as if I were talking to you – perhaps it was because of similar backgrounds, and you both wanted to use me in similar ways. Perhaps an establishment civil service or secret service figure, to put it bluntly.'

'Really?'

'I do not think he is an evil person – for instance, he took measures to ensure no one was injured in toppling Nelson.'

'I myself thought the same, but not everyone in government, certainly not the PM, agrees.'

'The distortion of his voice, fluctuating from deeply male to shrill effeminacy with the intercalation of computer-generated phrases, was very off putting and made it difficult to assess him. However, after a time I thought I could pick out the computer-generated words, as most were rather simple interjections – such as "like", "well", "actually", "come to think of it", "to put that into perspective" – obviously intercalated to prevent me noting mannerisms. He was certainly a highly educated individual.'

'You said he had a list of demands, so we shall have to wait for them, to get a proper idea as regards what he wants. Have you any idea what they might be?'

'All I know is that he was very concerned about the state of the country. He wanted to make England great again. He had me attend a Rethinking Democracy seminar on a mega-yacht called the *Vessos*, moored near Monaco. Many important people were there.'

'What did they mean by that?'

Holt explained the seminar's keynote speaker's suggestion that voting in democracies needed tweaking to give more weight to merit and intelligence. He had admitted the problem was how to allot full votes to people whose contribution to society could not be measured in monetary terms, such as intellectuals, writers, carers, voluntary workers and some housewives and single mothers.

'Do you think the Owl would like to apply that to Great Britain?'

'He might,' replied Holt, 'be seeking that in the long term but gave the impression that might be a bridge too far at the moment. I think he wants to push some pet policies. Of course, there is the possibility, as you mentioned when you asked me to work undercover, that all this might be a red herring, with the real aim being to make a financial killing on currency speculation.'

'Sounds a bit like super-UKIP to me,' commented Sir Charles.

'I actually suggested that to him, and he replied that UKIP were much too simplistic, though the fact that Farage sometimes stated obvious truths that the PM and others were afraid to mention or could not comprehend was refreshing. He said Farage was right in saying that the brouhaha with Russia was unnecessary in that the European Union in befriending Ukraine and trying to pull them into their orbit had provoked Russia stupidly.'

'From what you say, the only thing I think we can be sure of is that his – we assume it is a man – intention is to cause as little harm to people as possible. Probably our greatest problem will be preventing the government escalating it into a tragedy.'

'You may think I am suffering from Stockholm syndrome, in that I ended up sympathizing with the Owl – or rather, with some of his ideas regarding what the UK needs.'

'You are being frank with me, and I in turn will be frank with you. This is a unique, unexpected chance for Giraffe to be at the centre of things, and I recognize you are now the lynchpin. Jeremy, from now on I shall regard you as one of my protégés. In consequence, you will have the highest security clearance possible in Giraffe.'

Chapter 20
Captain Holt

Sir Charles had told Holt that in keeping with that security clearance he would have access to masses of material, even from the CIA, that other departments, let alone the prime minister, could never set eyes on.

'Please do not abuse my trust in you,' he had said before telling him to return to Sackville Street at ten the following morning so they could continue their talk.

In trying to ensure he would not be late, Holt arrived at Sackville Street much too early and to kill time decided to drop into a very well-known jeweller's in nearby Bond Street to see whether the bracelet Consuela had given him as an afterthought on their parting was of any significant value – he knew rich people very often wore imitations in public out of fear of being robbed.

'I was given this by a wealthy American friend,' he said, addressing the clerk, 'but cannot believe it is as valuable as it looks. It must be an imitation – though if it is, it's so good it's great to have. Plus it has great emotional value.'

The clerk examined it closely and raised his eyebrows. 'Please wait a moment, sir. I'll run it by our expert just to make quite sure.'

So saying, he disappeared into an office at the back of the shop, leaving Holt behind under the suspicious gaze of a well-built man in a morning coat standing at the door.

The clerk finally came out of the office and returned the item to Holt.

'Three hundred and fifty,' he said in an unfazed voice.

'Pounds?'

'No, thousand pounds – more than half a million US dollars.'

'I can't believe it.'

'According to our man, it's a unique piece. Of course that is the price he would recommend *we* try to sell it for. He said that

185

because it's unique, there's no knowing what it would fetch at an auction. If you ever do want to part with it that might be the better option, though I should not really be telling you this. You could always set a reserve.'

Holt stepped outside in a state of disbelief and walked the short distance to Sackville Street thinking how lucky it was that he had been too preoccupied to mention the bracelet to anyone at Giraffe. Doing so would have made people jealous. Also there might be some regulation that significant items received in the course of duty had to be forfeited. Perhaps he had meant more to Consuela than he realized. He regretted not having something to give her to show how much she had meant to him. But then there was nothing of equal value that he could have given her.

On arriving at 45 Sackville Street and entering through the double doors, Holt was as usual about to go straight ahead to the stairs on the left, only to find the elderly tailor blocking his path.

'It's your uniform, sir.'

'What uniform?'

'Your captain's uniform.'

'How come? I've never even been in the army or any of the armed forces for that matter!'

'You are now. At this rate of promotion, you'll soon be back here for your colonel's or brigadier's clogs.'

'I doubt that. The steps get steeper after the rank of captain. What is the old joke? "The higher they get, the thicker they get," meaning it's not only the stripes but the people inside the uniforms that are thicker, stupider. I'm not stupid enough.'

'You must,' said the tailor, 'at least try it on – though I am sure it will fit perfectly – just to see how my creation looks. You see, I had to invent it.'

Taken aback, Holt went into the tailor's just as he had done on that first day. The youngish assistant again took his jacket, but with less disdain than before, and hung it up in the cupboard as the tailor picked up a snazzy uniform with a captain's insignia from the bench.

The tailor insisted he put on the trousers as well.

'Not bad, eh? Sir Charles wants to see how you look in it too, so keep it on and leave your suit here with me. If you're too embarrassed to go out all dolled up, put it back on when you leave.'

'It does look great, I admit,' said Holt. 'What regiment is it?'

'Apparently, you are attached to, but not part of – whatever that means – the Special Reconnaissance Regiment, the SRR, which is based up in Hereford with the SAS. No one knows much about them.'

Holt was pleased to see how good he looked. He could have been playing an officer in a World War II film. Going upstairs with a spring in his stride, he even seemed to impress Cut-Glass. The words of the major came to mind: 'A great suit gives one a lift and makes one feel someone. Of course, a military uniform with several pips would be even better.'

How he wished the major were around so he could show it off, with three pips indicating he was a captain!

Sir Charles came out on the landing on hearing him talking to Cut-Glass.

'Don't you think he looks great,' said Cut-Glass to Sir Charles.

'Yes, Sandra, I certainly do,' he replied, pausing for a moment and then adding, 'You had better wear it in. You do not want to look like a tailor's dummy. Prince Charles has some flunky his size wear in his new suits and uniforms. Wear it around your flat, even sleep in it for a few hours. If it looks too new, you will not only look silly but risk those generals and top officials cottoning on to what we've done. Another thing...don't go around saluting people indoors. Pity there's not time to send you to Sandhurst for a couple of days. Then you could say you had been there without lying, just like Jeffrey Archer said he went to Oxford when he just went to some school there and not the university.'

'I'm worried I will ham it up, pretending to be Michael Caine.'

'Don't worry too much. They won't be seeing you face to face, at least for now. You will be at Farringdon, and we will be seeing you from the Cobra room via a video link on a smallish screen, so there will be no need for hamming. The reason I am making you a captain is that "Captain" will be more impressive than "Holt" in the presence of the prime minister, senior officials, and top brass. Pompous officials always put people into slots so they know how relate to them according to an established pecking order. Given time, we could establish your position in the hierarchy as a recognized expert, an intellectual James Bond. However, time is something we don't have, and by giving you a military rank we can slot you in and ensure you are respected.'

'I get it.'

' "Captain" gives the feeling of the go-ahead bright chap. "Major" sounds too staid, and anyway you are a bit young for that. This fits in well with the fact that you are now an "officer" in Giraffe, whereas before you were either a technician or undercover operative.'

'That's nice to know.'

'By the way, you are attached to the Special Reconnaissance Regiment, the SRR, who are even more secretive than the SAS, with whom they work, so it won't seem strange that no one has heard or even read about you. They will realize they can find even less about you in that you are only attached to them. Come into my room so we can review the situation.'

Holt followed Sir Charles into his room, while Cut-Glass went off to deal with other matters.

Holt and Sir Charles then discussed what would be likely to happen when the Owl contacted them after the weekend, and how they might handle the situation as it evolved.

'The top brass,' said Sir Charles, 'would very likely want to have the OwlPhone in the Cobra room, but apart from the fact that switched-on mobile phones are forbidden in there, I will be able to dissuade them from that by saying it almost certainly contains enough explosive to kill them all.

'I'm afraid, Holt, you will again be putting yourself at risk for the cause. If it blows up, it will be you who will be nearby. However, as the Owl has said that you personally should remain in charge of it, I don't think you are at any risk, as the Owl would gain nothing by killing someone, if I may say so, as low in the food chain as you, and would have a lot to lose thereby.'

188

Although calls from the Owl via the OwlPhone would be patched through to Sir Charles at the Cobra room, there would be a twenty-second delay to allow Holt to filter them if either he thought it necessary or the Owl insisted on confidentiality. That would give Sir Charles in particular considerable power.

Betting against the pound was continuing in the money markets and Sir Charles was certain that some form of attack on London instigated by the Owl was imminent. They both felt that the care the Owl had taken to see no one was killed, let alone injured, in the toppling of Nelson meant that that he would endeavour to avoid loss of life, and nothing as deadly as 9/11 was in the offing. However, the government was working itself up into a lather on the assumption that they were dealing with someone sinister or an al-Qaeda-related group.

'Of course, as I have said before,' said Sir Charles, 'all this political stuff may just be a smoke screen to hide the fact that the Owl and his associates are in it for the money they can make speculating against the pound.'

'Quite possible. His demands do seem rather outlandish,' commented Holt.

'Anyway, I'm officially putting it on record by notifying all the concerned departments, including Downing Street, that we at Giraffe think significant – a weasel word – loss of life is most unlikely.'

Giraffe's HQ at Farringdon would have feeds from the various news services and ability to see the same images from video cameras as those available to the government. They would also have the CIA feeds.

Here, Sir Charles let Holt into a little secret. Thanks to personal relationships built up when – like Kim Philby – he had been MI6's liaison man in Washington, he could access ultra-secret satellite images and intercepts from assets that the US did not want to share with the British security services at large. They even sent someone over to install equipment at Farringdon to ensure Britain's GCHQ could not spy on or even detect those communications.

'How many people know about that?'

'Just a couple at Giraffe. My let-out is that if I did not keep it from the government, the CIA would not let us have it anyway.'

'You seem to think of everything!'

'Not only that, I even have access to the memos and briefing material that the CIA prepare for US presidents before they receive foreign dignitaries. You'd be surprised at the titillating information they contain, such as that a French president was called "three-minute or five-minute X" because that was the time it took for consummation of his sexual conquests with party activists and secretaries in his younger days, and that allegedly included the shower afterwards! The CIA drafter's idea was that the US president should mention it to the French president to break the ice, as in France having sexual conquests is something of which to be proud and increases support amongst female voters.'

'Makes sense.'

'I told our prime minister at the time that I had a copy of a memo concerning him in particular, recommending the president build up his vain ego with the usual ceremonies on the White House lawn and trips on Air Force One, and then knock it back down in the course of prayers in the Oval Office.'

'Really?'

'Yes, and just like J. Edgar Hoover would do with senators and the like, I told the PM not worry, as my copy of the memo, which, although in the computer system and undeletable, was in safe hands with me. I would take good care to protect it.'

'That must have worried him.'

'Not only that, I said the memo detailed the procedure whereby the president could use prayer to show who was top dog by positioning himself so when they kneeled he would be gazing upwards towards the Almighty, and the British PM would have his view of God obscured by the presidential posterior. There were, I said, further unmentionable details regarding how the president could humiliate the PM even more that would make him a laughing stock should the press get hold of them.

'Though it started off as a joke, it gave me a free hand in setting up Giraffe with myself in charge! If you ever mention that to anyone, your life will not be worth living – not that anyone would believe you. Whistle blowers rarely come out of these things well. Usually, they are shunned by colleagues and suffer a fate worse than witnesses on witness-protection programmes.'

With these confidences having, as intended, tightened the bonds between the two of them, Holt thought it a propitious moment to ask something that had been troubling him almost from the very moment he joined Giraffe.

'Why don't you get rid of Blackwell? He's a pervert exploiting his position.'

'I know, but he knows everyone's secrets – not only here but in a number of other sensitive places where he previously worked. We could only risk terminating him if he committed an indictable offence and had been sentenced to a long prison term.'

'Maybe I should set a trap for him.'

'Be careful. He's no fool.'

Holt spent the weekend pottering around, aimlessly doing this and that. On the Sunday afternoon he went to Dulwich Park – seeing normal people out with their kids full of the enthusiasm of youth made him feel life was worth living. One reason he felt so low was that he missed Consuela, not only for the sex and the high life but also for the companionship she provided. He remembered how one of the rich women he had met in the course of his relationship with Consuela had said once you get used to the high life, it is impossible to renounce it, even when the money runs out. He could well believe it.

On returning to his flat, he had a simple meal literally washed down with what was really a very decent £8 bottle of rioja but that could never measure up to the £100-plus bottles he had shared with Consuela, her presence making them even more enjoyable. Nevertheless, the always-honest rioja sufficed to relax him enough to drop off to sleep quite easily.

On his way to Sackville Street on the Monday, Holt dropped into his office at Farringdon to find it now had a camp bed so that he could sleep there during crises. He also found that by virtue of his new security clearance, he had access to the sophisticated technical facilities, in addition to certain encrypted material in the computers.

These included video and data links not only to police operations rooms (and their CCTV cameras) but also a special booth for sensitive links with the CIA at Langley in the States and to their satellites, which could cover London, as well as any other place on earth. The links with the CIA were set up so that GCHQ could not decrypt them. If someone, even from security, should gain entry, the link with the US would automatically be broken, and the screens filled with innocuous material.

Chapter 21
London Alert

Holt arrived at Sackville Street with plenty of time to talk to Sir Charles before the OwlPhone would ring. They discussed the various possibilities as they saw them.

At precisely 2 p.m., there was a ping indicating an incoming text message. Although it could be read on the screen, they copied it to a computer as instructed and printed it out. It was very much along the lines of the suggestions made to Holt at the end of his interrogation.

LONDON ALERT

A series of disrupting events in London and England are imminent. They are to remind you to take the Owl's recommendations to improve the country seriously.

These alerts, together with the measures we wish to see imposed, will be sent to news organizations, the media, and tweeted to prevent the government withholding them from the public. All will be copied to this OwlPhone.

Let the games begin.

The Owl

Within minutes, the media and the internet were being bombarded with warnings citing the Owl's agenda for putting the country to rights. He told them to expect happenings to ensure the government paid attention and started taking action.

Strangely, though GCHQ had managed to link the Owl with people engaged in financial speculation against the pound before Holt's undercover mission, they were no longer coming up with anything. This suggested the Owl had learnt about GCHQ previously having found a link – perhaps from Holt during his interrogation.

A week and a half went by, and with nothing having happened there were suggestions that the whole thing had been a hoax. Sir Charles's enemies began bad-mouthing him in the hope that they could pounce and get Giraffe closed down and Sir Charles taken down a peg.

'Without Giraffe, he will be a eunuch,' said a senior general who in an argument six months earlier with a third party present had been accused by Sir Charles of being an incompetent buffoon.

Chapter 22
COBRA

The first sign that something was brewing came from the air. The first officer of an airliner arriving much earlier than scheduled from the Far East was requesting a priority landing, as some of the passengers and the captain were acting crazily. Ten minutes later, another aircraft called air-traffic control with a similar story, except that this time it was the Muslim copilot who was off his rocker, and an elderly rabbi had put his hand up a flight attendant's skirt.

Air-traffic control called the first aircraft to ask whether their captain was a Muslim, and was told he was Jewish. This added to the confusion. Was the common factor that none of the zanies had eaten the pork option for their meal?

Within minutes, dozens of aircraft were calling in with similar stories. All demanding priority, with several even having declared a fuel emergency, which meant they had to be given absolute priority, thus further delaying other arrivals.

Nearby countries were refusing to allow London-bound aircraft low on fuel to divert to their airports after receiving warnings that there were individuals on those flights infected with viruses developed for biological warfare.

With Holt already at his post in the special ops room at Farringdon, Sir Charles set off by special car to the Cobra room, somewhere below Whitehall. There were all sorts of ways to access this secret location, via tunnels from the prime minister's residence at Downing Street, the Foreign Office, and the Ministry of Defence, not to mention the Cabinet Office, at 70 Whitehall, which was the way Sir Charles chose. Using his swipe card, he went through the blast-proof doors to find the prime minister and the heads of MI6, MI5, the Metropolitan Police, and the military, and other officials such as the mayor of London, already there.

Some of those present were standing, others were already seated at the 30 ft polished burr-walnut table. Most of the far wall was taken up by a giant eight-panel video screen, on the right of which was a lectern for the chairman – in this case the PM. The side walls had four flat-panel screens high above the participants' heads for teleconferencing and TV feeds from the BBC, CNN, and so on. Each position at the table had its own microphone.

The term 'Cobra', suggesting something menacing that the government was taking very seriously, was not the brainchild of some consultancy but had been arrived at by pure chance in that it was simply an abbreviation for 'Cabinet Office Briefing Room A' – one of a number of rooms in the Cabinet Office used for meetings of the CCC (Civil Contingencies Committee).

The British government had again moved tanks, armoured vehicles, and troops to London's Heathrow Airport and other airports to try and show that they were in control, but there was not much that they could do, other than raise the fear level amongst the population.

Heathrow, with only two runways and operating close to its limit in terms of the number of flights it could handle, was in deep trouble, as prioritizing aircraft having declared a fuel emergency meant others were being delayed and circling overhead, burning up fuel, and themselves about to declare fuel emergencies. Soon the airport got to the point where it could no longer cope. The usual alternative airports were in a similar predicament.

Airliners were having to land at airfields with runways so short that the seats and everything else removable would have to be taken out to enable them to take off again, and then only with difficulty. Then, when it seemed the situation in the air could get no worse, mortars spewed spikes coated with adhesive onto the two runways at Heathrow and the single runway at Gatwick, making them unusable.

The pound sterling's value was continuing to drop.

Hoax calls were also coming in from people trying to exploit the situation.

Exasperated, the police at first dismissed a call from a woman saying she had seen a duck with machine-guns coming out of the River Thames. The official taking the call called out to a colleague, saying some crazy cow had reported seeing ducks with guns, only to be told the woman probably had her head screwed on the right way as she must have meant the amphibious motorized 'ducks' used to take families with kids around London, the excitement being that they could ride both on land and on the river.

Since the phone system had recorded the woman's number, the official was able to call back, apologise, and ask for further details.

In fact, the ducks-with-guns story was not daft at all, for a little earlier a woman with a revealing lace blouse had distracted the drivers of a couple of these motorized ducks parked at their usual pick-up point near the London Eye. While the drivers were occupied ogling her twin assets, a kindly man had been giving the children onboard their vehicles some *toy* Glock semiautomatic pistols, a couple of *toy* surface-to-air-missile launchers, and other *toy* weaponry. He also gave them masks, which made their faces look adult-like.

'You kids,' the kindly man had said, 'are lucky to have been chosen to take part in a game to be televised. When attacked by pretend policemen either on the ground or in helicopters, return the fire with your toy weaponry. Even though it's only a game, you will be famous.'

What the children did not know was that though they had not been given the real thing, what they had been given were not innocent toys either.

Holt later learnt from the Owl that he had come up with the idea after hearing from a woman at a reception of an incident in which she had been on one of those ducks with her two children when it was waylaid by fearsome-looking police toting machine-guns telling then them to lie flat on the ground. Only later did she learn that the police had been looking for armed robbers allegedly making their getaway on one of the ducks, following a hold-up in central London.

SWAT teams began stopping the motorized ducks taking tourists – mostly children – around central London. The two with the masked kids brandishing the 'weapons' they had been given were following each other up Regent Street when they were stopped. As instructed, and believing they were taking part in a TV programme, the children immediately 'opened fire', forcing the police to withdraw and call in helicopters with marksmen able to get a better angle of fire.

In the Cobra operations room, some officials, including Sir Charles, were urging caution, pointing out the danger of firing on armed terrorists in central London.

'Have we any better idea now as to who the Owl might be?' asked an admiral, feeling the senior service was being left out of things and wanting to make some contribution.

'Only that he, or she, could even be one of us,' replied Sir Charles. Those present began looking at each other suspiciously.

Chapter 23
Dangerous Ducks

As the helicopters moved in close to the two ducks, they came under 'heavy fire', with noisy rounds exploding near them with puffs of smoke, just like flak in World War II. As the pilots hesitated and hovered some distance away, rockets whizzed up from the ducks. Striking the helicopters on their windscreens, they spewed out a paint-like substance, producing a mist covering not only the windscreens but also the sights of the marksmen's weapons. One marksman did get a shot in but could not see whom he had hit.

Ironically, at that very moment the Metropolitan Police commissioner, adorned with insignia to denote his great importance, was reassuring the public on television.

'We have the situation fully under control,' he was saying. 'One of our marksmen on a helicopter has taken out one of the terrorists, and our SWAT teams are courageously exchanging fire. Our dedicated men and, I must add, women will overcome them in the end. That's all I can say for the moment. There's no need to panic. Thank you.'

Ten minutes later, TV footage revealed that the 'terrorist' they had 'taken out' – a fourteen-year-old girl – was being carried from the duck by some young boys, themselves no older than twelve. Believing the terrorists were, as President Bush used to say, 'hunkered down' amongst the children, the SWAT teams were caught in a tricky situation and ordered to pull back even further.

The country was running out of airfields, let alone airports where airliners low on fuel could land. Holt was telling Sir Charles over the video link that the Owl seemed to be attempting to provoke the government into overreacting.

'Not everyone here agrees, Captain,' replied a frustrated Sir Charles. 'Your job is to try and work out what the big one, if anything, is going to be.'

'I'll do my best,' Holt assured him.

'Remember we have put a lot of faith in you. Keep in mind what I told you about how giraffes should look down from a great height. I'm counting on you! That's all for now.'

Though it had not been Sir Charles's intention, the idea of looking down from a great height had given Holt an idea – he could try using the CIA's satellites to do just that!

He thought back over the things the Owl and his interrogators had focused on in the interrogation and the places he had visited during his time with Consuela. The only common thread, the only common line of questioning, had been the River Thames and the precautions the government might have taken to prevent Mumbai-style incidents with terrorists arriving by waterborne transport. He seemed to remember being constantly asked about the Thames when under the truth drug.

Was the Owl planning some Mumbai style of attack, with team members arriving by river? The authorities were sure they already had that angle covered, with police checking the occupants and crew of every boat and now even every motorized duck on the river.

He checked the tide for the Thames at London and found that it was just before high tide and that it was to be one of the highest predicted tides of the year. Perhaps the time and height of the tide were significant.

Holt pressed the key to open the link to the CIA liaison officer at Langley. He knew that although it was early in the morning over there, Sir Charles's 'pal' was already in his office because of the situation developing in London.

'Do you have a spy satellite over London?'

'Please do not refer to it thus,' replied the operative at Langley testily. 'Yes, we did move an asset into place, more to follow the action rather than anything else. A kind of voyeurism; just like people watched the Twin Towers in real time on CNN. By the way, we can see people sunbathing half-naked in their gardens – it's a nice day on your side of the pond. Our satellite is so good we can see the women's navels and sometimes more than that.'

200

'No need to go into detail right now, perhaps later. Can you wait a moment?' replied Holt.

He quickly noted the coordinates of the River Thames from the Thames Barrier in the estuary up to the bridge upriver at Windsor, where the Queen has a castle. He then spoke again to the CIA man in the US.

'Can you obtain a series of images of the River Thames, starting from an overall view between coordinates x and y, then then give me a series of very detailed images section by section between them, and repeat the process every ten minutes?'

The man at Langley agreed and said he would have them put up on the system so that Holt could download.

Holt and the two other members of Giraffe authorized to see the special CIA material studied the images as they came through. The amount of detail was unbelievable. No wonder they did not want other countries to know how much could be seen.

Small boats and especially speedboats were being checked by the river police, helped by the military, so the chance of a Mumbai-type attack seemed remote. The three of them at Farringdon could not see anything out of the ordinary. They must have missed something, and they examined the various boats on the river ever more closely.

'Let's reassess the overall picture again,' suggested Holt.

They looked at the large print-outs showing whole stretches of the river.

'Hey, there's a pattern!' exclaimed one of Holt's colleagues.

Holt saw that downstream of a number of bridges were tugs towing barges, all equidistant from the bridge in question. On examining detailed images, they noted that each train of barges had one with a peculiar hydraulic contraption on it.

'That's it,' shouted the colleague standing beside Holt. 'It would be statistically impossible for several bridges to have barges equidistant from them.'

Holt looked again at the CIA close-ups and zoomed in again on the barges with those strange contraptions. He then called Sir Charles on the video link.

'I think we're onto something, Sir Charles.'

'What have you got for us, Captain Holt?'

'Barges towed by tugs are going to do something to some key bridges over the Thames. To damage them mechanically in some way at this time, when the tide is exceptionally high. It can't be to blow them up, as all those barges have been searched repeatedly and nothing found. They have some form of innocuous-looking contraption – hydraulic, I expect – that they intend to raise under the bridge spans to unseat them from their underpinnings.'

Holt then listed seven bridges, saying they might not all be involved, as some normal barges might be there by chance. Orders were immediately issued from the Cobra room for the barges to be intercepted and prevented from reaching the bridges with care taken, as some might be quite innocent. There was more time than appeared to thwart attacks, as the barges had not only to reach the bridges but also needed time to raise the devices to a point where they would exert significant upwards pressure, bearing in mind that they would be floating and not on solid ground.

As police and security people were already engaged in searching boats on the river, the seven lines of barges were quickly intercepted. In five cases, a barge had a contraption that when raised under a bridge would heave up a section the roadway, making the whole bridge unusable until the span was replaced.

Had the centre spans of those bridges been unseated, vehicles and even trains in the London area would have been unable to cross the river at those places, causing incredible traffic congestion. North London would have been half-isolated from South London and the short-term financial consequences considerable.

Chapter 24
Tower Bridge

Like the end of a Hollywood film where calamity is averted at the very last minute, officials were patting each other on the back and congratulating themselves that the damage had been limited, all the while making out they themselves had played key roles in thwarting the Owl's plan when that had been largely thanks to Sir Charles and Holt.

There had been no loss of life, as the fourteen-year-old girl was out of intensive care and making a rapid recovery. The police were thanking their lucky stars that she and the other children had not been riddled with bullets like the innocent Brazilian at the time of the 7/7 London bombings. In his case, it had been a matter of mistaken identity, due to an officer watching his building taking a pee when the man left for work.

The long-term cost did not seem to be too great either. The airlines would have to go to considerable expense removing seats and galley equipment to allow those airliners forced to land at small airfields to take off, but it seemed only five airliners – a Boeing 747, three Boeing 777s, and an Airbus A340 – would actually have to be taken to pieces and carted away by lorry. A superjumbo A380 had landed at a small airfield with just enough runway to take off when lightened, with local people there very excited at the prospect of watching it take off.

Looking like the cat that got the cream, the prime minister was giving interviews to journalists avid for hard news, of which there was little. Many officials had already set off for home to celebrate with wives or partners.

Sir Charles had invited Holt back to Sackville Street to take stock over drinks.

'Reviewing the situation before anyone else is the key to keeping ahead of the pack and being able to steer it in the direction we want.'

Having made that pronouncement, Sir Charles was pouring Holt his third drink when the OwlPhone sounded, with the computer-generated voice on the line:

We must congratulate Captain Holt for having worked out our intentions.

We recognize that the changes sought will take time to realize, so we will give you time, even several years' time, before repeating the exercise. Key people in the country will perhaps need to be ready to take over, should you fail to implement the changes. In addition, we recognize that it will take two or more generations for the policies to result in material changes in the make-up of society.

However, our imbecile prime minister's declaration that the government has achieved a great victory over us suggests he might renege on his assurances and fail to endeavour to introduce the measures right-thinking people believe are needed to better the country. I have therefore arranged a final nudge. Call it a booster jab.

The target has been selected to highlight the sad fact that while Air Chief Marshal Dowding and Air Vice Marshal Park saved Britain during the Battle of Britain in World War II, Bomber Harris and Leigh Mallory and their cohorts at the Air Ministry subsequently not only killed many civilians in France as well as Germany but sacrificed thousands of our pilots and aircrew for little gain other than their egos.

Finally, you must remember that the equipment we have at our disposal thanks to our financial clout and supporters in the armed services is second to none. This includes antimissile devices that will not only foil any attempts to use them against us but also render the said missiles uncontrollable, at least by you. Firing missiles at us could cause great collateral damage and loss of life, especially in a city such as London.

The OwlPhone switched to stand-by without any intervention on Holt's part.

Sir Charles called the prime minister on the scrambler but could not persuade him to take the warning seriously. The PM reiterated the lie that the British government had never dealt with terrorists and said he was sure the Owl was bluffing. He would call his bluff – 'teach the bugger a lesson'.

'These are no ordinary terrorists, Prime Minister,' remarked Sir Charles before replacing the receiver in despair.

To cover his backside, and fearing what might happen if the PM had his way, Sir Charles sent an official memo to all concerned, and that included the service chiefs, the Cobra intelligence committee, and the commissioner of the Metropolitan Police, warning of the dangers of attacking any perpetrators or preventing their escape without due thought as to the possible consequences.

He even mentioned the possibility that while the Owl had up until then used simple techniques, he might not be bluffing regarding the technology at his disposal, and notably antimissile technology, which could result in any missiles fired at his people running wild. As the Owl had said, there was no knowing the magnitude of the disaster that could befall London.

The television Sir Charles had left on in the background to keep up with the latest news, consisting mainly of a recap of events earlier in the day, had switched to a BBC reporter waiting with a cameraman on the river embankment outside London's City Hall to interview the mayor.

'I am not sure,' the newscaster was saying, 'what is happening here. HMS *Belfast*, the decommissioned World War II cruiser moored to my left above Tower Bridge as a tourist attraction, is on the move. I cannot see how it can serve any useful function in the fight against the terrorists, for although its guns are trained so that any shells fired would theoretically hit a motorway service station some twelve miles merely to show schoolchildren the elevation required to hit such a target during a battle at sea. As far as I know, there are no munitions of any kind onboard, apart perhaps for a few fireworks.'

What the TV commentator did not know was that half an hour earlier a group of the Owl's men who had been eating at the riverside terrace of the Côte restaurant one hundred yards upstream from Belfast, had synchronized their watches before getting up in ones and twos, and walked casually towards the cruiser's ticket office. Once onboard, they had meandered around, looking like typical tourists, until ending up at their designated positions.

One of those positions was the cabin controlling the ship's public address system, where a couple of them were hovering around, pretending to be tourists interested in some detail, asking each other questions. At precisely 17.58, the two then moved into the empty cabin, with one guarding the door and the other seating himself in front of the microphone. At 18.00, the man at the microphone pressed the fire alarm, which started sounding throughout the ship and made the following announcement: 'Everyone onboard, including all Royal Navy personnel, must vacate the ship immediately. This is not a drill and applies to everyone. This is not a drill. I repeat this is not a drill.'

There was a pause to let the order sink in, before it was repeated, followed by the usual words of reassurance: 'Please proceed calmly. There is no need to panic.'

One veteran officer did try to make his way to the cabin with the PA system microphone but found the watertight doors leading to it were impossible to open. Apart from a party of schoolchildren, there were hardly any visitors onboard and the ship was 'clear' in as little as five minutes.

The visitors and six crew members gathered on the bank, wondering what was happening. The schoolchildren were larking around, much to the annoyance of their teachers.

Meanwhile, Sir Charles and Holt back at Sackville Street were also wondering what it signified when another message came in on the OwlPhone:

REPEATED WARNING!

As you can perhaps see on the television, we are now going into action again. If you try to attack us, we will attack the launching platforms. We will also render uncontrollable any missiles fired, with the result there is no knowing where they might end up.

Any loss of life will be your responsibility, or rather that of our demented PM.

Sir Charles immediately communicated this to the prime minister, who got wound up by the Owl's final remark about him being demented and shouted, 'They are bluffing. They have all along been trying to make us look fools.'

'Prime Minister,' Sir Charles insisted, 'don't you think he is trying to provoke you into doing something unwise? You should take them at their word. I must put it on the official record that I have advised you that any action you might take, and in particular one involving the firing of missiles, could result in a tragedy. The fact that I am advising you thus has been emailed to your office and the relevant departments, including the service chiefs, and I shall be following that up with a second warning in the light of the repeated warning from the Owl.'

Officials, some on their commuter trains halfway home, were called back to the Cobra operations room and to their offices. From Sackville Street, Sir Charles did not have far to go to the Cobra room, where he found key people, including the prime minister, already gathered and discussing what the threat might be.

Holt, with no time to return to Farringdon, stayed behind at Sackville Street with the OwlPhone.

Sir Charles again repeated to those assembled in the Cobra room the warning from the Owl.

'You do realize,' he said, 'the Owl may, as I have said before, be with us here in this room. We assume the Owl is a man, but it is not necessarily so. One thing I do know is that it cannot be the PM, as the only moment we are sure the Owl was addressing Captain

Holt in real time, the PM was never alone, except for when he was busy in the toilet or bath.'

This remark about the PM being in the toilet only increased the PM's anger, as all those present looked at him, imagining him doing his business.

Meanwhile, below decks on HMS *Belfast* other members of the Owl team were releasing the mooring chains, starting with those at the bow. An Owl diver who had been hiding underwater surfaced and clambered aboard a speedboat moored nearby that had been ignored by the police in their checks precisely because no one was onboard. The diver started the engine and eased the throttle forward, whereupon a hitherto unseen cable from the bow of *Belfast* to the launch rose out of the water as it took the strain.

As the cable tautened, the prow of the massive ship, initially pointing ten degrees leftwards towards the bank, was pulled to the right. At first, resistance was considerable, due to the strong current pushing the bow towards the bank, but once the bow reached the tipping point the effect was reversed, and the current pushed it out faster and faster towards the middle of the river. A couple of the Owl's men at the stern of the *Belfast* began releasing the cables attaching her to the mooring there.

The diver gunned his extremely powerful engine to haul the cruiser into midstream and hold it against the tide, and once it had straightened up in alignment with the centre of Tower Bridge, he released the cable. The fast tide was carrying *Belfast* stern-first towards the two centre bascules, which open and shut to allow ships with high superstructures or tall masts to pass through.

Meanwhile, a recording was being played over and over again on the public address system on HMS *Belfast*: 'Danger! Danger! Anyone remaining onboard should proceed to the bow and be two decks down, as the stern is about to collide with Tower Bridge, and much of the superstructure will be ripped off. This is not a drill. I repeat...'

This warning was not in vain, for a boy and girl some fourteen or fifteen years old had been smooching in one of the cabins, oblivious to the fact that the rest of their school party had left the ship. Looking out of a porthole, they could see it was no joke and quickly made their way to the bow and went one deck further down.

The diver on the powerful high-speed launch moved in to pick up the Owl's men, who had escaped from the *Belfast* in a rubber dinghy, and after they had clambered aboard, gunned the engine so that it shot off downstream at high speed. As all eyes were on HMS *Belfast*, not much attention was being paid to it, especially since the men onboard had peeled off covers on the sides to reveal POLICE written in large letters.

Nevertheless, the video feed from the BBC reporter at City Hall was being watched attentively by the PM and officials in the Cobra room. The PM had seen the launch making its escape and ordered that the two RAF Tornado fighter-bombers on standby over the Thames Estuary be sent to the scene.

'Prime Minister, I must strongly object. I think attacking the launch from the air with a missile would be a great mistake and would have possibly disastrous consequences,' interjected Sir Charles.

'You are not PM. I am, and I have had enough.'

The PM then gave orders that the Tornadoes were to engage the launch regardless.

Having guessed the perpetrators' intention to make *Belfast* collide with his bridge, the bridge controller tried to raise the bascules in the hope the giant ship would pass through, leaving the bridge unscathed. However, with insufficient time, he made matters worse, as the bridge would be even more vulnerable with the bascules slightly raised. Furthermore, in doing so he was blocking the path of the vehicles crossing it.

Drivers and a cyclist were surprised to see the road at the centre of the bridge rising up in front of them. A cyclist almost fell off into the water through the widening gap between the bascules, while the vehicles first stopped, then started slipping backwards, with the drivers behind not knowing what was happening and still coming on.

Cars were piling up on each other, and the occupants, seeing people fleeing, tried to exit their concertinaed vehicles and do likewise.

The massive cruiser was coming on relentlessly. The stern, slightly off centre, first ploughed into the left bascule, bending it back, and a fraction of a second later the ship's superstructure was crumpling as both bascules ripped into it.

A couple of seconds later it was all over. The ship was through, leaving the bascules at the centre of the bridge contorted into ugly shapes, as if hit by a bomb, and the gearing for raising and lowering them damaged beyond repair. A landmark bridge that had miraculously largely survived the Blitz was fatally wounded.

As one can imagine, the TV stations were having a field day. Though the Owl had failed to bring about the semi-paralysis of London by unseating the five key bridges, the more visually dramatic events, such as the blinding of the police helicopters by kids firing from motorized ducks and destruction of the centre spans of Tower Bridge by the *Belfast* – filmed live by the BBC crew waiting to interview the mayor outside City Hall – were being viewed by the whole country and millions abroad.

The Owl had waited for the *Belfast* to finish its task before again claiming responsibility and sending his 'political wish list' to every TV station, newspaper and press agency.

Chapter 25
Errant Missile

Tower Bridge was a mess of contorted metal, and HMS *Belfast* was not a pretty sight either as she drifted on downriver with much of her aft superstructure missing or contorted.

The two naughty teenagers had felt the shock of the ship's impact with the bridge and had heard the crumpling sounds. Realizing from the ensuing silence that the danger was over, they went up on deck to find considerable damage at the stern, while the bow was unscathed. They moved right to the prow and started waving at the armada of boats following them.

With so much attention being paid to the carnage taking place at the bridge and the sight of the wounded *Belfast* continuing on downstream, the escaping launch had for a moment been forgotten by those following the massive ship. Anyway, none of the boats were fast enough to catch up with it.

On learning that it had not been stopped and was fleeing downriver at high speed, the prime minister confirmed the order for the two RAF Tornado fighter-bombers to engage it. They were to take it out dramatically with a missile in a demonstration of the government's power.

Despite the warnings from Sir Charles and military officials, the prime minister refused to back down.

'Blow them to smithereens,' he ordered.

In only a couple of minutes, the Tornado pilots had Tower Bridge in sight in the far distance and, dropping down to five hundred feet, easily picked out the fast-moving launch from the great amount of wash it was generating. Only one of them would engage it, as they did not want to risk firing more than a single missile in the centre of London. If Flight Lieutenant Saxton, who was the one going to fire, was not careful, he would overshoot, and it would take at least six minutes before he or his colleague could turn round and line up for another run, by which time the launch might well have disappeared up a canal. There, with buildings and people close by, it would be a more difficult and dangerous proposition.

His controller had already confirmed his orders to fire on sight and not waste time requesting reconfirmation – the prime minister had said they would be court-martialled should they disobey the order to fire – so he simply locked on to the speeding launch and fired a single missile, which, with its sophisticated guidance system, could not miss. As he did so, there was a small puff of smoke from the launch, and he himself received a warning of an incoming missile.

He launched flares to try to confuse it. All to no avail, for just as he was initiating a climb, the missile from the launch detonated alongside his craft, crippling it. He was, however, able to point the nose downwards to ensure it would crash into the river, before ejecting himself.

Coming down in the river slightly concussed, he looked around but could not see the debris of the launch. A couple of minutes later, a couple of officers in a police launch pulled him out of the dirty Thames water.

'Congratulations, sir,' said one of them, making Saxton for a moment think he was a hero.

'You've just demolished Big Ben!'

No one was ever quite sure whether the fact that the missile hit Big Ben was down to bad luck or was the result of the Owl having such sophisticated equipment that he had been able to take actual control of the missile fired by the Tornado and direct it there. Many thought it was too much of a coincidence that it would end up hitting such a famous landmark when there were so many other places where it could have come down.

Meanwhile, the prime minister and his advisors, expecting the launch to be blown up by the missile from the Tornado, had told police launches and other pursuing craft to hang back at a safe distance. With no boat near enough or fast enough to pursue it, the high-speed launch had disappeared into a smokescreen generated by devices set up by the Owl on the windward bank of the river.

212

The pursuing vessels milled around haplessly in the smoke, hoping to find the launch but without success, and when the smoke cleared there was no sign of it. Its burnt-out hulk was found further downriver at the next low tide. The men onboard had doubtless got off at the bank, holed it, and set it on fire to erase fingerprints before releasing it.

The *Belfast* was still being carried downriver by the tide, with the authorities wondering whether they could throw a line to the two gesticulating teenagers. However, none of their boats were powerful enough to hold the giant ship against the powerful tide. Their greatest fear was that it would damage the Thames tidal barrier defending London against floods, but fortunately it went aground on one of the bends further down the river before reaching it. Shortly after, the chastened teenagers were taken off, very much shaken, with their parents shocked to see them on TV when they were meant to be in safe hands on a school trip.

Once again, Sir Charles came out of the affair honourably, having put the warning about not using missiles on official record. The value of the pound dropped even further than it had done earlier in the day, and the Owl and his associates had certainly made a financial killing, even though they had not brought London to a state of paralysis by destroying as many bridges as intended. Even so, the damage to Tower Bridge was so extensive that it would be many weeks before any vehicles would be able to cross, and as a result traffic jams on the south of the river continued for weeks.

But who was the Owl? Theories abounded.

'The Owl,' said Sir Charles, 'could be one of us, someone in the secret service. On the other hand, he could be living in luxury abroad, say in the south of France, where you possibly met him. Or amongst the high and mighty in the UK, in which case he might well be a Russian oligarch, senior politician, top civil servant, banker, hedge fund owner, or businessman.'

These were all people difficult to interrogate and investigate. The claim he made that he could have been prime minister, just like Sir Charles, was probably a red herring. Assuming it was not a red herring, the use of the term 'our country' would rule out Russian oligarchs. He also gave the impression that he went to the same private school as Sir Charles and other establishment figures, but again that would be easy to do, and it would be unlikely he would narrow down his background so much after taking so much care to ensure Holt did not know the precise time they had met supposedly, but not definitely, with him behind that mirror.

'The fact,' said Sir Charles, 'that the Owl mentioned pilots and aircrew being sacrificed in addition to French civilians suggests he might be someone whose family lost members as pilots and civilians in World War II. But there were so many of those, and again it could be a red herring.'

Sir Charles made it known that he thought it was ludicrous for the security services to concentrate their limited resources on looking for a relatively benign 'terrorist' – who, after all, wanted what many in those services and the country really sought – when there were so many evil ones posing much greater threats. Sir Charles maintained that Giraffe should be the unit responsible for seeking the Owl, with the help of GCHQ intercepts, of course.

The press was having a field day, running articles saying both the politicians and their parties should reveal all contacts with lobbyists and any donations or invitations to overseas conferences and seminars, with airfares and hotel costs included.

Chapter 26
Better for Having Waited

For Holt, there was one unexpected highlight – a visit to Buckingham Palace to receive an honour from Her Majesty the Queen. Because of the confidential nature of his work, it was all very low-key, with him only allowed to bring along someone with a high security clearance to witness it. Celia was the ideal candidate, and to his surprise he found she had a security clearance even higher than his.

Wearing his captain's uniform, more to impress her than anything else, he looked good, and with his confidence bolstered, asked Sir Charles, who was accompanying them to the palace in the official car, why he was not getting a gong too.

'You deserve one – you managed everything, made it possible.'

'I've already got my K, and it would only provoke my establishment enemies. Besides, at my level extra honours are only a balm to console you when you retire or are let go.'

The ceremony at the palace was a laid-back affair, and before he knew it, Holt was slipping back into the role at Giraffe originally intended for him. To his dismay, Celia was hardly ever in the office, as she had been parachuted into a job as PA to a high-profile VIP too often in the news. The idea was that she would nominally be keeping a daughterly eye on him while all the while sniffing out what some of the rich foreigners he was hobnobbing with were up to.

The colleagues betting on when she would lose her virginity were still convinced she had managed to retain it.

'Her face isn't relaxed enough,' they claimed. 'It does not have that satisfied glow showing she's getting it, or that look of frustration proving she needs it again.'

Holt did sometimes manage to meet Celia in St James's Park, out of the sight of colleagues but not perhaps out of sight of security, which meant they had to be watchful. Blackwell had programmed their platonic relationship so well that Holt was not in the least put out when, on one of their afternoon get-togethers in the park, she suddenly came up with a suggestion that seemed to indicate she still thought they should not be intimate.

'I am sure,' she said, 'you would agree…'

'Agree with what, Celia?' he asked as he turned away from the ducks on the lake to look into her eyes.

'That we do not want to spoil our relationship by doing something silly.'

'I quite agree,' he replied, wondering how far one would have to go for it to be something silly.

'I was thinking it would be great to do another trip abroad. Like the time we went to Japan, but just for our own sakes. We could go to some fantastic place. A honeymoon but not a honeymoon, if you get my gist.'

'I am not sure I do.'

'Like our first night at The Loughty, without the peep show. You wouldn't need the sedative this time. We managed without it on our trip to Japan, didn't we?'

'Only you know that. I take you at your word. Every time we had a bad coffee I wondered…'

'Well? How about it?'

'I think…it's a…great idea.'

While it indeed was a great idea, he had agreed without hesitating for fear that if he declined she might seek out someone else, who would inevitably exploit the situation. Losing her, particularly to a colleague, would be a tragedy of the highest order, and it would most likely be a colleague because of the security angle, which always concerned her.

The 'we do not want to spoil our relationship by doing something silly' stipulation was not of great concern, for after his pulsating trysts with Consuela he was not gagging for it. Besides, the added confidence gained through that experience would enable him to adopt a haughty attitude in that domain.

After consulting friends – or rather, acquaintances, as they had none working for the service – they opted for the Maldives.

216

Several had said if they were going all the way money-wise, even if as they claimed not otherwise, the ultimate escape was to have a chalet there perched on the sea, with a glass floor to watch the tropical fish milling about below while enjoying each other's company above with a glass of bubbly.

And so it was. Their Maldivian chalet was everything they had been told to expect and more. Each island had its resort and nothing else, so there was a sense of relative privacy and privilege. Of course, that did not apply to the ordinary citizens, and there had been troubling stories about a fifteen-year-old being raped by her stepfather and sentenced to a hundred lashes, to be applied on her reaching the age of eighteen. Eventually, the highest court had stepped in and overturned the judgment after representations from foreign governments and fears that it would damage the tourist industry.

Such iniquities were far from their minds as they enjoyed a great seafood dinner at the restaurant on the beach by the sea on their first evening. On returning to their chalet, they collected the bottle of champagne waiting in the fridge and went out to the veranda facing the sea, where a couple of glasses were already laid out.

They felt as if a charm had come over them as they sat silently, gazing reflectively at the water flecked with moonlight. There was no need to talk – after all, they had known each other and shared each other's company closely, if not intimately, for a long time. Resisting the temptation of a second bottle, they decided bed was the better option.

As on that unforgettable first night at The Loughty, Celia insisted Holt be the first to go to retire. Again, as at The Loughty, she emerged from the bathroom with a bath towel wrapped around her, but instead of allowing it to slip off right next to him and waltz in her birthday suit to her case for her knickers, she kept it firmly in place and made straight for the foot of her bed for her nightie. Only when the nightie fully encompassed her did she unclasp the top of the towel, extract it from underneath, and jettison it on the back of a rattan chair.

This time there was no gap between the twin beds, and consequently she had to get into hers on the far side and wiggle her way across.

'Gosh, what a place!' she exclaimed on arriving in the middle.

The schoolgirl language again took Holt back to The Loughty, adding to his guilt at thinking she must have nothing on underneath. A girl like her would hardly keep on the underwear she had worn during the day.

'Why...don't you come over here? It'll be easier to...um...talk.'

'Are you sure?'

'Sure of what?'

'Sure that you'll...be all right.'

What a stupid remark. Again he had forgotten the golden rule that one should never put too much into words.

'There's nothing,' replied Celia, 'to be afraid of. Or *is* there?'

'Of course not. Hold on. I'm coming over.'

Unlike at The Loughty, it was not only his resolve to behave himself that was stiffening.

Moving like a crab with an unwieldy pincer, he wriggled over to her side, glad not to have to untuck the sheets, which the maids of course had not tucked in between the beds.

On arriving by her side, he did not know what to say, let alone what to do, so accustomed had he become to behaving as her brother. Contemplating the fan gyrating languidly above them, she seemed oblivious to him. Or was she too shy to look at him directly?

As he was resigning himself to the idea that after the meal, wine, and champagne they would drop off to sleep like that with no word spoken, she rolled over and looked at him intensely.

'It's wonderful,' she whispered.

'Wonderful?'

'To be so close like this. Isn't it?'

'Yes, but...'

Raising her head, she gazed into his eyes, at the same time bringing her lips towards his in the obvious expectation of a kiss – an expectation he guiltily satisfied. Blushing and batting her

218

eyelids, she was behaving as if she had never been in such a predicament before.

Feeling like a college lecturer embarking on an illicit relationship with a student, he brushed his right hand up and down her back, noting with pleasure the protuberances along her spine. Emboldened by her quivering response, he slid his other hand towards her left breast, encountering what proved to be token resistance, for when she finally ceded he found her nipples had already hardened under the cool linen of her nightie.

As his fingertips wandered at will over other sensitive areas, he could hardly believe his reversal of fortune, except for one place remaining off limits, as her knees were squeezed so tightly together that further exploration was impossible. Using a technique Consuela had taught him, he placed the leading edge of his open hand between her clenched knees and began sawing away. The sensation made her grit her teeth and squeeze them even more tightly together to resist his attempted intrusion, but after he had varied the pressure and the rhythm, even stopped once or twice, she suddenly giggled violently as her thighs involuntarily sprang wide open. As they spread, her nightdress rode up, allowing him to snuggle down between them.

The two of them remained motionless for what seemed an eternity but what was in reality only a minute or so. Gazing at him invitingly, she locked her arms around him and attempted to pull him even closer.

All that followed was so spontaneous and natural they might well have been lovers accustomed to sleeping in each other's arms night after night. Even so, at the key moment Holt held back, only for her to shout out, 'Don't stop. Yes, no, no. Oh my…'

* * * * *

The next morning, after a repeat but more paced performance, they lay there in each other's arms, replete, not saying a word.

With Celia lost in her own thoughts, Holt got up, switched on the kettle to boil some water for the coffee he so desperately needed, and went for a shower. Letting the water trickle over his face, he savoured the moment. At last she was Miss Innocent no more, and the limbo he had been in for months was over.

Later they would further liberate their bodies by going diving together amongst the tropical fish. Could life ever be better than this? He had said the same thing to himself when on the Côte d'Azur with Consuela.

Either he had the best of both worlds or neither world was quite what he had imagined it to be. Was Consuela the innocent one, and Celia not quite the innocent she made herself out to be?

Having returned the pillows on what had nominally been her bed back to their proper place while she was away in the shower, he had raised the top sheet and was just tucking it in at the foot of the bed when he noticed a little red stain almost in the middle of the bottom sheet, right where they had been lying. He stood there contemplating it, wondering about the implications.

'Leave that to me,' ordered Celia, who had come up beside him.

Letting go of the top sheet, he went off to finish making the coffee, missing his chance to mention the presence of the red spot without making a big deal of it.

On coming out to the veranda to join him for coffee, Celia gave no indication she had noticed anything. Not only did she look fulfilled, she looked completely at ease.

Was there a hint of amusement in her eyes, or was it his imagination?

Later at breakfast, again outside by the sea, neither of them said anything of any consequence, aware that a postmortem might spoil things. Holt did mention a breakfast he had had at a resort hotel in Thailand where a baby elephant went around the tables putting its snout into women's laps in the hope of being able to share their breakfasts.

'Women sitting alone would give generously, only to be shocked to find the cute cuddly one had rough skin like sandpaper and was not the pleasure to caress that they had expected.'

'You know,' said Celia as if she were very knowledgeable in the matter, 'there must be something special about breakfasts on overseas holidays shared with someone one loves.'

'How do you know that?' asked Holt.

'You remember how we used to laugh at that couple who repeatedly told us how much they enjoyed that wonderful breakfast in Paris they had together with coffee and croissants?'

'Yes, only too well,' replied Holt, relieved she was not speaking from personal experience.

'Funny,' added Holt, 'how they hardly ever mention the expensive dinner they had the evening before.'

'We will have,' replied Celia, 'to be careful not to be like them and bore people with our stories. Anyway, we'll have to keep all this secret from our colleagues at Farringdon.'

'Especially them,' retorted Holt, wondering whether the two colleagues placing bets on when she would lose her virginity would be able to tell she was *different*.

With breakfast over, they sat in silence looking at the sea. To give himself a breather and allow Celia to go back to the chalet on her own and have free run of the facilities, Holt announced he would hop over to the resort office to see if there were any brochures about the activities, such as diving and catamaran trips. But just as he was placing his hands on the arms of his chair to heave himself up, Celia leant forward and stopped him.

'Wait! Promise not to be angry.'

'I promise,' replied Holt, thinking he knew what she was about to say.

'You remember that night at The Loughty?'

'How could I ever forget it, with you parading around in your birthday suit? You were so pure and angelic I was not in the least aroused – physically, that is.'

'Actually, my being so pure and angelic had nothing to do with you not being aroused.'

'What do you mean?'

'You couldn't have done anything anyway.'

'How come?'

'I slipped a powerful tranquiliser into your coffee on the terrace while waiting for you to return from the loo. Enough to calm a horse.'

'So that's why the coffee was so awful.'

'You must understand I was acting under orders from Blackwell. He said it would make things much easier for us both in the long run and that it was my duty. When I expressed my doubts, saying I did not join the service to be an exhibitionist and put drugs in colleagues' coffees, he said that if I refused, I would be replaced. As I both liked you and wanted to go to Japan, I accepted.'

Holt could imagine Blackwell debriefing Celia after their stay at The Loughty, laughing to himself at how he had watched helplessly as the Virgin Mary pranced naked around the room. Thank heavens The Loughty had refused to comply with Blackwell's request for the video.

'Blackwell insisted the first night was critical, and if it went according to his plan, you would get a mental block and no longer think of me sexually. And, to be fair, it worked a treat.'

'The tranquiliser – How many times did you use it?'

'Blackwell said it should only be necessary for the first night, but to be on the safe side I might like to top you up from time to time. He said that the tranquiliser had not been needed in the case of other agents, but then none of the women had been as desirable as me!'

'You were toying with me!'

'Not really. I never took advantage of the situation to wind you up or play cat and mouse with you. Though, to be honest, having a man dangling helpless before me was pleasurable.'

Holt wanted to tell her that dangling was an unfortunate choice of vocabulary and suggested she was more experienced than she appeared, but before he could do so she gripped his hand tightly and batted her eyelids, just as she had done in bed the night before.

'I have no regrets, though. For me, last night was all the better for having waited.'

How could he not believe her?

Chapter 27
No Pain, No Gain

The colleagues betting on when Celia would lose her virginity failed to do so when she returned to work after her secret trip with Holt to the Maldives. Yet it was they who some weeks later were the first to sense something different about her.

'She must be getting it – she looks so satisfied,' said one. 'More like beatified,' replied another. 'A bit strange if you ask me,' added a third

She was pregnant!

After waiting in hope for the red dragon and then doing five tests, a worried Celia met up with Holt in the St James's Park – she was working nearby, attending a meeting at the Foreign & Commonwealth Office between British officials and dignitaries from a South American country.

'We were careful. I don't know what went wrong,' she said after telling Holt the news.

'No point in a postmortem,' replied Holt.

'I know the service would prefer I got rid of it – in fact, they would never need to know.'

'But do *you* want to…?'

'Not really.'

'We could get married.'

'Yes…that's one possibility.'

'Of course, with your looks there would be no lack of men more than happy…'

'That's true.'

'No need to get married at all, come to that. I wouldn't tell anyone. Leave them guessing. The only trouble with that is that people in the service might think it was one of your VIPs…a cabinet minister or a fusty old general. That would not look too good.'

'You're right there. Tongues *would* be wagging.'

'No need to rush. Think it over. I'm always here for you…whatever you decide.'

'You shouldn't underrate yourself, Jeremy. I could do a lot worse than you. Please don't take that badly. I'm being horrible because I feel bad this has happened.'

They wanted to mull it over more but had to get back to work.

The next morning Holt left his mobile phone on his desk at Farringdon, hoping she would not call, for if she did it would surely be to decline his offer. To get it over with.

He therefore picked the phone up with a feeling of resignation when it indicated a call from her. Her voice was merely a whisper, no doubt to avoid others overhearing.

'...you are the father after all...I'll marry you,' was all he could catch, but enough.

Sir Charles, Cut-Glass and envious colleagues, including the always affable Farringdon bureau receptionist, attended the simple wedding some three weeks later. The only outsiders were Celia's parents, who were doubtless already aware in general terms of the secret nature of their daughter's work. Holt was not at all surprised to find they were middle of middle class, and decent enough people and not pretentious. Of course, the service would have probably checked them out too before taking her on.

His nominal boss, Peter, was there too, somewhat miffed that Holt had not heeded his order to avoid any hanky-panky. He had lost his 'daughter' but like all fathers had to reconcile himself to the fact that it must have been partly his innocent child's fault, which was indeed the case.

The ceremony over, Holt had to get right back to work, since the Owl had been upping the ante, angry that most of his or her demands had been kicked into the long grass. Something of which Sir Charles and Holt were only too well aware.

To avoid Holt having to carry around the bulky OwlPhone, they had come to an arrangement whereby, except in a crisis, the Owl would only use it to contact them for major communications twice a week, on Mondays and Thursdays at 2 p.m. At other times the Owl would leave messages.

Before the wedding there had been the relatively short message expressing the Owl's dissatisfaction at the lack of progress and announcing that there would be a major communication on the following Monday.

Bringing the phone with him, Holt arrived at Sackville Street slightly beforehand and went straight up to see Sir Charles, who stood up to greet him and congratulate him on the wedding.

'No ghastly relatives. You see, working for the service has some advantages.'

'Thank you, Sir Charles, for coming. It was nice you brought Sandra.'

'She wanted to come – seems to have taken to you in a motherly rather than a Moneypenny way. She feared we had lost you when you disappeared from sight while undercover and grew quite concerned.'

'Really,' replied Holt, somewhat surprised by this revelation, only to be caught off-balance by what Sir Charles was to say next.

'Sorry you and Celia only had Saturday night and Sunday for the honeymoon. Though I suppose your trip together to the Maldives had some of the trappings. It's said to be famous for honeymoons.'

Holt had not realized such close tabs were kept on staff, not difficult with them both having travelled on the same flight to the Maldives under their own names. The security people probably flagged up such trips as a matter of routine. They knew that double agents would often arrange to meet their handlers abroad, where surveillance was more difficult and extremely costly. He wondered whether Cut-Glass was privy to their report – she had given him a knowing smile with raised eyebrows on his return, even though that had been on a different day than Celia.

It was approaching 2 p.m. The OwlPhone rang on the dot, and Holt immediately pressed the Answer key, having made sure the Record light was on. As usual it was the synthesized voice that spoke.

Many of the problems in the country arise from short-termism. Well-meaning people trying to avoid, say, children suffering the consequences of their parents' stupidity, sloth or even extreme religious beliefs.

Thus impecunious mothers can blackmail society into supporting five or more children and themselves because we cannot make the children suffer.

Likewise mothers who allow their daughters to be mutilated cannot be put in prison because the daughter herself would suffer, though in that case political correctness may also be a factor.

Going to the extreme, one could say that when having AIDS was a death sentence, before the development of new drugs to treat it and even help prevent it, marking anyone HIV-positive likely to be sexually active – say by having the letter 'A' tattooed on their forehead – was an option no one dared contemplate.

Sounds awful and cruel, but it could have meant relatively few people would even have had an 'A' and many lives would have been saved. Of course, rather than the tattoo, one could have easily used a more subtle marker.

No pain, no gain.

More to follow in ten minutes.

'You know,' said Sir Charles, 'I am beginning to think the Owl must be a highly educated, intelligent person with a logical mind, like Enoch Powell or Lee Kuan Yew. Did you know that those two both got the exceedingly rare distinction of being awarded double firsts *with a star* at Cambridge?'

'No, I didn't.'

'Look what Lee Kuan Yew made of Singapore!'

'Yes, though when I was there,' replied Holt, 'I heard their government's campaign to persuade university-educated women to have more children had failed.'

'There's a limit to what you can do in a democracy – even in dictatorships – when it comes to procreation. Do you know that they found that the best way to get people to have fewer children in some underdeveloped countries was to provide electricity?'

'No.'

'Well, with electricity the people could have televisions, and consequently not while away their time fornicating.'

'That's unforeseen consequences being positive there, though not in England, where the welfare system results in people better off not working at all. But, to return to the Owl, do you think we should look for people with starred double firsts? I got a double first, but not a star.'

'I would not go that far. There are hardly any anyway. There's no reason why someone clever but without exceptional academic qualifications cannot be the Owl. He could be a hedge fund manager – or one of us.'

'The point is,' said Holt, 'that the Owl wants what many intelligent people more or less want. Can't we get the government to do more?'

'If nothing is done,' replied Sir Charles, 'the Owl may start thinking in terms of a coup, though making one work in this country, with the unions and the lower ranks in the services and the police unlikely to follow, would be virtually impossible. Also, there is no one of stature who could be made the figurehead. No one respects anyone these days – least of all politicians.'

'How do you mean?'

'Well, there was talk of a coup when Wilson was prime minister, and Mountbatten's name was put forward as a possible interim leader – not that he would have gone along with it. There is no one of his stature or calibre nowadays.'

Their discussion was cut short by the OwlPhone ringing again. As before, Holt pressed the Answer key after making sure the call would be recorded.

Though I believe in 'no pain, no gain,' I think we can start off by using the financial stick and carrot to make the changes we seek. After all, it is the financial carrot that is largely responsible for the hordes gathered at Calais.

There are some relatively painless things that can be done using financial incentives and disincentives.

The first is to tackle the obesity epidemic by taxing sugar and salt, doubling the tax when they are combined, as in breakfast cereals, soups, and tomato ketchup. The government, whether it be Conservative or Labour, must stand up to the food industry and refuse to deal with its lobbyists.

Soft drinks with large amounts of sugar would also need to be taxed.

That would be an incentive to reduce the amount in bread, which is far higher than people realize and means they become addicted and fatter.

Finally, child abuse needs to be more broadly defined to include the enslavement of children by devout parents who make them relentlessly study religious texts. This should apply to Jews and Muslims alike.

No one proselytising should enjoy any social benefit. Limits should be placed on faith schools to ensure pupils get a rounded education.

At least initially, the aim would be to bring about improvements using the financial carrot and stick, rather than coercion.

There were a number of other recommendations, some easy, and others virtually impossible to put into effect in a democracy, unless introduced forcefully. One of the most problematic was the idea raised at the seminar on the *Vessos* that there should be weighted voting, with the votes of pensioners and some of those on benefits having less weight. The Owl stressed his intention was not to victimise such sections of society but to ensure that they could not electorally sway society the wrong way.

The Owl said he would be conveying the same demands to the prime minister and the media, and that he was informing Captain Holt and Sir Charles as a courtesy and in the hope they could persuade the government to take the necessary action, even though he did not expect 100 per cent success.

With the prospect of less immediate activity on the Owl front and unable to exert any influence himself, Holt was continuing with his other work and was finally able to clock up a success, enhancing his and Giraffe's reputation.

The idea came up at one of their weekly Sackville Street meetings, when he said, 'Sir Charles, if I were a terrorist wanting to do something drawing a lot of attention, I would go for the Shard.'

'How would you go about it?'

'The obvious way would be to go up to the observation platform with a bomb. However, as everyone's bags and handbags are checked, an inside job would be virtually impossible. Anyway, bomb scenarios are not really my remit.'

'So what else would they do?'

'Use the window cleaners – or rather, take their places. Have a long banner made of extremely thin material so it would not be difficult to bring it up in the cradle without drawing attention. Then, when half the way up, attach the top of the banner to the glass and let it unfurl for thousands to see. There would be photos in all the papers.'

Sir Charles, rather than informing MI5, sent his men from Farringdon to keep watch on the off chance. One of them called in to say there was some suspicious action, with two suspicious-looking individuals having joined the window cleaners.

Sir Charles then set wheels in motion, informing MI5 and the prime minister. In the end it was quite dramatic. On the day the suspects came to work with a package, they were hauled up to clean the windows, but the ropes kept pulling up their trestle until they reached the top, where, to their surprise, they were arrested before they could achieve anything.

Holt still had to take time off from his main work to meet potential Owls in high society, often having to frequent private members' clubs, such as The Athenaeum. He began to realize just how influential the service was on being able to join these institutions with just a nod and a wink, despite their long waiting lists.

Truth be told, he did not feel really at home in such august establishments, where members tended to only interact with friends and others equally high up on the food chain. He knew that his socializing was largely for show.

Celia was allowed to stop work well before the due date, as obvious signs of pregnancy were not in keeping with the innocent girl image she so capably projected on her missions accompanying VIPs.

When the big day came, Holt waited nervously outside the delivery room. The wait seemed endless, but finally his reptilian fears were allayed by the doctor coming out to congratulate him on his 'beautiful little girl' – something he probably always said to soften the blow when it was not a boy.

Holt's life with a new baby was made easier than it would have otherwise been by the Owl having granted the British government eighteen months to show they were serious.

Chapter 28
Time to Try for Another One

When twelve of the eighteen-month respite the Owl had granted were already gone, Celia and Holt had taken a much-needed summer break with one-year-old Claire at Saint-Jean-de-Luz on the Atlantic coast in southwest France. Their thoroughly relaxing two weeks were over, and they were making the most of their last afternoon on the beach. The sun was getting low and there was a slight chill in the air.

Supported by her proud father holding her by the shoulders, Claire giggled with delight as another wave rippled over her tiny toes. Tired of bending over, Holt lifted her up and took her over to his wife, who dried her lovingly before putting her down on all fours on the canvas sheet laid out on the sand beside her.

To Holt, his still-young wife looked almost as innocent as she did when he first cast eyes on her in Peter's office at Farringdon. But had she really been as innocent as she seemed then? Had she been so innocent on that first night in the Maldives, declaring the next morning that 'it was better for having waited'?

The question was by no means academic, for later that Maldivian morning she went out to get something from the resort shop, leaving her suitcase half-open, with the MI6 honeymoon kit clearly visible. Even though he had suspected it had been intentional, he still felt guilty on examining it and finding one of the reds to be missing.

Ashamed of her virginity, had she wanted him to believe she had used it? Or was it just to introduce a touch of mystery to spice things up? Or was she simply trying to pay him, the renowned practical joker, back in kind?

Whatever the case, she would have had to have already known what her intentions were when packing her case back at the flat in London.

Her angelic chic and elevated status as a special operative fraternising with the high and mighty made exploring certain avenues off limits. Whenever he questioned her, she would smile and put a finger to her lips, and this applied to personal matters as well. 'Mum's the word' was her pet expression. One she would also trot out to cut short domestic arguments, itself no bad thing.

With no explanation proffered, she would disappear for a few days or even a week or more at a time. Then, on returning, she would put him on his back foot by saying, 'Let's look at you,' followed by 'Mum's the word' and a conspiratorial wink, before they embraced.

Happy but not overjoyed to be back was how Holt would describe these situations. Pretending to be overjoyed would of course have been a sure giveaway she was having an affair. While that was something she could have worked out for herself – it probably featured in her training. The service was careful regarding such details, since in the field they could make the difference between life and death. Irate partners can stir up trouble and bring unwanted attention.

In her absence, there was always more than adequate financial provision for an au pair girl to look after Claire. Some had almost certainly been specially selected to keep an eye on him, even to test him. He was especially wary of the nubile and flirty ones most likely briefed by Blackwell on how to entrap him. One, who had behaved very suggestively right from the moment she arrived, later came out of the bathroom clutching Claire to her naked bosom, with only skimpy knickers on below. That one had been very tempting indeed.

Agents like Holt working independently, like the genius cryptologist seconded to MI6 from GCHQ in the spy-in-the-bag case (his naked body had been found in a locked holdall placed in the bath at his London flat), had come to expect regular monitoring. As already stated, he even wondered whether Celia's selection as his partner had really been to ensure he did not go off the rails. They did not want him ending up like the cryptologist, dead in a room with the heating turned up so high in summer that his body would putrefy, thereby making the cause of death impossible to determine.

However careful Holt was in his dealings with the au pairs, Blackwell could still get to him through Celia. Despite claiming to be too busy to deal with agents' personal problems, the psychiatrist-cum-physician had always found time to debrief Celia mentally, and even on the first occasion physically. Should she ever let slip that he had once mentioned that Sir Charles could be the Owl, Blackwell would exploit it to have him committed to a mental asylum as a crazy loose cannon.

Holt was well aware that once a psychiatrist decides you pose a threat to others, you can say goodbye to your life, and trying to disprove it only makes matters worse, since your rage at the injustice of it all is seen as confirmation of the original diagnosis and of your mental instability.

A psychiatrist working in the secret world would be doubly dangerous, as he could have you committed not only as danger to society but also as a threat to national security, all the while making your medical file a state secret so no one could ever help you. To think hate preachers, with their bevy of human rights lawyers, would be better off.

Holt knew he had so far been saved firstly by the Owl's insistence that he – via Sir Charles – be the intermediary in all dealings with the government; and secondly, by virtue of being the only person who just might be able to identify the Owl, in that he might pick up on a turn of phrase or manner of speech, or engender a reaction on meeting him.

He had met bankers, hedge fund managers, top civil servants, academics, and even a bishop, all to no avail, at conferences and the already mentioned private members' clubs he had joined. It seemed the only noteworthy personages he was not going to meet were the royal family and the prime minister. The latter had been ruled out, because he had never been alone for any length of time when Holt had his face-to-face session with the Owl.

Holt had not pointed out that the Owl might not even have been behind the two-way mirror when they talked.

The sun was getting low in the sky, and the few families with children remaining on Saint-Jean-de-Luz's sweeping beach were packing up their things. It was time they too headed back to their villa at Cibourne on the other side of the harbour.

When they had first arrived at their villa, perched on a hill with a view of the Saint-Jean-de-Luz beach curling round the bay, Holt had been struck by how the high-pitched screams of the children playing in the waves on the beach wafted upwards and over to them. Always the secret agent, he had wondered whether, with the latest equipment, he could have picked out individual snippets.

Exhausted by her exertions on the sand, tiny Claire had fallen asleep even before they got back to the villa and was placed comfortably in her bed. Having covered her to protect her from the evening chill, Celia stayed around to clear up her playthings and put her clothes away, while Holt readied the drinks and nibbles downstairs. Having checked her mobile phone, and with the toys dumped in a cardboard box, she came down to join him on the veranda.

'To us...and to Claire,' said Holt and Celia as they clinked glasses.

Hardly exchanging a word, they felt at one with each other as well as with nature in the cool and quiet of the early evening. There was only the lightest of breezes. Not wanting to spoil the mood, Holt used the pretext of going back indoors to replenish the drinks to check his phones.

Although he had to check the official Giraffe phone routinely, he doubted there would be anything important, as he was due back in the office on the Monday. This proved to be the case.

Checking his other phone – a cheap device he regularly replaced to make it difficult for GCHQ to monitor his personal communications – he found to his surprise a message from the Owl. He had only started using that particular phone a couple of weeks or so before, but of course all the Owl had to do was to monitor that of his closest friend to discover the number.

His face darkened and, on reaching the end of the message, he stood stiffly, as if his feet were glued to the ground.

'To think I stupidly never realized,' he muttered to himself.

After a couple of minutes, he gathered his wits, shuffled to the counter to pour the drinks for which he had ostensibly come and, trying to put on a brave face, went back out to rejoin Celia on the veranda.

'Bad news?' she asked on noticing his change of demeanour and the way he uncharacteristically plonked the drinks noisily down on the metal garden table.

'Mum's the word,' he retorted to gain time, using her pet expression for evading questions.

'Touché,' she replied with a wry smile.

While that had stopped her pursuing the matter, the evening would be spoilt if he left it at that. He would switch terrain. But what on earth could he think of to put her in a better mood?

'Darling,' he murmured, 'let's make tonight a honeymoon night.'

'Don't be ridiculous. We had that in the Maldives...in a kind of way.'

'I know, but it would be even more complete now we have Claire. When I say honeymoon, I don't mean wild abandon but doing it in the same way – gently, innocently, as if it were the first time. We could just pretend. You pretended a bit then, didn't you?'

Celia looked at him intently as if weighing up her response.

'We *could* make it *even* more complete.'

'How could we ever do that? Crikey, you didn't bring the MI6 honeymoon kit?'

'No. I gave it back. Couldn't see any possible use for it now we have Claire.'

'Then how could we make it more complete?'

There was a pause, with neither of them saying anything. Celia turned towards Holt.

'Don't you think it's about time?'

'Time...?'

'Time to try for another one. A little Jeremy would be nice this time around. Don't you think?'

'That would mean you giving up your special missions, at least for a while.'

'Good excuse for a break. I could do with one, not that a bawling baby and changing nappies represent much of a break.'

'Is this a new idea?' asked Holt.

'Not really. Seeing all those couples holidaying on the beach with two or three little ones in tow made me realize how nice it would be to at least have one more. The parents looked so contented, though that's not to say we're not lucky to be blessed with our Claire. I know it is a bit soon, but then one does not get pregnant that easily when one wants to.'

'I never told you this, even when you were pregnant with Claire, but the mere thought of a woman giving birth scares the hell out of me. When I was younger, I used to watch a US TV drama series called *V*, in which lizards from outer space able to morph into human-like beings came to colonize the earth.

'In one episode, one of the handsomer young morphs has an affair with a nice young earthling, gets her pregnant. All seems to be going well and normally, with her going into hospital to give birth to a lovely baby girl. Then, while a couple of nurses are busying themselves cleaning the baby up, a third nurse tending the mother shouts out, "Wait! There's another one!"

'After a pause, with anticipation growing and growing, out from between the girl's thighs clambers the most hideous reptile one could imagine. That image always haunts me whenever anyone talks about a woman going to have a baby – more so when it's someone I love. While that TV drama was somewhat over the top, it made me realize something can always go very wrong.'

'It can but is unlikely, with the proper tests. You were happy enough about Claire.'

'Only when I knew she wasn't a lizard – I'm partly joking. Anyway, Claire was a fait accompli. We didn't do it on purpose, did we?'

'No, but...'

'Okay, I have to admit it would be nice for Claire to have someone to play with – I missed out on that, being an only child. In the secret world, we do not associate with many friends with young children. Okay, I agree. Let's go for it.'

236

Chapter 29
Go On, Tell Me!

Holt gave his wife a desultory pat on the shoulder and, feeling terrible, disappeared inside to refill their glasses for the toast to the hoped-for new baby...boy.

Even though the Owl's message had been clear enough, he reread it to make sure there was no mistake.

My dearest Jeremy,

On checking to see how C was getting on, I discovered she had given birth to a boy nine months after you two parted.

Her husband insisted on bringing it up as his own in the knowledge that that the father (you!) is highly intelligent.

For the sake of your darling Claire and any further offspring you and Celia may procreate, you should keep this to yourselves. One never knows what impediments could be put in their way should you be indiscreet.

I will never mention this in the context of our official dealings, or indeed in any circumstances.

You will probably have the pleasure of seeing the growing boy's photo from time to time in the media, but do not let that tempt you to make contact either with him or his mother.

The Wise One

Now he knew what Consuela had meant when she thrust that half-million-dollar bracelet into his hand, saying he had perhaps given her something worth far more. He was glad he had kept it. Looking at it would remind him of his little boy.

The Owl had obviously used terms such as the Wise One and C and avoided trigger words like 'secret' to prevent GCHQ or the

NSA (US National Security Agency) computers flagging up the message.

It was uncanny. Had the time-stamp on the message not been prior to the conversation he had just had with Celia about trying for a son, he would have suspected the Owl of bugging the villa, though surely he would have better things to do.

Officers and operatives were supposed to report any situation laying them open to blackmail, but how could he? If he did admit a woman linked to the Owl had had his baby, he would no longer be entrusted with the pivotal role in the negotiations with him. Gone would be his high status, not to mention his coveted military rank, now that of major.

When should he – when could he – tell Celia? Wouldn't it be better to wait until she had her baby? But what if it were yet another girl?

He had to consider her distress at seeing him partnered with Consuela at the US embassy reception. Admittedly, he and Consuela had made an outstanding couple on the dance floor, not to mention their being seated with the ambassador at the top table, with the ambassador telling Celia how prestigious it was for Holt to have such a glamorous partner.

Even so, as someone who herself went on missions that looked sexually compromising to outsiders, she *should* have been more understanding. There surely had to be another reason for her over-the-top antipathy towards Consuela.

To make matters worse, in the taxi on his way to Sackville Street to report to Sir Charles on his undercover mission, he had in a moment of weakness reassured her that he had not been with Consuela long enough for anything *meaningful* to have happened between them. Now to admit it had been meaningful enough to result in a baby would prove him a liar, when his honesty was the one thing she claimed she truly liked about him.

The truth was he loved them both. Consuela had made him grow up socially, sexually, and emotionally, to some extent becoming a substitute for his late mother.

Having been in her company for little more than a week, he knew much more about her than about Celia. This included her overly strict upbringing in the sticks by her Baptist foster parents and the abusive husband, from whom she had been liberated at the doing no doubt of her current multibillionaire husband.

Even after having known Celia very much longer, marriage and a child together, he still could not fathom Celia's inner being and could only guess at her background by her accent. Her role-playing, rather than any rules forbidding agents discussing their backgrounds, was what made it so difficult.

With a heavy heart, he poured the drinks, a stiff one for himself and a weaker one for the mother of his next child. A prayer rather than a toast was what was needed – a prayer *for a boy*.

'Here's to him.'

'Or her – it may be another beautiful girl,' intoned Celia as they again clinked glasses.

If he reassured her that she had been uppermost in his mind while undercover, that might soften the blow when she learnt about little Jeremy in the States.

Leaning forward, he took his wife's left hand and squeezed it hard.

'I want you...to know...Celia...that in risking my life undercover...I was thinking of you, my darling. You were always there in the back of my mind.'

'Really?'

To his surprise, her voice had taken on a hard edge. What's more, she forcefully extricated her hand from his grip and looked at him with a look of sheer distaste he had never seen before.

'Yes, yes, believe me,' he insisted, nonplussed.

'I do believe you – only too well.'

'Then why are you so upset?'

'The very thought of being there in the back of your mind while you were relishing that slut's pulsations is gross.'

' "Back of my mind" was only a figure of speech. Come on.'

'It does not alter the fact,' insisted his wife, 'that it was her falling-domino pulsations that rang your bell.'

'Whatever gave you that idea?'

'Blackwell.'

Holt remembered bragging to a colleague about having made love to a woman with sensational, rippling, falling-domino pulsations. The guy had obviously served the titbit up to the Snake. Still, he had to deny it.

'Blackwell must have made it up. I didn't even mention Consuela to him. Peter told him I was not allowed to give any details regarding the mission other than that it was undercover, with a woman whose name could not be revealed.'

'Blackwell would dream up something like that,' admitted Celia.

Thinking he had regained some ground by persuading her that Blackwell made up the rippling, falling-domino pulsations scenario, Holt sought to capitalize on it.

'Of course, when I said you were in the back of my mind, I really meant those terrible moments under interrogation when I was half expecting to be bumped off and that my body would be dumped somewhere where no one would ever find it. Thinking of you, Celia, gave me the will to survive...made all the difference.'

'Jeremy, I have always admired you for accepting to go undercover like you did – amazing really, considering you were only meant to be a backroom boy, an ideas man. And even though I suspect you were an accidental hero just like Dustin Hoffman in *Hero*, I believe you deserved your medal from the Queen.'

Unable to leave well alone, Holt ploughed on unthinkingly.

'I certainly wasn't thinking of you when...'

'When what?'

'When...'

'Go on, tell me! Tell me!'

'I mean when...'

'When what?'

'Er...'

'When? Go on, tell me! I'm waiting. It must be something big.'

'It was – I mean, is. Her baby, I mean.'

'You mean she had *your* baby...and kept it?'

'Apparently. Except that it's no longer a baby.'

'And you've been hiding it from me all this time.'

'No, no. I only found out just now...that text message was from the Owl.'

'You didn't take precautions?'

'She said there was no need.'

'So she did it on purpose, the bitch!'

'We don't know that, do we? She wouldn't be the first married woman of a certain age to fall pregnant after doing it for years with nothing happening and believing it never would.'

'How come you're so knowledgeable about married women of a certain age *happening* to fall pregnant?'

'I'm not. A couple of my friends got caught out that way. That's all.'

Holt was being disingenuous, for Consuela's sudden change of attitude on learning he had an exceptionally high IQ signified it was no accident. The lying in bed for breakfast at the Hotel du Cap and languishing there in the mornings on their return to England had been for a reason. Though he was not a Nobel Prize winner, she had evidently deemed him a worthy donor.

'A boy or a girl?'

'A boy, apparently.'

Celia grimaced at the word 'boy'.

'What do *you* plan to do?'

'Nothing. Absolutely nothing.'

'I can't believe that. You're the father, for God's sake!'

'You *can* believe it, because the Owl said it would be in everyone's interest, including I might say Claire's, to keep it secret. He even put it stronger than that. He said revealing it could be detrimental not only to Claire but also to any future child you and I might conceive. I am not sure what he meant by that – better we don't find out. Her husband is a very powerful man with a long reach.'

'We mustn't let the Owl have us dangling on the end of a piece of string – could prove dangerous professionally.'

'Now you know the truth, he has less leverage. Anyway, he promised not to allude to it in our official dealings. I think he told me not to pressure us but because he likes us. Though it does make me feel a bit awkward, as if we owe him something.'

'For Claire's sake, we will keep it to ourselves. She is more important than anything, even the service, to me. But that does not make what you did with *that woman* right.'

'In a way I *had* to do it. Sir Charles specifically chose her from the rewards menu for me. I had to follow it through.'

'Don't give me that just-doing-your-duty crap. You knew we meant everything to each other. More perhaps than if we had consummated our idyllic relationship. You betrayed me. You betrayed yourself.'

'How can you sit up there on your high horse when you exploit your feminine charms on your missions? I've seen you stringing along your VIPs with coy glances and batting eyelids.'

' "Stringing along with coy glances and batting eyelids", as you so crudely put it, is as far as it ever went, though you'd be surprised how effective batting eyelids can be. It brings out empathy. Makes people think you are vulnerable, with the result that they drop their guard and open up. But just like Mossad's females – the top professional ones that is; for sexual blackmail or entrapment they simply use prostitutes – I never go all the way. We get what we want and sometimes more by flirting, admittedly sometimes so outrageously that we have to fight them off. Once you go all the way, you've lost the plot. The information spigot runs dry...or so I am told.'

'I did not mean to imply...It's just that I cannot understand why you react so strongly to Consuela. It's irrational. You're a big girl out in the wide world, rubbing shoulders with socialites and politicians who are having affairs all the time. Surely you are above all that.'

'You would say that, wouldn't you? You don't realize that while I have sacrificed myself for queen and country, along comes Her Royal Kentucky Highness, gets a baby boy out of it, and then, as the ambassador said, carries on with her high-society lifestyle as if nothing had happened. She's free. She's her own man – or rather, woman. Unlike me, she can be herself, have real friends. Have a life. I too could have had it all.'

'You have friends.'

'Only the cat, and he only thinks of himself.'

'If working for the service was not for you, why ever did you join up in the first place?'

'You want to know?'

'Yes, of course I do.'

'I was young, naïve. I was at RADA, the famous school of dramatic art in London, in my second year, with a promising acting career ahead of me, when out of the blue I received a letter saying I had the exact profile for a job that would help my country and save lives. How could I refuse to save lives? Besides, I thought it would be an exciting adventure, but apart from our Japanese junket, that has hardly ever proved to be the case. Now I'm stuck with accompanying boring old farts to conferences and receptions, without being able to personally exploit any situations that do open up. Unlike *her*.'

'You have a top security clearance. That must mean something. Shows they value you.'

'No, not really. That's only to allow me to be privy to the secrets of top civil servants, cabinet ministers, generals, and admirals. Since I don't analyse the material I dredge up, or any other material for that matter, I'm a mere dogsbody. I know it is sound policy to separate the spooks from the analysts and officers, but in my case I am only an operative like you, not a real insider, not commanding or managing anybody. I don't see the overall picture. What's more, I'll soon be too old to play the naïve ingénue, and they'll take that clearance away. Where will I be then? I've missed out big time.'

'Maybe they will find you something more in keeping with your talents. More your age. Exploit your experience. *You* could be a trophy wife, an even better one than Consuela.'

'That's a joke. The service does not have the funds for that. Anyway, they would rather spend their money exploiting cheaper, eager-to-please ingénues like I once was. Apart from the first year in the service, I have not even evolved personally like I would have done as an actress.'

'You had Claire.'

'That's my sole blessing, but I could have done so much more with my life had I finished RADA. Interestingly, the academy website quotes one of their alumni as saying,

> *My RADA training is the bedrock of my acting life. It*
> *allows me to change from one kind of person to another.*
> *There is not a job goes by when I do not rely on it.*

Yes, RADA allows me too to seamlessly change from one person to another at the service's behest.'

'So RADA *was* useful.'

'Yes, but had I continued as an actress I could have proved myself. Had real adventures rather than pretend ones – for better or worse, really lived. Here in the service, one cannot risk anything personally; one only takes risks for them. Except for not having to get up at five in the morning, I feel like a nun – duty, duty, duty.'

'You're exaggerating. You can't imagine, I am sure, what being chaste like a nun would be like.'

'My looks would have taken me far, if not in film or the theatre, then with a younger version of Consuela's husband. Whichever way it went, I would have had a real life, been living. As it was, I just stagnated and married you, with the service's blessing of course. Not that they were at all concerned about what was best for me personally.'

'So your relationship with me, all that innocence, was an act? A sham?'

'Not exactly, though role-playing became so second nature that it would switch on automatically, even with you.'

Holt wondered just what parts, if any, of their relationship had been genuine. His whole life was crumbling. A couple of hours earlier, everything had seemed so rosy. Damn the Owl. Not only was he the lynchpin of his professional life, he was becoming the fulcrum of his private life.

Chapter 30
What If...?

Dinner had passed in virtual silence.

With Celia upstairs looking after Claire, Holt tried to gain a few Brownie points by doing the washing up, gulping down the leftover wine to ease his anguish. By the time she did finally come back down, his senses were so numbed that he failed to realize her mood had completely changed.

'Hi,' he said in a depressed tone of voice, surprised that she had taken his hand.'

'Jeremy, don't take it too badly.'

Her voice was quiet and soft, even tender. Another act?

'I can't help it. You mean – meant – so much to me.'

'Trophy Wife stirred up feelings in me of what might have been. From what you say, Consuela really did have a hard time when young. Life for her was not always the bed of roses I imagined. She used you, though.'

Remembering how much he had enjoyed being used, Holt felt another twinge of guilt and did not quite know how to respond.

'I'm sorry,' he replied lamely as she released his hand and sat down on one of the wooden kitchen chairs.

'Don't be. I could have ended up like a crumb from a Warren Beatty table, with no baby, like so many. Take Diane Keaton. She had everything, and yet...'

'Diane Keaton was more than a crumb. She was at least a crust for Warren Beatty – they had a full-blown, longish affair. She had romances with many other celebrities, not to mention Woody Allen and Al Pacino.'

'That's true, but recently I read she told *People* magazine that she regretted not having married. I remember her exact words: "...I really wish I had bought myself a man! A good man who would be a great father – I really do. I think it's a better way to go." Like I did with you, Jeremy. Marry a good, simple man.'

'I'm not *that* simple.'

'I meant it in the sense you're unpretentious and lead a simple life, not a glamorous one, like those celebrities in the limelight she was so beholden to. Like her, I had – have – the choice of many men with my looks. I admit it did not work out too bad for the two of us. You might not be rich, but at least you're highly intelligent.'

'Life,' replied Holt, regaining confidence, 'is like a railway train. Someone flips the points, and off you go on another track, with getting back on the original line well-nigh impossible. Just think, had the Owl not found out I had forewarned the government about the Nelson thing, I would have passed the initiation test and be still working undercover, with even less a life of my own than you have with your à la carte escorting. I could never have risked meeting up with you, let alone taking our relationship further!'

'And to think I played a key role in your getting rumbled.'

'I must say, you played the hotel room maid to perfection. At one point I was worried you would overdo it.'

'Five minutes of real action in a four-year career! I felt I was really living – and you there into the bargain.'

'Having had your five minutes, why don't you pack it in and return to proper acting? We can easily get by on my salary.'

'Who would protect you then?'

'What do you mean by that?'

'Many in the service and beyond resent you being the intermediary in dealings with the Owl, as it cuts them out and enables Sir Charles to keep them at bay by telling them only he, via you, can interface with him. Many are convinced the wily bird turned you in the course of those interrogations and you are a double agent, wittingly or unwittingly. What's more, they also say the freedom Sir Charles grants you to roam at will – as was accorded to the genius spy-in-the-bag cryptologist – means you could compromise yourself and embarrass us all, just as he did.'

'I was aware of a negative undercurrent but didn't realize it was that strong.'

'I protect you by submitting reports on what we do together so *they* do not start thinking you might be playing away, getting your pleasures in situations where you could be compromised. I show that there is not much chance of you participating in quirky sex and having a double life.'

'It's pretty obvious I don't.'

'More importantly, I keep them abreast about what you are thinking. Or so they believe. That is why they retain you, despite your hobnobbing with the Owl. Knowing you had a baby with a woman who once worked for him would cement their suspicions. They could use that info to finish you off. That is not to say you don't have your powerful supporters who share the Owl's view that radical action is needed and think the country has gone to the dogs.'

'In future dealings I'll try not to appear so friendly with him, but he makes it difficult, demeaning us in front of others by insisting we address him as Your Wisdom.'

'Of course,' continued Celia, 'I edit the things I tell them about you.'

'That's some consolation, but to whom do you report?'

'The security wallahs, of course. Sir Charles occasionally, who by the way refers to you as if you were his son, despite your faults or perhaps because of them. Sometimes even Blackwell.'

'The Snake. How could you?'

'No big deal really. I found out that he keeps details of everyone's sexual peccadilloes to himself to use as ammunition to protect his own position.'

'But why give him any ammunition at all?'

'For fun partly, and to keep him sweet. I have to tell him something anyway, and winding him up is one of the few pleasures I have – his contorted face as he imagines what we are getting up to is something to be seen, especially when I drag it out, with the ups and downs, like some shaggy dog story.'

'You're joking – the ups and downs, I mean.'

'That was just a figure of speech, like you saying I was in the back of your mind when you were screwing...'

Having left the sentence unfinished, she picked up her glass – untouched since the toast to the new baby – and took a couple of sips, before carefully putting it down as if she were weighing up what she was going to say next.

'Jeremy,' she said, leaning towards him.

'Ye-e-e-s,' said Holt, afraid that a faux pas issuing from his lips would result in another dramatic outburst.

'What if...what if...half of what I told Blackwell *were* true?'

'What did you—?'

'You were proactive in bed. That really got him speculating as to what that meant.'

'It would. Even makes me wonder.'

'Of course, we both know it's not true, but let's just suppose you started showing me the zing and zip you must have shown undercover with Consuela when you were doing your duty for queen and country, and your life – or so you thought – was at stake. If you did, we too could end up with a little boy. Time to really spice our sex life up, don't you think?'

'Christ. Whatever happened to Miss Innocent?'

'Who?'

'The Miss Innocent I married. The virtuous mother of my daughter. The one the Snake said was the Virgin Mary for the likes of me.'

'You mean the one in the Maldives who told you it was better for having waited?'

'Yes, that one!'

'She never existed.'

'What!'

'Playing her was fun, though. Proved I could have been a serious actress.'

'Couldn't you be serious, honest with me just this once?'

'I'm not sure you'll like it. The whole truth, I mean.'

'Try! What can there be left for you to tell me?'

'For starters...that His Wisdom sent me a message too.'

'You're having me on!'

'Not in the least. It was here waiting for me when we got back from the beach.'

'Seems we can never get away from him. He's up there watching over us, like God.'

'No, not God, but he would make a great godfather. You see, he suggested I have another baby. Hopefully a boy, and that you had something important to tell me. That's why I insisted so much.'

'One would have thought being the country's godfather would be enough for any man, assuming of course he is a man.'

'Godmother...is fine with me.'

'Either way,' contended Holt, 'a godparent is usually someone you expect might be able to help the child in the future, someone of substance.'

'The Owl must surely be someone of substance, great substance. Besides, I think he has a sweet spot for us, another requisite for a godparent, don't you think?'

'You are changing your tune. I thought you owed your allegiance to the service.'

'In a way, but as I said before, I am not really an insider, not an officer, expendable.'

'I would have to agree with you there, though they do not seem to be writing you off just yet.'

'Promise me one thing, Jeremy. If you ever do think you recognize the Owl by some turn of phrase or otherwise, don't ever let on.'

'That's crazy.'

'If you do, no one will thank you – most of what he wants is what we all want. If his identity is revealed, with him having to be arrested, Sir Charles will lose his leverage, Giraffe may be closed down, and where will you be? Sir Charles's enemies will have a field day, and you will go down with him.'

'I hadn't thought of that.'

'Now hear this! I've definitely decided to take your advice and resign from the service. Strike out for better or worse. Be myself.'

'You can be sure I'll do my best to support you.'

'To do that, you will have to avoid doing anything silly and keep your powder dry, and not wind up the Snake just for the kicks. I'll be having a hard enough time and don't want it made more difficult by my husband moping about his demotion, not to mention his reduction in salary.'

'You're making me nervous. Ever since that unforgettable night at The Loughty, I've worried that I might end up there myself if things went tits up.'

'Just imagine...' said Celia, her face lighting up.

'The tits?'

'No, you fool. A washed-up spy doing the washing up.'

'Better,' retorted Holt, 'than the fate that so often befell those parachuted into France in World War II. Gestapo and all that.'

'Actually, Jeremy, in this business it has always been two different worlds – the operatives on the one hand, and the officers, either with diplomatic immunity or sitting in London, like Philby, orchestrating operatives and informers at no risk to themselves.

'You yourself, Jeremy, took a great risk going undercover like that. You were not to know the Owl was relatively benign. How could you?'

'I suppose so, though to be honest I did it partly for you, Celia – maybe because of you.'

'Thanks for saying that, though I presume you also had some higher motive?'

'That did figure in it, but how much, I'm not sure.'

She stood up, looked at Holt endearingly, and kissed him on the cheek.

'Jeremy,' she muttered, almost as if speaking to herself, 'it *is* great to have a husband one can respect as if he were a James Bond, even if he does not rise to similar heights in bed or in high society.'

'Point taken,' admitted Holt ruefully, wondering what the future held once Celia branched out and started meeting a whole new range of people. He tried to express his concern without making too much of it.

'You will be starting out on a new life as an actress, meeting people in all walks of life. You will inevitably meet someone much more glamorous than me.'

'Stop worrying about that. I'll be too busy climbing the acting ladder and...with luck looking after our next baby. You, Jeremy, will have to deal with the Owl again.'

'I don't think,' Holt replied, looking at her with a half smile, 'he will do anything grandiose like Tower Bridge again.'

'No?'

'More likely he will target individuals and organizations. He must have built up quite a list. Would be great if it included incompetent school teachers that our Claire might soon have to suffer. They could be exiled to the Falklands, together with the families of the teachers' union officials protecting them so those officials' children would end up being taught by them.'

'You're joking? That could never come about.'

'Yes, sorry, I am beginning to sound like the Owl. He did suggest the Falklands be used as a kind of dumping ground for those wrecking the country.'

'Let's hope that at least thanks to him the country will one day deserve to have Nelson back on his column.'

Holt's face turned serious.

'Celia, I need to anticipate what fanatics might do – the ones that will stop at nothing. That's my real mission. Make a difference that would have made my parents really proud and save lives.'

Almost for the first time ever, Celia looked straight into his eyes with no hint of artifice. No play-acting any more. She would keep acting for the stage or film set.

An exception might be made were the service to come to her asking her to play a particularly challenging one-off role.

Acknowledgements

Peter George, the officer in charge of our language course in the RAF and author of the novel *Red Alert*, on which the film *Dr. Strangelove* was based, inspired me to try and write a similar novel.

Frederick Forsyth's *The Day of the Jackal* reinforced that notion, and far too soon – almost totally lacking experience – I wrote one, which I binned on being told by a US editor that there was far too much philosophizing about physical relationships.

London Alert, written many years later, benefits from more profound experience at home and abroad, and not least from insights and snippets of information gained from people whose names I cannot cite for fear that readers might jump to wrong conclusions. I hope those still with us will realize how much I appreciate their unacknowledged contributions.

There are therefore only three individuals whose encouragement and assistance I can properly acknowledge.

Hilary Tucker, my proofreader, who, besides checking, commented from the female vantage point.

Marcus Trower, my copy editor, who not only corrected and improved the copy, but also made invaluable suggestions regarding characters and scenes that needed treatment in greater depth.

And finally James Denny, a friend from way back, who made me believe the book was good enough to merit going that extra mile to get it really right.

Christopher Bartlett

The Author

Christopher Bartlett initially trained as a mining engineer.

As a teen he was a member of the British Interplanetary Society, where Patrick Moore and Arthur C. Clarke figured prominently at a time when believing in space flight was thought by many to be crazy. He completed his two years' military service in the British Royal Air Force.

After taking a degree in Modern Chinese and Japanese at the School of Oriental and African Studies, London University, he became, among other things, a professional translator of Japanese technical material. He also wrote for magazines in the Far East.

His presence by pure chance in countries when and where headline air crashes occurred enabled him to add local colour and extra details to a number of the sixty narratives in his 'classic' - and in its genre best-selling - *Air Crashes and Miracle Landings*.